Fire on Mount Maggiore

Fire on Mount Maggiore
A Novel

John Parras

The University of Tennessee Press / Knoxville

TENNESSEE BOOK AWARD | PETER TAYLOR PRIZE FOR THE NOVEL

Co-sponsored by the Knoxville Writers' Guild and the University of Tennessee Press, the Peter Taylor Prize for the Novel is named for one of the South's most celebrated writers—the author of acclaimed short stories, plays, and the novels *A Summons to Memphis* and *In the Tennessee Country.* The prize is designed to bring to light works of high literary quality, thereby honoring Peter Taylor's own practice of assisting other writers who cared about the craft of fine fiction.

This is a work of fiction; it describes imaginary persons and situations.

The lines the protagonist invokes on page 168 are the opening words of V. S. Naipaul's *A Bend in the River.*

This book is printed on acid-free paper.

Parras, John, 1964–
Fire on Mount Maggiore : a novel/John Parras.—1st ed.
    p. cm.
ISBN 1-57233-445-2 (acid-free paper)

1. Forest fires—Fiction.
2. Fire fighters—Fiction.
3. Americans—Italy—Fiction.
4. Arson investigation—Fiction.
5. Italy, Southern—Fiction.
I. Title.
PS3616.A7655F57 2005
813'.6—dc22   2005011129

For family: **M., V., & M.,** and Mother and Father

Contents

Acknowledgments

It is my pleasure to thank the National Endowment for the Arts for a fellowship that made the difference. And gratitude is due to Paulette Alden, for clearing the way in an early draft, to Gina Perfetto, Martine Bellen and Lisa Bankoff, to the Knoxville Writers' Guild, and to all who advised me on writing and helped me break through. I am also indebted to Norman Maclean's inspiring book *Young Men and Fire*. Special *grazie* to the Italian fire squad in Caserta, with whom it was an honor to serve.

Part One
Survival

Chapter 1

I have seen fire do many strange and terrible and wonderful things. Among the groves of alder and spruce stringing the slopes of Monte Croce, I've seen flames leap from branch to branch as though the trees were relaying giant torches hand to hand. At the sea flats of Marina di Minturno, I watched stands of umbrella pines burst into plumes of fiery smoke that churned across the treetops on the strong inland wind, the great orange flames rolling and breaking, storm waves of fire atop the canopy. I've seen fire burn upside down from towering limbs of willow and ilex and have heard pine trees explode from the pressure of their own volatile sap. I've watched flames put their heads together to pause and confer, seen them rock their shoulders back and forth, witnessed their spectacular jump across the foliage-cleared firebreak. I've raced searing heat through tangled understory, chased quick curls of smoke as they scurried across grass fields like swarms of mice. I've beat back the ranked onslaught of blazing broom and shied from crucibles of flame thronged in bramble. Once, in the Parco Regionale della Campania, I watched fire hitch a ride on a fallen snag, float across the Sangro River and spread to the far bank. I have seen fire resurrect itself, seen it rise and stretch its limbs after smoldering underground along tree roots for three summer days. I have trod dirt as hot as barbecue coals, marveled at glowing birch bark ashes floating down out of the night sky like big orange snowflakes, listened to fire's snap and hiss and whistle and roar and tasted its bitter funereal ashes. I have felt fire singe my own skin like a flank of steak, inhaled the putrid odor of my own charred flesh. I have seen and smelled and felt what fire can do to a human body, to my own body and to the bodies of my closest friends, burning alive.

They are dead now—Enzo, Saverio, Massimo, Pietro, Renato—all burned dead, their remains interred beneath white marble slabs on the manicured grounds of the military cemetery in Casabasso. Neat ends to messy lives. Below the names and dates of birth, each slab reads:

> *Perished heroically in the service of the country.*
> *Mount Maggiore, August 16, 1999.*

Some forty kilometers from the cemetery, high on the slopes of Maggiore, bright orange surveyors' flags now punctuate the scorched ground, marking the sites where the bodies were found. Massimo and Saverio, their limbs entwined in a harrowing embrace just above the tree line. Enzo further up the slope, his leg wedged in a rock crevice, the left tibia and fibula snapped at the boot top. Pietro, his jawbone still locked open in a final gasp for air, entangled in thorns at the foot of the stone bluff that stood like a fortress wall at the summit of the ridge. Pietro was but meters from a rocky trail that led up and over the bluff—a path to safety that in the roiling smoke and fumes and confusion of fear he hadn't managed to find.

Luchetto and Cesare, luckier, stumbled upon an escape route. Pursued up the slope by the roaring blaze, they scrambled through a narrow pass in the bluff and managed to cross the mountain's crest to the safety of the far slope. When the fire caught up with them moments later, it was met by a strong counterwind blowing up that far slope, met and pushed back by that wind and by the same rocky bluff that had prevented the others from crossing the summit to safety. The fire reared in the face of the counter-current, it grasped for fuel among the rocks, but, finding only the sparse maquis, couldn't top the crest. Here the flames flickered in the weeds and powdery dirt and spent themselves, while the main body of the fire turned its fury toward the fuel-rich stands of oak and birch and tamarack lining the eastern hills.

Safe astride Maggiore's thirteen-hundred-meter summit, Luchetto and Cesare watched the blaze move eastward. They didn't speak—they had just sprinted up several hundred meters of mountainside and were breathless, stupefied, utterly exhausted with their own survival. Crouched over against the cramps in their guts, they panted for air. The smoke shifted, momentarily enshrouding them in a brown cloud, and when it lifted again they spotted a figure wandering downslope not fifty meters away from them. Someone else—one of the fire crew—had made and crossed the summit.

Cesare called out but got no answer, so he and Luchetto descended toward the figure, their boots slipping and scudding on the loose soil and rocks. When they got close enough, they noticed the tattered uniform, the raw outstretched arms, the skin scorched black. A thick gold chain, remarkably untarnished, hung on the blistered chest. The burned man was Renato, their squad commander. Renato—seared hairless, disoriented, barely recognizable. He looked at his two comrades briefly, emptily, his lashless eyes two red stab wounds, then returned his gaze to the ground's rubble. He seemed to be looking for something. He was busy, he indicated with a curt wave of his hand. He didn't want to talk. He seemed upset that they were interrupting him at some task. He made angry gestures with his arms, then suddenly dropped his chin as if embarrassed. He pointed at his feet. He was searching for his boots, he told them.

"But," Luchetto replied, astonished, "you're wearing them!"

"Are you an idiot?" Renato spit out the words in a burst of frustration. He had lost his boots scrambling over the ridge. His feet had gotten caught in the rocks, and his boots had fallen off somewhere along the slope. Had they seen his boots? Would they not help him find them? Did they not see that he had lost his boots?

There were other ways of survival, but not many—and other survivors, but few. Tonino somehow wove his lifeline through the woof of the burning woods, while Tancredi dug a shallow foxhole with his hands and fingernails in a patch of soft dirt. We picked ourselves up like soldiers who had lasted the fray by hiding behind the bodies of our slain comrades.

I too survived. I emerged from the ashes with the American still clinging hotly to my calves. We were twin phoenixes reborn on the blistered clearing where he had tackled me down. Nicolas Fowler—Nico, we called him—eccentric Americano, volunteer firefighter, epicurean of flames, poet, friend, enigma. He now sits in a federal prison cell near Pisa, scribbling on scraps of newsprint. His pencil stub has a dull tip. I can picture him there crouched behind the dented cage bars, a goatee coming out in a wiry tangle on his chin, his gray eyes brooding, his bony body contorted over the scrap of paper he writes on. The guards flick him charred cigarette butts and he smokes them down to the filter. Ashes to ashes.

He is the one I have come to this shore, this hot, frivolous beach, to forget.

I have not been to the seaside in a long time. Coming down the stairway to the beachfront crowded with canvas chairs and umbrellas, I find myself abruptly reintroduced to this peculiar flat terrain, the shoreline. A wide, sharp, gleaming sheet of sea. A steady inland wind blowing across a narrow strip of sand the color of ash. Harmless waves lapping at the land. And high up overhead, blindingly forthright, the sun—a raging ball of gas and fire stretching its rays 150 million kilometers to blanch the Italian coast.

The women strip down to neon bikini bottoms, confident, holding their shoulders back, baring their breasts, at ease in this scene. But on this sandy terrain crowded with avid vacationers, I am unsure of myself. Having fought fires in the mountains almost since I graduated from high school, I am accustomed to wild hillsides, to jagged slopes and rocky cliffs, rough cobblestones—not these shifting, sandy grounds and wet shallows. My feet, bootless and exposed, drag in the uneven sands. I step across the hot grains to splash around in the sea's tepid shallows, my nearly naked body oddly unwieldy and vaguely shameful in nothing but a pair of old trunks I haven't worn in ten years. I squint into the noonday sun. The sky is perfect forget-me-not blue.

But how forget? How get on with the mundane business of life? Whenever I close my eyes I am taken back to Maggiore, to my unlikely survival while others perished. I hear the vast roar of the fire behind us, relive the squad's desperate scramble up the slope. I see my comrades flinch at the stings of flame, reenvision their exhausted and ignoble collapse. My only reprieve is to convince myself that the fumes suffocated them before they were burned. Maybe, I tell myself, they were unconscious when they hit the ground—before the flames tore like hyenas at the muscle and bone of living men. Maybe they were spared that end.

Renato was not. The last time we saw him on the mountainside—this was right after that nasty one-sided fistfight between him and Nico—Renato's feet were so mangled he could barely take a step, his hands so burned he couldn't drink from his own canteen. By the time a rescue crew arrived to carry him off the mountain his feet had swollen horribly, and they were forced to cut off his half-melted boots with a hunting knife. We had stupidly, unforgivably neglected to remove or untie the boots ourselves. His feet bloated like two hunks of spoiled meat.

We thought Renato wouldn't survive the stretcher trip down the rugged terrain or the helicopter flight to the special burn unit at Santa Maria di Novità Hospital in Napoli. But the body can be stubborn, and Renato's lingered on, degrading from third-degree burns and anoxia for fifty-six agonizing hours after the blaze. Immobile, intubated, swollen with sores and bandages and trussed by medical machinery, Renato crept steadily from life to death, virtually unresponsive to treatment, until his lungs failed. When the doctors finally covered the corpse's bloated eyes, Renato's mother thanked God for her own son's death.

So what am I doing here in my bathing suit with my toes in the sand pretending that today matters, that tomorrow is something to look forward to? Though I've tried to withdraw into a mute patch of sunlight and turn my chair toward the future, my guts are still twisted with yesterday—twisted with past decisions, past mistakes, with unspoken motives and gestures and lies (possibly my own) that led to five burned corpses, five comrades dead on the mountainside.

Six corpses, actually. There was the *contadino* farmer too. His remains were discovered near the Punti Cliffs, far to the west of the other bodies, at an altitude of about a thousand meters. What the farmer was doing so high on Mount Maggiore that sweltering afternoon nobody knows—not Nico, not Renato, maybe not even me.

Truth is, I cannot choose what to remember, and unexpectedly, even amid the ravage and loss, my memory is drawn to thrilling glints of beauty. There were the Polish girls smelling of mint and Chanel on those languid August afternoons, there were red-syrup sunsets from thousand-meter summits, there were times you thought you glimpsed the protean flux of higher powers in the flaming trees and hillsides.

I recall one particular June afternoon when the squad walked through an olive grove that seemed to float on a cloud marbled with veins of flame. Tonino and Enzo were there, I remember, and Saverio and Nico the Americano and me. It was out near Pratolungo. The olive trees were strung out along a cliff on the side of Monte Lantere. The fire wasn't burning up in the trees but skittering along the ground, smoldering in the ankle-high grasses. There were hardly any flames at all, only low white tufts of smoke hugging the earth like clinging vapors of dry ice at our boot tops. You couldn't see the ground, it was so fogged over, just a thick white carpet of shifting smoke. This was something we'd never witnessed before, and we found it beautiful and couldn't find words for it. None of us spoke, nor did we try to put out the fire. It was as if we were hypnotized. We followed the path blazed by the flames as you would trail in the wake of spirits. Each step we took kicked up another little puff of smoke, as though our boots were fuming. And each time we stepped forward, we weren't sure whether our feet would touch the ground again—whether the cloud would hold us up or whether we would step right through the whiteness and find ourselves free-falling down through heaven back earthward.

Will such transcendent moments ever again be mine?

When we reached the edge of the olive grove, we all took off our boots and socks and stretched out our feet in the weeds. We could see the Vesuva Creek gleaming brightly in the lower valley. Rays of sunlight shot through the clouds like lines lightly sketched by an artist in the sky. Tonino was whistling. Saverio closed his eyes. Enzo caught a brown cricket in his hands, looked at it, and let it go. Nico recited something in English that none of us understood; it might have been poetry. When we finally turned back to the olive grove, the fire had gone out.

The pinkish scars streaked down my neck and arm—burn wounds I received not on Mount Maggiore but at a similar blaze several years ago—begin to tighten and itch in the sunlight. Though a breeze is blowing shoreward off the sea, the sun is still strong. I am not used to exposing my skin to heat, an element against which I instinctively cover myself. I drag my beach chair into the shade, installing myself securely beneath the umbrella, and drape a damp towel over the scars on my arm. Nearby, a young woman has taken off her bikini top and splayed herself out on a recliner in the sun and I am suddenly thinking of Lyn, the Polish *ragazza* I met and desired and lost in the space of fifteen intense August days. I close my eyes and see Lyn's unbuttoned blouse, I remember the thin chain of gold that hung from her neck, her hazel eyes shining in bonfire light. I remember her face and the faces of the other Polish girls—the face of Katja, glancing with sorrow and astonishment at Nico—when we visited the destroyed statues in the gardens behind Palazzo Sangiusto. The Polish *ragazze,* volunteers in art restoration, had spent two weeks under the August sun hand-scrubbing those terrific Renaissance statues until they gleamed, but the night the fire broke out in the palace gardens, their painstaking labor was undone by the heavy smoke in minutes. The marble had been scorched black, ruined by the poisonous fumes. The once-proud face of Il Carpiglio's *Prometheus,* the most famous statue of the series, was besmirched with a charcoal smear, reduced to an ignoble wince. That image was the last the Polish volunteers had of our little southern town of Casabasso. And short of reversing time itself, there was nothing we in the squad could do about it. Their stay was over; they headed back to Warsaw.

After the van pulled off to the airport with Lyn, Katja, and the other Polish girls, Nico did something strange. Without a word, he scampered up onto the ruined statue of Prometheus. I thought he was going to try to wipe the statue clean or something, but instead he reached out and snapped off one of the demigod's marble fingers and slipped it into his own pocket. Maybe we guessed what Nico was trying to get at with that symbolic gesture, because no one in the squad intervened. Anyway we were still reeling with the loss of the Poles, reeling at all that perfume and beauty being torn away from us. And besides, Nico often did things like that, things that are difficult or impossible to explain. When I think about him, my thoughts are bumblebees loose in my brain. Still, I think about him a lot. About my friendship with him, about my confusion when he tackled me down on the slope of Mount Maggiore and dragged me into the ashes of his fire, saving my life. How did the American volunteer ever conceive of such a thing as backfire? To light a fire in the roaring midst of fire, to lie down in ashes like a log beneath hot coals and then to rise from ashes and walk again upon the earth—how did such strange and wonderful and terrible ideas take root and blossom in his mind?

Chapter 2

Nicolas Fowler showed up at our firebase about six months ago, in late April, on a morning as cloudless, hot, and fire-prone as any other morning. He'd signed on through the International Youth Volunteer Network to serve out the summer with our *Vigili del Fuoco* brigade—a squad of forest fire fighters. It wasn't unusual for us to take on interns once in a while, but I'd say that as far as international volunteers went, Nico came across as disappointing. With his sneakers and his ponytail and his fancy backpack, the American struck me as your typical saccharine cowboy—some lost undergraduate doing Peace Corps penance to assuage the guilt he felt about being a privileged rich guy. He looked jet-lagged and strung out, and right away I found him petulant. When I asked him if he spoke any Italian he said dully that he did, a very little, but that he was too tired to just then. He didn't apologize or smile or look me in the eye. He asked where his bunk was, and when Renato pointed to the barracks Nico went straight over and lay face down on one of the bunks and fell asleep. This was before lunchtime even. I thought he'd brighten up in the afternoon, but when I saw him later he was still taciturn, even downright haughty. Instead of sitting at the common table with the squad, Nico dragged a chair over to one side and began scribbling intently in some kind of journal or diary. He barely spoke to us and behaved this way for the whole next day too, and I began to resent him the way you resent guests who don't know their place. I found an even better reason to hate him when, at his first fire, he almost got Renato killed.

It was a minor burn out in a field of grass and birch running along some freight tracks near Báia Domízia. Renato, Massimo, Saverio and Enzo, along with Nico and me, responded. The fire had taken hold in the reeds along the rails and spread across the weed-strewn embankment to the open field. We began by snuffing out the flames in the grass meadow and clearing a firebreak to prevent the blaze from reaching the nearby stands of birch trees, whose flaky white and tan bark was beautiful in the strong sunlight, and by the time we turned our attention back to the train tracks, the fire was all over the line. Tall weeds and poppies were growing in among the ties—it seemed to be a freight line that wasn't used much—and the flames were jumping from flower to flower and weed to weed like a swarm of bumblebees.

Saverio looked up and down the tracks. "Trains run these lines, anyone?"

We all shrugged. "Guess so," Massimo said, "at least once in a while."

Renato, our squad commander, tapped me on the shoulder and pointed to my two-way radio unit. Because I knew the difference between cathode, anode and diode—I'd taken a science class or two at a local university—I was usually the designated radioman for the squad. "Call the *carabinieri* at the Báia," Renato ordered, "and tell them we've got a situation." He turned to the others: "The rest of you move up the tracks. Buddy up and watch out for the third rail."

"I thought they ran the electricity up there," Tancredi said, pointing at the electric cables running overhead.

"Do you want to find out the hard way?" Renato answered.

"Piece of toast," Massimo said, "that's what you'll be."

"A burned marshmallow impaled on the end of a twig," the American offered lamely. No one knew what he meant.

"Pork on a spit is more like it," said Enzo, who was trying to balance-walk a train rail. He lost his footing and fell hard onto one of the wooden ties. When he stood up, there was blood and a big splinter in his palm. "This assignment's a real piece of shit," Enzo spit.

"Stop playing balance beam and get a move on," Renato said sternly, waving his forearm. Enzo cursed and moved toward the fire.

As I tried to get a radio transmission to the *carabinieri*, the others headed up the line. The tracks split into four separate runs as they approached Báia Domízia to the west, and the fire had spread out among all the lines, burning haphazardly in patches of grass and weed between the tracks. Some of the wooden rail ties were beginning to smolder as well.

"Americano," Renato called to Nico, "you spray water on the smoking ties—and keep an eye for trains coming from the east."

We'd given Nico the only portable water pump in the jeep. We thought he'd do better with that than with a *flabello*—a switchlike firefighting tool made by nailing strips of rubber to a wooden handle. With a *flabello* you had to go right up to the flames and whip them into submission, physically smother them to the ground. It was tough work that often grew nasty, and we thought we'd save the American the trouble, at least for today.

Nico hoisted the strap of the water pump over his shoulder. It looked heavy for him. Then he put his head down and began examining the train tracks—a bit too minutely, I thought, considering how much track there was to cover.

After I'd explained our situation to the *carabinieri* at Báia Domízia—which took a while, since for some reason they hadn't been alerted about the fire—I hurried to catch up with the others. When I passed Nico, it seemed he'd hardly moved. He was hunched over, soaking one of the wooden track ties with water. It didn't look to me as though the tie had even been smoldering.

"You probably don't want to waste water on that," I advised him. "It's not burning. Some of the wood is black from sitting in the sun all these years."

He didn't even glance at me, just nodded his head and kept spraying.

"I called the town to stop the trains," I told him, "but keep your eyes peeled."

Nico shrugged as if I'd said something he already knew. Without looking at me, he lifted his head, found another charred tie less than a meter away, and stepped toward it.

I moved on to help the other squad members, though in terms of size it wasn't really much of a fire. We'd already stopped its momentum in the fields and now it was nothing but a bunch of small patches burning here and there among the tracks without any pattern. The main problem was just picking your feet among the railroad tracks and ties and loose gravel. We kept stumbling, and the rails were hot as cooking pots in the sunlight. We weren't sure which lines carried electricity and which didn't, but there was a loud buzzing sound coming from one of the voltage transformers nearby and the air reeked of burnt wires and charred wood and tar. The smoke wasn't thick, but that just made it worse—it was one of those thin, hazy smokes that drags its nails along the inside of your throat and goes way down into the bronchioles. Some of us wet bandannas with our canteens and tied them around our mouths and noses.

We were so busy tripping on the ties and choking with the noxious smoke and watching the third rail that no one saw or heard the train coming until it was right on top of us. Nico was still in the rear, and I guess he'd had his head down examining the ties when the freight came along. He ended up on the other side of the train, and if he was yelling, Renato couldn't hear him. The engineer sounded his horn at the last second, a huge blast of noise you could feel wrenching your guts. We'd all been concentrating on the weeds and ties underfoot but raised our heads at the sound of the horn. Renato was on the tracks in front of the locomotive. When he turned and saw ten thousand kilos of iron and steel bearing down on him like a huge wave about to snap him in two, he half jumped, half fell off the tracks onto the rocky embankment at the last moment. As the freight rumbled by, we heard the conductor's voice yell from the engine room: "Get the fuck off the tracks, you damn idiots!" The engineer never bothered to halt the train.

Though nobody reprimanded him, we all thought it had been Nico's fault. He'd been in the rear and should have warned us about the train. But Nico, he just mummed up. Didn't talk about the incident or admit his guilt. And for the next several days he was aloof, replying to inquiries in suspicious monosyllables and seeming to desire above all else his own solitude—an odd mannerism, considering he had decided to join a firefighting brigade.

Worst of all, for me, was that he spent most of his free time writing in that black notebook he carried with him at all times. Even right after the train incident, as soon as we got back to the firebase, Nico immediately poured his heart out into that small black book. He guarded it with a ferocious eye, wouldn't let it out of his sight. During downtime, while the rest of us played soccer or Neapolitan card games or just goofed around during the long afternoons, the American would sit hunched in a chair scribbling away in his notebook, ignoring us, dangling a cigarette in his mouth and wearing a scowl on his face as though he were angry at the very paper on which he wrote.

Still, he was a volunteer, and despite myself I actually felt a little bit sorry for him. I tried to see it all from his point of view. At Báia Domízia we'd put him in the midst of a confusing fire situation without any training, expecting that he'd just get the hang of it. For us, fighting fires came as easily as joining pickup soccer games. It was part of our very Italianness. But this was obviously not so for Nico, and I thought perhaps I might give him the benefit of the doubt. So one day not long after Báia Domízia, I experienced a momentary feeling of goodwill—or perhaps I felt guilty at my own poor manners as a host—and I was stupid enough to try speaking with the American as he was writing.

I walked up to him boldly. "Ciao," I said. "I'm Matteo," I added, reminding him of my name and stretching out my hand.

"How's it going," he said in English. He reluctantly extended his hand and let me shake it. It was lifeless—sweaty yet cold, even in the punishing heat of the afternoon.

"Have you fought fires before?" I asked, also in English. (At my father's urging, I had chosen English as my required foreign language in high school, and I was suddenly glad of it; my father had wanted me to become an electrical engineer and said that all engineers studied English.)

"Don't need to," the American answered me, narrowing his eyes, "I know enough about it." He looked down at the page and read. I stood there for several awkward seconds, slapping a pair of dusty work gloves against my thigh. You couldn't tell what this one was thinking.

I tried again, politely: "Which part of the States are you from?"

"The East Coast," he said.

"Which state?"

"The one where you find Pittsburgh," he said, looking up at me and squinting.

I just nodded. I couldn't remember which state that was.

"Have you ever been to America?" he asked. The way he said it sounded like an accusation.

"No," I said awkwardly, "but I plan to go one day."

"It's a big place," Nico said, inclining his head back to the page he was writing on. "I wish you luck."

So that's how it's going to be, I thought. I turned and had started to walk away when I heard him clear his throat. I stopped and turned back to face him.

"By the way," he said, looking me straight in the eye, "you told me there were no more trains."

I was suddenly aware of the sunlight striking my forehead. The heat seemed to boil my blood. I opened my mouth. "No," I replied. "I only said I had called the *carabinieri* about the trains."

"Whatever," Nico answered, inclining his head to read again. "Really, whatever."

My face flushed and I began to sweat heavily in the armpits. I was angry, confused. I couldn't believe he was blaming me for this. But I was never good at confronting people, I get too easily flustered. I felt dizzy, the ground seemed to tilt, and my thighs were shaking as I walked away, but I tried to keep my back straight and my shoulders steady.

I went to the canteen and stood in front of the stove to make a pot of coffee, my heart twitching like a cricket in my chest. That American, I muttered to myself, is a real bastard. I switched on the gas and touched a match to the burner. The blue flame was pale in the afternoon light. Not knowing why, I extended my wrist above the circle of flame and steadied it there, holding it over the heat, struggling against the flinch of the body. A cousin of mine could light a cigarette half an arm's length from the flame of a match simply by steadying the tip of the cigarette directly above it, in the line of heat, and I thought of a boy from my neighborhood who could put out a cigarette on his own forearm, and of others I've read about who are able to walk barefoot over red coals. But my arm, a coward, jerked back from the flame by itself. There was a lesson in that perhaps: the body knows enough to protect itself. On the other hand, the skin on the underside of my wrist showed a small red welt. I had inflicted harm upon my own body, and there was a lesson in that as well.

Just then Saverio walked into the canteen and noticed me rubbing my wrist. "What's up?" he asked.

"It's that American volunteer," I said dejectedly. I turned off the stove burner.

"What about him?" Saverio asked, knitting his brows in concern.

I'd learned over the years to trust Saverio's honest assessment of life's matters, and as I put away the coffee—I didn't feel like making a pot anymore—I told him about the conversation I'd just had with Nico. To tell the truth, I had been looking for Saverio to confirm my opinion of the American's repulsive nature, so I was taken aback when Saverio came to Nico's defense, saying that the American was simply "his own type of person" and that we Italians were too quick to judge foreigners by the clothes they wore.

Like Saverio, the other brigade members were taking the American's behavior in stride. Nobody, except probably Renato, seemed to hold anything against him. But even so, I utterly couldn't fathom this one. I couldn't shake my resentment at his presence. It was a visceral hatred that rose inside me like bile. The American made me feel uncomfortable even here in my own country, on my own turf. I got the feeling that he was criticizing our every move, that in his minutely scripted handwriting he was recording each and every of our foibles and shortcomings. What did he mean coming here with locks of greasy hair and sullen looks of insult and impatience? No, this volunteer wouldn't last long. Two weeks, three at most. He would soon tire of the heat and dust, of ashes in the mouth and tepid showers, of endless afternoons spent kicking at pebbles and staring dumbly at mute shadows crawling across the firebase compound. He would tire of our inane conversations. He would learn just as the rest of us had that fighting fires was no boyish adventure, that it was a joyless occupation corroding the lungs, that it was nothing but filthy, punishing labor performed under harsh working conditions. Scorched by flames, depleted from smoke inhalation, bored by waiting, utterly broken by the physical demands of the mountain terrain, the American would depart a thoroughly drained and disillusioned young man.

I was wrong, of course.

Chapter 3

I once saw fire burn the pants off a man. It happened a few years back in a valley near the Lago di Vairano. The terrain is fairly flat over there, but it was windy that day and the flames were getting fanned by a lot of oxygen. The fire was moving fast and kept changing direction, first heading up the foothills toward Presenzano, then shifting over toward the Volturno River, then following the channel of the valley and charging down toward the farmlands in the south. The weather was so blustery it seemed the firesmoke was being whisked right off the earth. High, high above, cirrus clouds etched chalky hieroglyphics in the pale blue sky.

Despite the winds, the squad basically had a grip on the situation. We met the fire head-on, using our handheld *flabelli* to snuff out the flames in the shorter grasses. But as we deployed our wide arc, slowly closing the two forward points of our crescent rank to surround the blaze, something strange kept occurring. We noticed as we moved forward through the grasses and broom that spot fires kept igniting behind us. Tonino, the squad commander, thought Enzo was doing a sloppy job, and every time a spot fire flared up Tonino would order Enzo to the rear to put it out. The third or fourth time it happened, Enzo got mad. He claimed it wasn't his fault. Tonino thought it was, he insisted that it was, and again ordered Enzo to the rear. But Enzo wouldn't budge. He jammed his shovel into the ground and said something abusive and stood there like a chess piece with his arms crossed while Tonino yelled and cursed at him. It was nothing new to the rest of us. Those two, always bickering or mocking, insulted each other as casually as they drank their morning cappuccino.

Just then, not far from us, some movement caught our eye. A piece of fire broke free from the main blaze and moved toward us. It was a small chunk of flames, about as large as a loaf of bread, and it moved as though it were a soccer ball that had taken aflame and been kicked toward us. It bounced right past our position and rolled into the unburned grasses behind us.

But it wasn't a ball, we realized. It was a jackrabbit—a burning jackrabbit. Making an eerie screech that sounded like a baby being torn limb from limb, the rabbit hopped in a wild zigzag pattern and collapsed in the grasses to die.

So then we knew. The fire was scaring the animals out of their holes and into the flames, where they caught fire and then raced blindly into the unburned fields.

We laughed at that, laughed and laughed like kids at a birthday party, laughed until we saw the farmer. He was alone. He had seen the fire blowing toward his land and had come out to stop the flames before they reached his fields. He'd made a makeshift *flabello* from a tree, simply cutting off a big long leafy branch and using it to smother out the flames in the grasses. But the winds had been too much for him, and the grasses too tall, and the fire had moved faster than he could. We were still standing there scratching our heads and laughing in wonder about the rabbits when another screech came from over a nearby rise. We were quiet for a moment and the noise ceased. All we could hear was the sound of the flames at the top of the low rise, a rustling and crackling sound like a column of soldiers shuffling through a field of dry leaves. We thought the screeching sound must have been another jackrabbit.

Just as we were about to move on, a burning man tore through the wall of flames and careened toward us. It was like an act you'd see at the circus, a clown or daredevil bursting through a burning paper hoop. But the man was no clown or daredevil. He barreled into Saverio, knocked him clean over and kept going, running in frenzied circles and screaming horrifically, "Where's Volturno! Where's the river!"

The man didn't know enough to stop, drop, and roll. He was trying to outrun his own skin, and we had to hunt him like a pack of hyenas. Finally Enzo, kicking hard at the man's shins, tripped him down and smothered him in the dirt some hundred and fifty meters from the main blaze. The man had been burned pretty bad. His pants had been scorched off and his legs were covered with open wounds and ashes. The flames had eaten off the entire back of his shirt and most of the hair from his head. He looked like the survivor of a nuclear blast. When Enzo grabbed at the man's forearm, the skin tore and slipped at the wrist, revealing the red steaklike flesh beneath.

So how forget, how forget?

It's been a season of memorable fires, and I don't mean only Maggiore. All around the globe, grassland plains, conifer forests, dry savannas, entire mountain ranges have burst into flame at an astonishing rate. In Mongolia, two enormous conflagrations—each the size of an entire Italian province—raged uncontrolled for several weeks in April and May, destroying a mind-boggling two and a half million hectares of forest. In Texas, rangers in jeeps had trouble keeping up with grass fires that swept across the panhandle plains at fifty, sixty, even seventy kilometers per hour. Devastating burns tore through Indonesia, Mexico, the boreal forests of Ontario, Sweden's famed conifer stands, Brazil's rain forests, vast expanses of Siberian evergreen steppes.

Closer to home, a series of fires up north along the Riviera di Levante made headlines early in the tourist season. These burns didn't occur out in the remote countryside but erupted at the brink of populated areas, in fields and forests on the outer edges of towns, the meeting place of the city and the countryside that in fire parlance is called the rural-urban interface. The landscapes of picturesque villages like Argentario, Punta Ala, and Forte dei Marmi—some of the poshest seaside vacation spots on the Mediterranean, not far from Pisa and Firenze—were marred by ugly burns. In June the popular government news channel Rai Uno televised images of bikini-clad bathers covering their faces with beach towels as plumes of black smoke drifted over La Maddalena, one of Sardinia's choicest beaches. Up and down the western coast, vacation crowds stood thigh-deep in the sea gawking landward at once-verdant cliffs now burning out of control.

The worst part was, most people couldn't have cared less. They said *boh* and shrugged their shoulders—or if they did show interest, it was only because they were morbidly drawn to the destruction as a source of perverted entertainment, the way you slow down at a car wreck along the *autostrada*. Wildfires have become part of our national routine, simply another inconvenience of Italian life, like municipal kickbacks or traffic jams. In mid-July, I remember, beachgoers fed up with the noise and disruptions of firefighting operations spit obscenities at Corpo Forestale helicopters filling their buckets in the Mediterranean sea.

A few spectacular fires early in the season did manage to capture national attention for a few decent media bites. On May 3 a fire tore through La Spezia, Liguria, and destroyed several trillion lire worth of property. And on May 14 a blaze swept up the La Cervara cliffs in the night, killing a family of four vacationing in Portofino. Shortly following that disaster, the ministry of the Protezione Civile began televising infomercials starring an Italian version of Smokey Bear. Special signs—images portraying a hand flicking a cigarette from a car window, with a big red line slashed across the picture—began appearing on major thoroughfares considered particularly at risk. Soon enough the newspapers jumped into it with the passion of a crusade, publishing sensational accusations of forestry mismanagement, insurance fraud, serial arson, and organized conspiracy—and politicians took note. The head of the Piedmontese section of the Communist Party dramatically announced a "War on Fire." The Greens, too, reasserted themselves, plastering walls from the Alps to Sicily with posters of burning trees and introducing into the legislature a law that would increase the penalties for arson by rendering it a federal offense. In early June an army of Green Party supporters ran a water hose up and down the entire length of Tuscany.

Nico entered into this maelstrom, this wholesale burning of the nation, like a mild annoyance, a headache that adds to the general malaise. The American was nothing but a pesky idealist who, though trying to help, was actually getting in the way. At least that's how I thought of him at first, before I came to care for him. I dismissed him as a moth about to perish in the flame. Who contemplates one single tree when the entire forest is afire? Perhaps that was my mistake. I didn't realize it at the time, but Nico was actually an ambassador of bigger powers, a symptom of some more widespread dysfunction that threatened the very marrow of the country.

There's more than one map to Napoli, as we say around here, and the same goes for the fire on Mount Maggiore. Though Nico and Renato and I and the rest of the squad all found ourselves on the same slope that afternoon of August 16, we'd each come spinning toward it along our own private vectors. I wish I could say it was sacrifice or bravery or some moral imperative that sped me along, but this is no place for more lies. There have been enough lies. My road to Maggiore began with thieves and brigands.

A few days after Nico arrived at the firebase, Renato showed up at my apartment early one morning. I was still in the T-shirt and boxer shorts I used for pajamas.

"Put on some jeans," Renato told me when I opened the front door. "I want you to come somewhere with me."

"Where?" I asked.

"To have breakfast and fix your life," Renato replied.

I got dressed quickly and followed Renato outside. The streets were quiet at this early hour, the air cool and gray. The sun had still not come up over the eastern mountains, but the sky above us was cloudless, a sheet of metal waiting for the sun.

I was looking for the brigade jeep but Renato had driven his own car, and as he unlocked his door I noticed he wasn't wearing his *Vigili del Fuoco* uniform either.

I settled into the passenger seat and said, "I haven't even had coffee yet."

"Mezzasoma asked me to pick you up before you signed in at the firebase," Renato said.

"Mezzasoma?" I repeated. That would be Cavalier Mezzasoma, district commander-in-chief of the Casabasso *Vigili del Fuoco* fire brigade. "So this is official business?"

"I didn't hear that," Renato said.

"I said, *Is this official busi. . . .*"

"I'll tell you what this is about," Renato interrupted. "This is to find out what kind of man you are."

When I didn't answer, Renato added, "Today you'll see."

He drove toward Céllole. You'd never find it on a map. It was neither here nor there. Between Casabasso and the sea, was all. As we wove down out of the hills I got a glimpse of the Mediterranean—the water broad, silver, calm—then it was lost in the trees. When I rolled down my window, the smell of brackish tides floated to me on the intermittent gust.

Near Céllole, Renato pulled up on a dirt shoulder near a two-story building with a yellow sign that read *Osteria Il Grappolo* in red letters. The building was set so close to the road you had to check for passing cars before opening or closing the front door. That was the new Italy and the old Italy in a nutshell: an ancient building beside a newly widened road, and neither the new nor the old giving up a centimeter of ground.

Inside, a woman in a blue smock—the kind *contadini* used to wear—stood behind the counter rubbing a glass with a rag. At the bar an elderly man in a black suit and hat leaned forward and put his lips to a coffee cup. Renato walked past the bar and out into a rear courtyard. The courtyard was enclosed by leafy vines of ivy entwined on chicken wire. The worn flagstones were stained with old spills. Two men—pilots of the Airborne Fire Protection Squad by their uniform—sat at one of the tables, licking the bottoms of their cups. An empty stem of grappa stood on the tabletop. Renato walked over and stood beside the table.

"What's the word from Casabasso?" one of the men said. He was a heavy guy with red blotches marring his face and light brown hair beginning to gray. He fingered the empty stem of grappa. The other man was younger, black-haired, fit with muscular shoulders. A small piece of paper was stuck to his chin where he'd cut himself shaving.

Renato pulled out a chair for himself and sat down. "The word is, Time's up."

"Same here," the blotched man replied. He turned to me with blue, penetrating eyes and said gruffly, "Sit down, man. I don't like having people looming over me when I'm eating."

The younger guy jerked a chair out for me with his foot. I sat down.

The waitress came up to our table. "You want something?" she asked.

Renato ordered coffee and brioches for both of us.

The blotched man scratched at a sore on his face, then stretched out his hand and poked at a newspaper that lay on the table. "That boy's got his foot up his ass," he said in a rough voice, pointing to a picture of Carlo Scarlini, a forward for the Napoli soccer team. Scarlini had recently been brought down south from AC Milan in an urgent and expensive trade, but since joining Napoli three months ago he hadn't scored a single goal.

"He's a Buddhist, isn't he?" I said, just to say something.

"I don't care if he's the Dalai Lama, man," the blotched one said. "Petro"—the head coach for Napoli—"should send him back north where he came from."

"Or he can pray with Buddha for the Chinese team at the next World Cup," the younger one said with a guffaw.

Renato forced a smile. The waitress returned to serve our coffee and brioches, and after she'd gone back to the other room Renato took a manila envelope out of his pocket and said, "Here's another word from Casabasso." He placed the envelope on the table.

"Your taxes?" the blotched man said with obvious irony.

"No, your report card," Renato answered.

"Ha, ha," the younger man said, sitting up to his full height.

"Same to you," Renato said.

The blotched man put his hand on the envelope and pulled, but Renato kept a grip on one corner. "Don't wear your uniforms next time," Renato said. He waited a second to get his point across, then let go of the envelope.

The blotched man took it and tucked it in his pocket. "I'll wear what I fucking wear," he said, looking straight at Renato.

The younger guy stretched his neck menacingly. He had the neck of an ox.

Still looking at the blotched man, Renato simpered: "I think your red house dress would be much nicer, actually."

The younger guy scraped his chair on the floor and gripped the armrests like he was going spring out of his seat, but the blotched man found the humor. "You're a real fucking asshole, Renato," he said with a grin, "a real piece of shit." He shook his jaw from side to side with a broad smirk.

The younger guy lit a cigarette and tossed the matches onto the table. Printed on the match cover was an image of a red umbrella and big yellow letters spelling out *Sabbiadoro*—some local beach club.

"It's not Scarlini," Renato said, going back to soccer. "It's the midfielders' fault."

"Do you think so?" the blotched man said, interested.

Renato leaned forward and poked his index finger on the tabletop as he answered. "Yes, the midfielders—Ferrenzi, Alvo, and Ottolino. Won't give Scarlini a decent pass. They're doing it on purpose, everyone knows that."

"Maybe," the blotched man considered, picking at something on his chin.

Renato sat back. "When will it be done?" he said.

"As soon as the word is said."

"The word is said."

"Soon, then."

"Fine." Renato leaned forward again. "You guys got any more of that?" He nodded to the empty stem.

The blotched one yelled over his shoulder, "Marienza, another grappa!"

Back outside, I watched a hawk tacking on hot-air tides high in the sky. Barely moving his wings, he kited around up there at what must have been twenty-five hundred meters. You'd be able to spot a lot of fires from that altitude, I thought.

I lit a cigarette and waited for Renato to finish up business with those Airborne Fire Protection Squad pilots. I guess I knew the gist of what they were talking about. I guess I realized what I had just witnessed.

We called them *transazione*, or assignations. Say you were a farmer who wanted to graze your livestock on government land: you might send the right politician some homemade sausage or a case of *fragolino* wine. Or for instance, if you ran a liquor business and wanted to open a storefront on the same street as another liquor store, you might persuade the owner of the other place to relinquish his right to commercial-competition protection. I couldn't see how terribly large amounts of money would be involved.

Renato came out the front door and put on his sunglasses. We both got in the car.

"That's how it works," Renato said to me, punctuating his sentence with a slam of the door.

"It's nothing," I said casually.

"Oh, it's something," he said, starting the engine. "You better be sure it's something."

I nodded, settled into my seat.

Renato put the car in gear. "We're not just fucking around here," he said.

"No," I replied.

Renato churned the tires on the dirt shoulder, made a tight, quick U-turn, and headed back to Casabasso.

"Speaking of fucking," Renato said down the road a bit, "maybe you can buy a piece of ass with this." He groped in his pocket, pulled out a wad of notes, and tossed it over to me. I bobbled it, and the wad almost went out the window.

"What's this?" I asked. Then I saw. The bills were twisted tight in a thick red rubber band, the kind fishermen use to hold lobster claws shut. I wrestled off the elastic and flipped through them. It was more or less a million lire—about five hundred dollars.

"You want an exact count?" I asked Renato.

"I don't want any count. Just put it in your pocket."

I opened my mouth to say something but didn't know what. I wasn't sure if I understood. We passed a small farm and there was a pig lying in some mud in its pen. I thought the pig looked happy. I said, "Renato."

"It's from the Cavalier," Renato said. "He told me to give it to you. I didn't even look at it. I don't even know what it is."

My blood raced, suddenly hot. I felt as though I'd been running at full speed and had just skidded to a stop at the edge of a cliff. It was strange, almost lewd, to be paid for nothing more than taking a drive and having breakfast. Yet here was the money, right in my hands. I gently fingered the bills. They were well worn, as soft as flower petals, but the cliff's edge where I imagined myself dropped off into a gorge of jagged rocks, and I instinctively pulled back from the precipice. "I can't accept this," I said, handing the money back over to Renato.

But Renato wouldn't take it. "It's yours," he said. "I already told you, the district chief, Cavalier Mezzasoma, wants you to have it."

I bounced those words around in my mind for a few seconds. I had a glimmer of hope that the district chief had me earmarked for promotion, that he had an eye on my future. The Cavalier had known my father, they'd worked closely together on a few projects; and I thought that perhaps the Cavalier was watching over me for my old man.

Renato went on, "Don't think it's this way every time. This is special because it's your first time. And because of your father, what he's done." Renato paused, steering a tight curve, and I imagined my father sitting in his old office, signing and stamping papers. Though he'd been a tireless worker, he'd sometimes complain that the government never gave a man his due.

The car swung out of the curve at a healthy clip. Renato continued, "That's a lot of money, but you deserve it. You've been with the brigade for a long time. You can buy something for your moms."

I guess this is where I should have protested again and handed back the money, but my hand fell limply into my lap. I watched the trees racing by on both sides of the road. Birch and oak, sycamore, olive, fir and ash and chestnut, larch. Trees like these existed, I thought, partly because of me and my work as a fire watcher, a *vigile del fuoco*. It's not like the brigade was mixed up with the Camorra or anything. There were no drugs or prostitutes—of that I was almost certain. The transactions involved nothing more than a bunch of small southern businessmen networking together, proffering deals and, truth be told, doling out some trivial bribes, but primarily just watching out for each other's interests. The *Vigili* brigade was simply used as a kind of messenger service; we had great mobility, we were always driving all over the countryside and could easily deliver a letter of recommendation or a crate of fresh mozzarella or what have you.

I gripped the money tightly in my hand and then, just to get it out of sight, stuffed it in my pocket.

When we reached Casabasso and were driving through the main square, Renato suddenly slowed down the car and craned his head. "Isn't that the American?"

"Where?" I asked.

"There by La Buca, the billiards dive."

There were several guys standing in front of the pool hall, so it took me a few seconds to spot him—his thin frame, his brown hair, that blue polo shirt he often wore. His back was turned to me, but as Renato drove by I looked back and was sure it was Nico.

"I wonder what he's doing at La Buca this time of day," I said.

"Not fighting fires, that's for sure," Renato spit.

"You don't like him?" I asked.

"I don't trust him."

"He almost killed you, huh?"

"What, the train thing?" Renato said. "No, that's not it. That could've happened to any of us. Fucking engineer should've stopped the train when he saw the smoke. Instead the idiot went right on through like a bull on the run." Renato wrestled the car around a triple-parked truck. "Plus, Matteo, you were the one who was supposed to have made the call to the Báia to stop the trains."

That last comment stung me, and I protested, "I *did* call them. The *carabinieri* assured me. . . ."

"Oh, never mind about that," Renato interrupted. "I'm not blaming you."

"So, Nico?"

"I'm not blaming him for that either. Actually, I heard him screaming something and looked up right before the train blew its whistle."

"But I thought. . . ."

"No," Renato continued, "I said it's not that." He hacked a gob of spit out the window. "The American is trouble of a different sort."

"What do you mean?"

A traffic light turned yellow on us and Renato stopped; he was the only driver I knew who stopped for yellow lights. "I once knew a guy who could steal the rear window from a Fiat Spider without leaving a single scratch or fingerprint on the car," he said. "He was truly *furbo,* crafty. Pilfer the wedding ring right off your finger. There' s a lot of guys like that around here, so I grew up knowing how to keep my things safe, you know what I mean?"

"Yeah, so?"

"So on the day this American arrives I lose fifty thousand lire—you get my drift?"

"Kinda," I said.

"What are you, a moron?" Renato said. The light turned green and he jerked the car forward. "I've never lost a *centesimo* in my entire life."

"So you think Nico stole money from you? How?"

"If I knew how, I'd beat the shit out of the guy first thing."

"So you're not sure it was him?"

"You're a true genius, Matteo," Renato said. The rear wheel hit a curb as we turned a corner, and Renato cursed. Then we eased onto a straight-away and Renato floored it. "Just keep your eye on him, is all," Renato said, tapping his finger in a sinister way under his left eye. "He may be American, but he may be devious too."

The wad of lire bulged in my pants all day long like an unfamiliar limb. I felt like a man who had stuffed his pockets with stones before jumping into the river.

Chapter 4

As I've said, I disliked the American. He was unspeakably rude and had tried to blame it on me that the train almost crushed us at the fire along the railroad tracks. He might've stolen money from Renato. And as the days and weeks passed I noticed something else: Nico was a malingerer. He seemed to take off as many days, afternoons and evenings as he pleased, and rarely did he bother to give us any advance notice. During his first few weeks with the brigade he must have taken off as many hours as he put in. Tonino, Saverio, Enzo, and others in the squad shrugged it off—the Americano was a *volunteer,* they reminded Renato and me, not a full-time *vigile del fuoco* like the rest of us. Let him sightsee, visit museums, take some hikes in the countryside. We've got a beautiful country and he might as well enjoy it, they said. When he wants to fight fires, he'll fight fires. If not, we can handle it anyway.

But Renato wouldn't hear them. He scowled. The last thing we needed around here, he'd respond, was another unemployed slacker—and a foreigner at that—bumming off the Italian government.

About the time we first had these conversations—it was mid-May—there was a huge Class-C fire along the shore near Marina di Minturno. It was a Sunday, I remember, and it just so happened that it was one of those days the American had decided to take off. He'd left the firebase early that morning with his daypack and journals, saying he was going sightseeing. Renato wasn't around that time to stop him either—unless there was an emergency, Renato kept strict bankers' hours—and there was no protest from the rest of us. Since I wasn't a squad commander, I didn't feel like confronting him myself. What could I say? But the fact was that because Nico hadn't given us any advance notice, his absence left the squad one man short for the day. And sure enough, about three hours after Nico had gone, the radio crackled with a 10-13 at the seaside. As I climbed into the jeep with the rest of the squad—Tonino, Enzo, Saverio, Cesare, Luchetto and Pietro—I grumbled something about needing one more set of legs and arms, and everyone knew what I was talking about. Pietro grunted and said the American was only like one arm and one leg when it came to fighting fires anyway, and we all laughed and kind of shrugged it off.

Our attentions turned to the fire. It turned out to be *un casino,* a real whorehouse extravaganza. We could see the smoke, a thick white haze blowing inland from the Mediterranean, as soon as we crossed south of the city limits, and as we approached the *autostrada,* we saw traffic backed up for kilometers on the opposite side. It was a perfect Sunday for the beach, and it must have been packed; lines and lines of cars and campers were forcing their way north and west away from the blaze, and there was a tangle of angry drivers at the choke point leading to the Aurelia intersection. It seemed like no one was moving, and even at this distance, several kilometers from the flames, large white ashes were floating down from the sky like lost confetti.

As we exited the *autostrada* toward the marina, the host of cars got even worse and we had to muscle our way through. The drivers were using all traffic lanes—even those going the opposite direction—to flee the scene. Tonino was driving the jeep along the shoulder of the road and we were having a tough time of it. We could see heavy smoke pouring off the trees two or three kilometers to the south, and to crawl so slowly toward the fire was infuriating.

"*Brucia la pineta*!" Cesare suddenly realized. "It's the pine grove!"

This new bit of information made our skins itch. The pine grove was environmentally sensitive land, and federally protected at that. If the pine trees were on fire, it could be a national disaster.

Enzo stuck his head out the side window of the jeep and yelled at a driver who refused to make way. "*Ao!* Blockhead! Get off the shoulder!"

"What do you want!" the driver screamed. He hung his arm out the window and moved it up and down in a gesture of insult. Then he pulled over a centimeter or two. Tonino inched the jeep forward but still couldn't get by.

"Let's go, move that vehicle!" Enzo ordered the driver again.

"Can't you drive! Watch the mirror, guy!" the other driver yelled.

"Fold it in or lose it!" Enzo threatened.

"You know where you can go!" the driver said, folding in his side mirror and cursing.

After much time wasted in this way, we finally we made it to the edge of Marina di Minturno. At the main intersection we drove up to a municipal policeman who was lazily directing traffic.

"What's going on?" Tonino asked from the driver's window.

"There's a fire," the policeman replied. There was a bored expression on his face.

"Genius!" Tonino said. "What's the plan?"

The policeman looked up at us and thought about responding to the taunt. "How do I know?" he said instead, shrugging his slouched shoulders.

"What do you mean?

"I'm just directing traffic for Christ's sake!"

"Where's the brigade commander?"

"How should I know!"

"Have fun, officer!" Tonino said in parting, giving the policeman a mock salute.

We moved on, forcing our way as far as we could against the traffic. We finally pulled into a parking lot at one of the camping grounds near the beach, where the air was acrid with smoke.

"Tool up!" Tonino ordered as we piled out of the jeep. "Massimo, make sure the chainsaw is full of gas. Spread out but maintain visual contact."

There were no Corpo Forestale or city firemen or *Vigili del Fuoco* in sight, and among the citizens there reigned a strange mixture of panic and indifference. Most vacationers were rushing about gathering together their belongings in preparation to flee the area, but some had towels wound around their necks and were carrying day bags and floats toward the beach as though it were just another lazy Sunday.

The wind was sucked strongly inland off the water, feeding the flames, which were still about two kilometers to the south but moving steadily north toward us. Judging from the heat and smoke, we figured the umbrella pine groves all the way from Marina di Minturno south to Castèl Mondragone must have been a single wall of flame. Tucked among the groves were numerous seaside resorts, beach bungalows, villas and camping sites. Our job would first be to pound on all the doors to make sure every last soul had evacuated the premises, then think about finding a place to establish a firebreak to prevent the fire from sweeping north past us.

We moved laboriously south toward the main fire, keeping the sea road to our left and passing several families walking in the opposite direction, wet towels slung over their heads and shoulders. They had apparently abandoned their cars.

"Did you park your vehicles to the side of the road?" Enzo asked these people.

"The whole place is a parking lot!" one man answered roughly.

"How about your keys?" Enzo asked. "Did you leave your keys in the ignition?"

"Are you crazy, *vigile*?" the man responded.

"What if a fire truck needs to get through?"

"What fire truck?"

"Any fire truck!"

"I don't see any fire trucks here, *vigile*!"

We shook our heads and moved on, checking each door at all the villas and bungalows as we went. After a couple hundred meters we reached a tourist village which marked the very tail of the traffic line that stretched several kilometers all the way back to the Aurelia. Here we found a dozen cars and campers still trying to reach the main road—they didn't realize that vehicles had already been abandoned in front of them—and chaos reigned in the village. Tourists were running around screaming for their families and scrambling to pack what few items they could. To the south was nothing but smoke and heat, and the fire was rapidly shifting closer. The fumes grew dense and stung the eyes, orange-edged ashes floated everywhere and the roar of the fire was some rough beast skulking toward us.

A woman cradling a bundled-up infant hurried up to us. "It is true there are boats?" she asked.

"We don't know, Signora," Cesare answered her, "we just arrived."

"What should I do?"

"Walk the road north—to the left, understand—as fast as you can," Tonino advised her.

The woman hurried on. Her figure soon disappeared north into the smoke.

Finally we came across some *Vigili del Fuoco* from another brigade. Their badges indicated they were from Mongibello.

"What's the word, *compare*?" Tonino hailed them. "Where's the firebreak?"

"There's no firebreak," one of the *vigili* said. "We're evacuating the coast. By boat. Off shore. Send all civilians to the beach, the exit road is impassable. They're sending crews to the east to stop the fire at the sea road—if they can—or else at the Aurelia."

"Who's to the north?"

"No one, as far as I know."

"We'll check doors here and establish a line to the north, then."

The *vigile* turned up his palms and shrugged. "This place is toast anyway you turn it," he said.

We continued running from bungalow to bungalow checking doors. In one suite we found a little blonde girl sleeping on a cot. She was wearing a bathing suit with a neon-bright flower pattern and must have been about five or six years old. Saverio took her in his arms and carried her outside, but as we were walking away a brawny man came out of nowhere and asked us where the fuck we were taking his daughter. The girl said *Papi* and jumped into his arms, and the man, casting us a swarthy glare, turned and began walking toward the beach.

"You're welcome, you bastard!" Enzo yelled after him.

We checked the rest of the doors and, satisfied that everyone had been evacuated, regrouped the squad at our rendezvous point and decided to get the hell out of the area ourselves. The fire had moved up from the south to the edge of the village and set the entire canopy of trees aflame. I'd never seen anything quite like it. Flames poured downward out of the treetops like Greek fire. Pine cones as big as wine bottles were crashing down everywhere, and now and then we heard explosions we supposed were gas canisters many campers used for cooking. We weren't too happy about that, and to get out from under the trees and stay away from the campgrounds, we decided to follow the shore back north and look for a spot to dig the firebreak. At the sea's edge, large groups of evacuees were waiting in huge queues for the coast guard boats. The scene reminded me of clips from wartime Kosovo I'd seen on the television news.

We circled around to pick up the jeep. As we drove out to the main road we had to push two or three abandoned cars off the drive. We went northeast and stopped near a marsh, which at that time of year was nothing but a huge field of grass and reeds. Though it didn't look it, the field was actually more dangerous than the pine groves (where the fire burns over your head), but we had to stop the fire somewhere, and there was a little brackish inlet nearby that would help us contain the blaze. We positioned ourselves along the edge of the marsh and hoped the pines wouldn't send live ashes across it and luckily we were right that time and were able, several hard hours later, to stop the fire at the edge of the marsh.

Later on, through the firefighters' grapevine, we learned that the marina's underground sprinkler system may have been tampered with before the fire, and it seemed—though no one could be sure—that gas canisters had exploded in three dangerously key locations meant to maximize the fire's spread. It didn't take a genius to put three and three together: at the center of that triangle stood *Sabbiadoro*, a tourist village that had accumulated sizable debts.

Because fire is both an arsonist's method and his accomplice, arson is never a simple matter. Like a magician, fire erases its own footsteps even as it destroys what is to be destroyed. Here the justice system encounters an abyss. Lawyers can wag their tongues all they want about motives and modus operandi, but their threats have no teeth if the fingerprint on the matchstick cannot be submitted as evidence.

When we finally returned to the firebase from the marina late that afternoon, we found the American lounging on the command post steps writing in his journal. The clouds were pink and purple in the western sky, and orange sunrays slanted sharply across the compound.

"Eh, Americano, you missed a doozy!" Enzo said as soon as he climbed out of the jeep.

Nico looked tanned and relaxed. He closed his journal and stood up to stretch. He was wearing a bathing suit under a long black T-shirt. "What happened?" he asked.

"A fire, Americano! A big fire!" Enzo said, tossing down his tools wearily. "Where did you go?"

"I took the day off," Nico shrugged.

"I know that, Americano, but you missed a good one," Enzo said, shaking his head.

"A good one?"

"A big one," Pietro chimed in, "monstrous."

"Too bad," Nico said.

"Yes, too bad," Enzo echoed. He pointed at Nico's swimsuit. "Did you go swimming, Americano?"

"Sure I did."

"Where?"

"At the beach, of course."

"At the beach? Didn't you see the smoke? The fire was down at the marina! Huge flames! Smoke clouds! It was good training for you."

"Would have been," Pietro put in, "if he'd only shown up for duty."

"Cut him some slack," Saverio interrupted.

Nico glanced at Pietro without answering, then said to Enzo, "I was up at Cerveteri, it was *molto bello*. I didn't see any smoke."

Cerveteri was a good hour's train ride north. We nodded our heads; he probably wouldn't have seen anything from up there.

"Well next time," Enzo said ironically, trying to invoke an upbeat mood, "don't disappear when we have a nice fire planned. We've got to train you somehow."

Nico didn't get the joke. He gave us all a dark, hurtful look. "I don't need any more training," he grumbled. "I know what I'm doing." He abruptly turned his heels on us and shuffled off toward the barracks, obviously offended. Enzo tried to call him back to explain, but Nico just waved his arms in the air dismissively without bothering to turn around. I thought his reaction was puerile, all out of proportion. The sun was hitting the far horizon now, and his shadow stretched all the way across the compound. I put my boot on the shadow and ground my heel into the dirt.

I'm not sure what prompted me to look into his bags and steal the knife. I guess I felt in some twisted way that it was payback for the rude way he treated us, for his poor humor, for the way he insulted us by walking off. After turning his back on Enzo, Nico disappeared inside the barracks, only to stomp out a moment later smoking a cigarette and storm out the firebase gates.

From the steps of the command post, we watched him go. We all knew he'd gotten into the habit of hanging out some evenings at La Buca, the local billiards hall where Renato and I had spotted him the day I completed my first assignation. I watched him now marching along the dirt shoulder of the road toward town until his limbs became as small as matchsticks. Then I lost him.

I slumped down in one of the plastic chairs in front of the command post with the rest of the squad.

"Why do you think he goes over there?" Cesare asked no one in particular.

"What?" Massimo asked.

"The American," Cesare said, "why do you think he goes to La Buca?"

"Why shouldn't he go?" Enzo asked. "Maybe he likes to play billiards."

"I don't know," Cesare said.

"So there you have it," Enzo said.

Though that sounded a bit like a challenge, Cesare didn't take it up. We were too tired to bicker. We just sat there rubbing the stubble on our chins. Enzo lit a cigarette then changed his mind, carefully stubbing the butt out on the sole of his boot and slipping it back into the packet for later. The last of the daylight was slowly leaking out of the sky and I tried to enjoy the deepening of the twilight, tried to savor the satisfaction of having just conquered a horrendous blaze, tried to look forward to dinner at the Trattoria Tramontano—the restaurant where, thanks to Cavalier Mezzasoma's administrative finesse, the fire brigade ate its meals. But the breeze was blowing badly—it carried a rich, disquieting odor over from the cisterns and, worse still, the acrid smell of the disinfectant meant to quell the stench of the feces. I slapped at a sting on the back of my neck; the mosquitoes were coming out now. They breed in an open bucket fill (a water tank for helicopters) that sits in the center of the firebase, near the cement slab that serves as the helicopter landing pad. It was better to move around, force the insects to find you.

I got up and tried to walk off my low mood. A small dirt track skirts the firebase perimeter, and I made my way around that twice or thrice, until I realized I had a callous on my left ankle and knelt down to look at it. I guess a hot coal had gotten caught in the neck of my boot during the fire and eaten a hole in my sock. I stood up. I had stopped in front of the barracks where Nico kept his things. A lizard scuttled across the cement block steps, paused to look at me over his shoulder with a green eye, and disappeared. I glanced over my own shoulder; the rest of the squad was still lounging around on the command post steps. Tonino had opened a six-pack of Nastro Moretti, a local brand of beer, and they were passing around the warm cans. No one was paying me any attention. I slipped inside the trailer.

I had to wait for my eyes to adjust to the dim light. The barracks were hot, the air completely stifled. Large beads of sweat dribbled in my armpits as I stepped forward. Twelve bunk beds, their mattresses bare, were lined up in a military row. Lying on one of the mattresses was a sleeping bag and a large duffel bag made of blue waterproofed canvas. The bag was packed so tightly it resembled a huge blue pill. It was extremely heavy, and when I shook it I heard something that sounded like coins inside a metal thermos. There was a U-shaped zipper on the front of the bag where you could secure a daypack, but Nico had taken that with him. Two long outer pockets ran down along either side. I opened them; one was filled with socks, the other with underwear. The main compartment had a lock on it and the lock was secured, but attached to the zipper by a key ring hung a small penknife. I eased the knife off the ring, slid open the blade, and ran the tip along the seam of the zipper. It wouldn't give, no matter how I jiggled it. If I wanted to get into the bag I would have to cut at the threads that held the zipper in place, but I decided that would be too obvious, so I let it lie. I folded the blade closed and put the penknife in my pocket.

I thought I saw a shadow in the window, but when I spun around no one was there. The empty bunks near me loomed hauntingly, and I slumped down on one of the mattresses and thought about all the volunteers who had slept here over the years. As I've mentioned, the *Vigili del Fuoco* sometimes took on interns like Nico, yet since we had extra barracks on the firebase, we also hosted various volunteer groups, mostly youths, who were engaged in local projects not related to firefighting—thus the Polish girls, who came to restore Il Carpiglio's rococo statues in the gardens of Palazzo Sangiusto.

Though I remembered some of our international visitors quite fondly, lately I had tired of being a host. Over the years I'd become disenchanted with most of the volunteers. Like naive Peace Corps enlistments, they would arrive callow and starry-eyed, quixotic youths who thought they could put right the environment by digging some ditch, or who hoped they could rescue the *contadini* from poverty by installing an electric pump on a water well. And then, supersatisfied, they'd head off to complete their university studies. In short, they'd come for two weeks, pretend they were doing their good deeds for the planet, then simply depart. And perhaps I envied them their freedom to come and go, to have their excitement and when it stopped being exciting, to pack their bags and catch the next train to Roma without really having learned anything about what it's like to live on the edge of indigence, without prospects beyond grocery retail or crime, mired in the mistakes of the past, amid the same provincial people, the same complaints and narrow-mindedness. . . . Maybe these were some of the reasons I resented this American volunteer so much. But District Chief Mezzasoma had plans for me, I remembered. Mezzasoma would help me rise above all this.

I stepped back outside. Over by the command post the guys were laughing about something, and their voices floated to me in the evening air. I knew it was almost dinnertime and I suddenly felt ravenous. I hurried over to join the squad. As I drew closer, however, I noticed someone sitting in my seat. It was Nico. He hadn't gone into town after all. He must have taken a walk and come right back, and I knew he'd probably seen me coming out of the barracks where he kept his things. The penknife was right in my pocket. Nico stared hard at me and said my name as I stepped up to the edge of the group. I thought for sure he was going to ask me what I'd been doing in the barracks, but he didn't. Instead he leaned forward, wrestled a can of beer out of the case, and handed it to me with an unreadable grin like he knew something I might or might not want to know.

Chapter 5

Despite what Nico had said about not needing any more training, he wasn't exactly the kind of guy you were happy to buddy up with in the field, to stake your life on him. Partners are supposed to watch each other's backs, but with Nico you were forced to watch that he didn't get himself killed—or worse, endanger the lives of others. And it being an unusually hot spring, with late-May temperatures regularly topping thirty degrees, there were plenty of fires. Most were routine burns out in the low hills, ugly scars in the Mediterranean maquis, virtually all of which we were lucky enough to contain to about ten hectares or less. And while conflagrations like the one at Marina di Minturno might have overwhelmed a novice like Nico, we would have thought that fighting these other, medium-sized burns would make good practice for the American. That didn't seem to be the case, however. Nico was having serious trouble getting the hang of firefighting.

It wasn't a physical incapacity. Nico wasn't slow or out of shape—just the opposite, in fact. But he seemed—how can I put it?—*timid* in the face of fire. Not that he was scared of the flames. No, I didn't see fear in his behavior; indeed, he would often put himself in dangerous situations to try to stop the forward momentum of a blaze. So it wasn't fear—nor even timidity, now that I think about it. It was more that the American showed an unusual *respect* for fire. He sometimes seemed unwilling to disturb the activity of burning. Like a camper staring at a campfire, he would observe the flames in a kind of philosophical reverie, as if they were pages in a book he was trying to read. Such behavior struck me as something like daydreaming during a plane crash.

Observing how poorly Nico comported himself at burns, we thought that giving him a lesson on how to wield a *flabello* wouldn't hurt, so one evening while we were all lounging around on the dirt clearing at the firebase, Luchetto pulled a *flabello* from one of the jeeps. The *flabello*, shabby from much use, looked like a long branch of driftwood with a head of dried seaweed.

Luchetto demonstrated a slow-motion version of the correct swing, then handed Nico the tool. The American took a few lackadaisical swings at an imaginary flame.

Enzo jumped up from his seat. "Not like that!" he yelled, grabbing the *flabello* from Nico's hands. "Americano, you hold this thing like a virgin with a broom! But this no a broom! You're no a poking at mice, here, you're turning off fire. Look—"

Enzo dragged the wooden handle of the *flabello* across the ground, scraping a line in the dirt. "Try that!" he challenged, shoving the *flabello* back to Nico. "You must erase line."

Nico walked up to it, looked at us all with a smile, then swept the *flabello* across the line like he was mopping the barracks.

"He thinks he's playing golf!" Pietro jibed.

Enzo ran over, snatched the *flabello* from Nico's hands, and slapped vigorously at the line three times. The line in the dirt was gone. "That's how you do it, Americano! With feeling! With gusto, spirit!" He redrew the line and thrust the *flabello* back into Nico's hands. "Now you it again try—and put some energy in!"

Nico slapped three times, somewhat harder this round, at the line. When the dust settled, the line was still visible. Nico shrugged his shoulders.

Enzo was quiet for a moment; he scratched his head. Then he walked over to Nico and put a hand on his shoulder as if to console him. "That was better, Nico," he said gently, trying another tack, "just a little bit better. But you must remember, this is not *una frusta*"—he turned to me—"Matteo, how do say *frusta* in English?"

"Whip," I said.

"Weep," Enzo said. "This no weep. You no weepa the flames, you *sbatti* them *cosí*, like this!" Enzo wielded the *flabello* and pounded the ground. He was right, actually. Nico had been pulling back too much at the end of his swing. "You start here," Enzo demonstrated, swinging all the way back, "gather momentum here," he slowly swung over his head, "and smother the flame," and he showed how you twisted the head of the *flabello* across the ground for a fraction of a second. Then he handed the *flabello* back to Nico again. The American was about to give it another shot when Tonino, who had been following the entire lesson with much amusement, rose from his chair and took center stage.

"Wait!" Tonino said. He tugged Massimo on the sleeve and whispered an order in his ear.

"What, what?" Enzo was saying.

Tonino grasped Nico by the arm and began pushing him toward the weedy field at the far end of the firebase compound. Evening was coming on, and the weeds looked blue in the fading light.

"What's going on?" Enzo was saying.

"I'm going to teach the Americano how to *flabellare*," Tonino said. He turned to Nico. "Trust me," he said.

"*In Italia, non ci sono problemi*," Nico answered with a grin, echoing one of Tonino's favorite quips: "Nothing's a problem in Italy."

Tonino removed the orange bandanna he always wore around his neck, stood Nico in the middle of the weedy field, and blindfolded him. "You tell him when to take it off," Tonino instructed me. Then he handed Nico a *flabello*.

"Don't worry," I said flatly in English, "I'll tell you when to take off the blindfold."

Massimo rejoined us. He was carrying a gasoline canister. Tonino took the can and, with a live cigarette hanging between his lips, began pouring gasoline in a circle around the American. There were shouts, murmurs, protestations, agreements—all of which Tonino interrupted with a wave of his hand. When he'd completely surrounded Nico with a circle of gas, he took out his lighter, bent over and lit the ground. "Not until I say so, Matteo," Tonino said to me sternly.

The gas immediately flared up, followed by the surrounding grasses and weeds. We had to back up to avoid the fumes of burning gas that swirled toward us. The acrid black smoke rose into the dark sky, blotting out twilight.

"Say it, Tonino. Give the signal."

Tonino took a long drag from his butt. "Not yet."

Nico hadn't said a word. He stood in the center of the circle of flames like a sacrifice. He'd probably figured out what was happening—the smell of the gas fumes would certainly have given that away—but he didn't show any sign of nervousness. He gripped the *flabello* with both hands and spread his feet into a ready position. I thought I could discern the outlines of a smile on his face.

Tancredi yelled, "Say it, Tonino!"

"Wait," Tonino said.

The fire spread outward, pushing us back as though we were a crowd at a crime scene. The weeds were thick in patches and the flames reared up menacingly. Somewhere in the middle of the smoke stood the blindfolded figure of the American. I was sure he would faint in the thick fumes.

Tonino removed the cigarette from his lips and tossed it on the ground. He said, "*Adesso.*"

"Now!" I yelled. "Take off the blindfold!"

"Pretend the fire's your mother-in-law!" someone screamed.

Nico flung off the mask and threw himself at the flames with a feral energy that astounded us. Who would have guessed he could transform himself into a fire-eating beast? He beat down the flames as though he were revenging himself against some unforgivable wrong done to him, and yet there was a precise, almost scientific methodology to his movements—his bursts were full of passion and yet coldly efficient. He stopped the fire in its tracks, except that the ground where the gasoline had originally been poured wouldn't go out. Soaked into the dirt, the gasoline there burned low but steady, like the blue flame on a stove. When he'd put out the rest of the fire, the Americano stepped back into the circle of the flames, brandished the *flabello* above his head, and belted out a savage roar of triumph. We joined in the yelling. The twilight air was vibrant with a confetti of charcoal and ashes.

The next day, when Renato arrived at the firebase and saw the burned field, he said, "What the fuck happened over there?"

"Training exercises," Tonino answered with a grin.

That fire seemed to have cleansed Nico. He no longer went around all day with a scowl on his face, and he stopped writing so much in his journal and began showing some small interest in our activities at the firebase—chores, cards, soccer, practical jokes. Though he still kept a measured distance, I began thinking that maybe he wasn't as rude or asocial as I had thought at first. Maybe he was simply a reserved and introspective person, the kind of guy who liked to keep to himself for whatever reasons. We all have our reasons for doing things, for behaving the way we do, and really it's nobody's business to judge strangers, even if they're standing on their head in a rainstorm.

One quiet afternoon not long after the *flabello* lesson, I was surprised when Nico struck up a conversation with me. We were on the firebase and the barracks were clean, the hoses rolled, the jeeps swept out. Everyone in the squad was simply lounging around, finding ways to pass the time. I was sitting on the terrace of the command post flipping through an electronics magazine when Nico, who was stretched out reading in the sun nearby, said, "Do you know Ezra Pound?"

I looked up from the magazine. The rest of the brigade was absorbed in a game of *scopone*. The Americano was talking to me.

"Who?"

"Pound, Ezra Pound, the American poet who supported Mussolini and wrote the most difficult and damned beautiful poetry ever written."

I'd never heard of the writer; I shook my head.

"He supported D'Annunzio's independence movement up in Lago di Garda" —(I knew about that episode in Italian history—the failed attempt to found La Repubblica di Salò)—"and was captured by the victorious American troops and held in a detention cage on the via Aurelia near Metato to be prosecuted for treason. That's where he wrote his greatest work, *The Pisan Cantos*."

It was probably the longest sentence I'd ever heard him utter, and it seemed interesting, I wanted to see where he'd take it. "Songs?" I asked.

Nico's eyes widened and he sat up. "Not songs, poems. Beautiful poems." He tapped his finger on a page of the book in his hands.

I put down my magazine and was about to ask what about it, but Nico fired off another question.

"Do you know about Roman history?"

"A little bit," I said. Every Italian schoolboy and -girl went over that in middle school, but I didn't remember much.

"There's a guy named Numa Pompilius."

"I might have heard that name before," I said carefully.

Nico continued, "He was a Sabine king, famous for his founding of the vestal virgins, guardians of the eternal flame symbolizing the empire—who, if they let the fire go out, were buried alive. I forget the century, a long time ago. But what interests me is that Numa Pompilius is said to have been born of fire."

"How so?" I asked, still wondering about the virgins.

"Just born of fire, like a phoenix, I guess," Nico shrugged. "Emerged from the flames and was born."

"Where?"

"That's what I want to know. I've done some reading, you see"—(that didn't surprise me)—"and I'm pretty sure that Pompilius was born in and about these parts."

"Caserta?" I guessed.

"No, but not too far by. Nobody seems to know for sure." He put his hand up to shade his eyes and looked at me and said seriously, "I want to find the place. Do you know where Apollosa is?"

I knew. It was in a godforsaken stretch of countryside about eighty kilometers east of Casabasso.

"I'd like to head out there one day."

"Is that why you came to Casabasso?" I asked, trying to steer the conversation around. Everyone in the squad was curious about why the Americano had come to our small town and whether or not it was true, as rumor had it, that he'd had an Italian girlfriend. But Nico easily evaded my question.

"That's one reason," he answered casually enough. He placed his book on the ground and dropped a pen on it.

"And the other?" I asked.

"Who said there's only two?" he said, looking up at me and grinning mysteriously, almost coyly.

"So what are the others?"

"Well," he said with a full-blown smile—I think it was the first time I'd seen him smile like that—"this should be *quid pro quo*. If you'd like to know about me, then you'll first have to tell me"—here he paused and squinted his eyes—"why you guys tried to set me on fire the other night." He held a straight face for a second, then laughed. He was talking about the *flabello* lesson. I laughed with him.

"I could hardly believe it myself!" I exclaimed.

"That gave me some kick," he said. "You guys are totally nuts. *Gasoline?* I mean, do you do that to everyone?"

"No, that was a first. Consider yourself special."

"Done." He ran a hand through his hair and straightened his collar, made like he was a dandy grooming himself. We both smiled. Nico said, "I thought I was going through some kind of pagan initiation ritual."

"It was kind of like that," I agreed. "You've become one of us."

"Which means?"

"Which means . . . you're certified," I said.

"Certified?"

"A regular firefighter. *Ufficializato*. And now we can let you in on our secrets."

"Now *that*," he said emphatically with a broad smile, "is something I would like."

There was something in his voice that brought up my guard for a moment. I thought about my rides out into the countryside with Renato. I'd fulfilled one or two assignations while Nico was around, but I seriously doubted he had any notion of what was going on. Then I remembered the penknife I'd stolen from his luggage the previous week. I'd carried it in my pocket for a few days, then got nervous and stashed the thing behind the shelf clock in the radio room at the command post. I resolved now to get it back to him somehow. Maybe I'd drop it on the floor of the barracks when he wasn't around.

When I didn't say anything, Nico added, "You know, in English when you say someone is 'certified,' it means they're mad."

"Mad?"

"Insane, senile, crazy. We say, 'So and so has got their papers,' they're *certified*—the doctors have written them up."

"That's not what I meant," I apologized.

"I know, I was just saying . . ." he answered. He got up from his chair in the sun and moved onto the shaded steps near me. "*Fa caldo oggi*," he said, fanning himself. Then: "So anyways, where did you learn such good English, Matteo?"

"By listening to the Beatles," I answered with a grin.

Nico cocked his head. "Really? That's great!"

"Actually," I acknowledged, twisting the magazine in my hands into a roll, "my father pushed me into it." I suddenly recalled how once in a while my father would buy me English-language magazines—*Popular Electronics, Science Systems, Mechanics Journal*. He always told me I should study to become an engineer, but the most I'd made of his advice was a hobby in electrical tinkering and shortwave communications. The thought of my father immediately made me sad.

"That's cool too," Nico said matter-of-factly. "What's your father do?"

"He was a government official," I said, not hiding my emotion. I raised my face and looked Nico in the eyes. "Regional level, here in Campania. He died a while ago."

"I'm sorry," Nico said. He hung his head down. "Mine too." I thought I heard his voice shake. "Died when I was ten. Smoked himself to death."

It was as if his words shattered a pane of glass in front of me. The air seemed to fill up with palpable emotion. Nico and I studied each other's faces warily. Then I drew a breath and said, "Same with mine," and as soon as the words scraped across my throat I felt the tears well up and tried to push them back. I don't know what it was, exactly, that moved me so profoundly. Perhaps we've all experienced such moments, when you say something to a relative stranger that for whatever reason resonates unexpectedly within you. To be honest, I don't think it was so much grief over my father's death—that flock of birds had flown by close to a decade ago—but more of amazement, even sorrowful joy, that I had met someone whose father had died the same despicable death as mine. "Lung cancer," I managed to say.

"Yup," Nico nodded, his lips pressed together tight in a straight line. "That's a cruel reality."

I turned away from him and surveyed the firebase. The rest of the fire crew was silently absorbed in a card game, but the air around us seemed to be wavering with heat and humidity, and my heartbeats were footsteps pounding up a flight of stairs. Without saying another word, the Americano and I knew each other. We heard the racking coughs, the hiss of the oxygen tanks, we saw the black spots on the x-rays, the gaunt eyes and sunken cheeks and chest, we smelled the rank nicotine on our fathers' fingers.

To dispel the disturbing visions, I stood up and said, "Nico, I've got something to show you. Wait here a second." The penknife, after all, was just inside the command post, and I could always say I'd found it lying on the ground or something. I went into the radio room and reached behind the clock where I'd stashed it. All I felt was dust. I poked around with my hand, then removed the clock altogether. The penknife wasn't there. I tried to think where else I might have put it. I looked behind the radio, checked to see if it had fallen on the floor or onto one of the other shelves. . . . It was nowhere to be found.

I heard Nico calling my name. He appeared in the doorway a second later.

"What is it?" he asked.

"Nothing," I said, "I was just checking the shortwave radio."

"What did you want to show me?"

"Another time," I said.

He didn't ask, just shrugged politely. "That's fine." Then he put his hand on my shoulder and said, "Hey, *acqua passata,* water under the bridge, huh?" I was still thinking about the penknife, and it took me a second to realize he meant my father's death. I couldn't find words and just nodded.

There was some loud commotion outside and when Nico and I went out we saw Massimo, who'd been playing cards with the others in the shade of the medlar tree, rise up and push Enzo backwards off his chair. Enzo yelled, just breaking his fall with one arm. He immediately jumped up, angry but smiling with thoughts of revenge. He opened his canteen and shoved the flimsy card table aside to get at Massimo. Cards and paper cups flew in the air, chairs tipped over, there was a bedlam of shouting and cursing and movement and Enzo emptied the canteen over Massimo's head and ran off. Massimo took off after him. Then everybody else picked up their own canteens and ran and splashed and chased after one another, and when we weren't looking Saverio turned on the spigot hose and sprayed Nico and me. The water hit me like an alarm clock, shattering the tension and awakening me, at least fleetingly, to the jots of joy and laughter in our little corner of the universe, our simple, small, pre-Maggiore world.

To cry, to mourn, to repent—all are unsatisfactory. And just what kind of satisfaction do I expect, after all? I am alive, others from the squad are dead. It might have been prevented. We fly flags at half-mast, we play brass instruments at funerals, we erect marble monuments and white crosses and inscribe brass plaques with heroic words. Grandmothers tear out their hair. The devout march the streets, wailing shrilly and flagellating themselves with leather whips. Cherokees sever a finger for every son lost. The widows of India have the right idea, consuming themselves on their husbands' pyres, mingling ashes with ashes and ashes. . . . I yearn, but do not have the courage for that kind of sacrifice.

Chapter 6

I currently live in a garret not far from Casabasso's old city center. The main room is narrow and long, the ceilings sloped low to a row of curtainless windows. At one end is a niche that fits my bed and a shelf with some books and a lamp. The books were my father's—mostly literature: Balzac, Hemingway, Verga, Moravia, that sort of thing—as was the lamp. The lamp is brass and has a long clear bulb I've never changed because it's never given out. My father, too, used it for years. After coming home from his job at La Regione Campania, the regional government headquarters where he served as a minor official, he'd lie in bed and devote himself to reading. It took his mind off business, he told us. As a child I never grasped the import of that statement, but after fighting fires with the brigade, after getting to know District Chief Mezzasoma, I understand my father more. The way some Italians do business, it's better not to think about it.

Later on, while Father was ill, he devoured one novel after another until his lungs gave out on him. As soon as he finished reading one book, he'd send me or my sister, Patrizia, to the bookstore for another, scribbling titles and authors down on loose scraps of paper. When we'd return with the book, he wouldn't let us keep the change but dispatch us summarily with a wave of his hand. Then, propped on three pillows, he'd read well into the night, the small brass lamp glowing brightly beside his bedside spittoon. My father has been dead seven years now, and it's a wonder the light bulb hasn't spent itself yet. A thousand times have I inspected the filament—a tiny perfect spiral of silver suspended between the circuits like some graven image on a diminutive throne. As for that spittoon, my mother cradled it for three days after the funeral, as though it held my father's ashes. Then she set it on a high shelf in her bedroom and seemed to forget about it. A week later, one cloudy afternoon when all else was quiet, she lugged it out back and smashed it against the metal garbage bins, cursing foully.

I guess I owe it to my father that I've read a few decent books myself. He'd leave novels lying about the house haphazardly and it was inevitable that they'd catch my interest. One of the first books of literature I put my mind to was a Japanese work called *The Temple of the Golden Pavilion*, about a student who performs poorly in school and, in the end, sets fire to a famous Buddhist temple. I've always thought the student regretted what he did, that he wanted to put out the fire immediately after he'd set it, except that the flames had too quickly spread beyond his control. When I finished the book, I said to my father, "If only someone had been around to help him put out the fire!" At first my father laughed, but seeing that I was serious he changed his mood and, nodding his head thoughtfully, replied, "Beauty can be overwhelming." He'd say things like that from time to time—puzzling things, things that would jostle around in your head for days or years. My father always kept me thinking. I miss that about him.

Next to my bedroom lies the small kitchen, which has a bachelor's stove with two burners and a refrigerator so low I have to crouch to see into it. In the fridge is a bottle of water, the butt end of a salami, two cans of Peroni beer, four olives floating in brine, a carton of old milk, and a bag of espresso. I grab the salami, but it smells bad. Maybe I'll go to the grocer tomorrow; for now I'll make do. I take out the espresso, rinse and fill the small metal coffeepot, and put it on the stove. The blue gas flame hisses and breathes. I stand close to it, as though worshiping, until the coffee is forced up through the filter. It smells, beautifully, like sifted earth and wildfire ash.

I fix my coffee and sit down at my desk to flip through a pile of unopened letters and bills and that's when I see it. My heart jumps and blood flushes my chest. The return address indicates the Tribunale dell'Interno; it's from the federal courts in Napoli. When I slide a finger beneath the flap and open the envelope, my hand flinches at the sharp sting of a paper cut.

The summons states that in three weeks' time Sig. Matteo Arteli of via della Veretta, number 23, zone 00364, Casabasso, is to report to the chambers of the Honorable Filippo Ceruta-Levitas regarding possible criminal conduct allegedly occurring on August 16, 1999, in the township of Ruviano, Province of Campania. . . .

The blood has drained from my head. The roof of my mouth is dry. I lean back heavily in my chair. The tribunal inquest is under way.

I guess I shouldn't be surprised I've been called in to testify, though I already said everything I have to say about Maggiore during the seemingly interminable postfire reports and debriefings a month ago. That phrase about *possible criminal conduct* worries me some, but I try to convince myself it's standard legal language. The inquest is likely to be routine, pro forma. It's the deaths, of course, that warrant a fuller investigation than is normal. Five firefighters—Lorenzo Donetti, Saverio Da Silva, Massimo Carrone, Pietro Posini, Renato Chiarine—have lost their lives. And the *contadino*, the farmer found halfway up the Punti Cliffs, I forget his name. Anyway they'll want to get my version of it, is all. The squad's method of deployment, our reaction time, the strategy we formulated in the field, wind conditions, on-site terrain, and the like.

As for the origin of the fire, I know as much and as little about that as the next guy. *Non è dal fiammifero che nasce l'incendio, ma dalla foresta,* as we say around here. It's not the match that starts the fire, but the forest itself—which is to say, fires are the fault of droughts and high temperatures, the wood on the ground and the oxygen in the air, the volatile, ready triangle of wind and fuel and heat. Fire is nature cannibalizing itself for inscrutable reasons all its own.

I light my third or fourth cigarette of the day and blow a breath of warm smoke into the warm air. My lips pull hard on the butt. Ash crumbles off, gray and weightless, into my lap. The corners of my mouth and chin collude in a profound frown. I am alive. It must be past ten. The coffeepot is empty.

I tilt my cup up at an unreasonable angle and stretch out my tongue, yearning for the deep brown dregs.

I tape a large map of Mount Maggiore to the wall of my living room. Though I stare at the map for long hours, it tells me little—and in fact raises more questions than it answers. Where, exactly, was the fire started? Did the squad descend too far down into the gorge before turning back up the slope? Would the two-way radios have made a difference? How was the wind blowing when Nico lit the backfire? What was the *contadino* doing at a thousand meters on the Punti cliffs? On paper, the cliffs look like accidental scratches and random dots. I stare at the map for two days straight. The topographical lines swirl in my vision, and the air in my apartment grows stale, choked with cigarette smoke.

When I can keep myself cooped up no longer I venture out onto the streets of Casabasso—any street that doesn't lead to the firebase, because when I think about the brigade my heart sinks like leaded fishbait. I haven't been back to the firebase since the disaster on Maggiore—almost a month ago. Maybe I'll never go back. I've heard that Tonino and Cesare have already returned to duty, but—like Tancredi and Luchetto—I don't feel I could face up to that. There'd be a new crew on duty—replacements—and it just wouldn't be the same without those who were lost, without Enzo, Saverio, Pietro, Massimo, Renato. Besides, how could I possibly explain my own presence? What words could I say to hide my self-disgust and shame? I miss them, I miss sitting around with them watching the shadows creep across the ground. I miss our bad jokes and unwitty conversations, our common hungers and our petty tiffs, I miss our shared exhilaration at the unpredictable fire calls that broke the monotony of our long afternoons. But for complicity, for cowardice, for grief—I cannot go back.

Loath to encounter anyone from the brigade on the streets, I steer clear of the main boulevard and avoid the shortcuts and back roads I know the fire squads like to take on their way through town. Instead, I wander for hours along obscure side streets and alleyways and frequently find myself in unfamiliar parts of town: decrepit shopping districts crowded with magazine kiosks, tobacco shops, cheap shoe stores and discount clothing retailers that choke the sidewalks with racks of gaudy fabrics. The old Jewish ghetto with its Hebrew signs and the buzz of Yiddish in the air. A bustling neighborhood of meat markets and metal workshops, the streets littered with metal scrapings, scraps of animal flesh cooking on the cobblestones in the heat. I explore sunny residential areas teeming with schoolchildren or navigate a vacant maze of blind *vicoli* leading to cobblestone plazas filled with Gypsies and North Africans. I realize with mild astonishment that I too can now be counted as one of the forgotten and displaced. I haven't yet told Cavalier Mezzasoma, nor anyone else, that I've decided to resign from the *Vigili* brigade. I turn a corner in the street and angrily kick my way through a smatter of pigeons.

I've walked similar streets with Nico. As we became friends we spent some time together exploring parts of town I rarely visited. It's funny how you can live in a city for half your life and think you know every inch of it, only to have some visitor arrive and give you an eye-opening tour of your own stomping grounds. But that's exactly what Nico did for me one day at the end of an afternoon shift. He tugged me on the sleeve and whispered, "Hey, Matteo, I want to show you the most beautiful woman in the world," and who could resist? We walked downtown and he guided me to a place I had never paid much attention to before—the Teatro di Giulia, our famed regional opera house. As we stood in front of it, Nico pointed up at one of the building's wings, a glass atrium with neoclassical trappings edged in gold, and said, "That's where they filmed *Star Wars*. You know, when they rescue the princess."

I nodded. I didn't tell him I hadn't seen the film. But I remembered when George Lucas and his crew had come to Italy a few years back. I'd read about it in the papers but had never actually seen the production. Despite all the American stardom, it had all been conducted pretty low-key.

Nico then steered me beneath the front portico of the opera house and stood me in front of a poster and she was indeed beautiful: *Cecilia Bartoli, mezzo soprano,* the poster read. Her eyes were lowered seductively and her lashes were long and curved. A blue velvet gown fell off her shoulders and you could see a strong cord in her neck, the bold line of her collarbone leading down to the white shadows of her breasts. I'd always thought of opera divas as chunky, but this one was indeed pristine. I whistled softly.

"Not such beauty since Maria Callas," Nico said. "I actually saw her in Milano—Cecilia, I mean. She sings like a siren. Divine coloratura."

"La Scala?" I asked.

"The one and only," he said dreamily.

Still now, I can only try to imagine Nico at Milano's world-famous Teatro alla Scala. His best American clothes—a button-down shirt with clumsy breast pockets and large seams—among those baroque flourishes, the tuxedoed men straight and stiff as bourbons, the ladies floating in chiffon dresses cut low on the breasts, the tentative murmurs of the orchestra coming from the pit. What arc of events and triumphs, I wonder now, led the boy named Nicolas Fowler from a basement in Pittsburgh to the great cosmopolitan halls of opera? I heard they burn torches along the theater's garden pathways at nighttime, for their fêtes champêtres. And I can picture the garbage cans out in the back alleyway, those big green plastic boxes like they burned at the Genova summit. I realize now there must have been lots of paper in there, costume scraps, wood torn down from the Verdi set. Plenty of combustibles. That small fire at La Scala happened . . . nine months ago, I think it was. It could have been him.

That afternoon as we toured the city by foot, Nico told me about some of his other travels in Italy, about his visit to Salò, Lago di Garda. He visited D'Annunzio's decadent mansion, with its dark fascist stylistic flourishes, the bathroom with a thousand blue bottles. D'Annunzio wrote a book called *Il Fuoco,* and Nico said he was writing a book too—a series of poems on the burning of heretics. Bruno Giordano. Beatrice. Joan of Arc. The Salem witch trials, the Waldensians. Galileo, almost. He wrote on the train going down to Rome—which was a beautiful city, he said, especially all the travertine, *and*—he added enthusiastically—he'd had a chance to toast Bruno's statue in the Campo dei Fiori with a glass of Sangiovese. But above all, it was in Firenze where he found heaven. He learned in Firenze all there was to know, he told me. There was a woman, of course—*una italiana* who was studying to be an ecologist. Adina was her name. They crossed the Ponte Vecchio holding hands twice a day and traveled to Tuscan beaches and the Umbrian mountains, as well as to industrial sites, mines, power stations, nuclear plants—Adina was an active protestor on environmental issues. They went to Genova for the World Summit, and this girl's friends, to prove to Nico that they were serious, torched a Porsche right in front of his eyes. Nico almost got hit in the head with a tear-gas canister when the *carabinieri* showed up. From there it was west to Venezia for cooling off, then back to Firenze and her museums, cafés, musical soirées. As we walked and spoke, I tried to imagine his whirlwind travels, tried to picture him hoisting a picket sign in Genova, sipping wine in Verona, lighting matches in train compartments zipping along the Po at 150 kilometers per hour.

"You people," Nico was saying—something about Bruno Giordano again, how he addressed the crowds in Campo dei Fiori before he was burned at the stake—"you Italians practically have a monopoly on fire—and I mean that in a good way. You put it to use—know what it's good for, and put it to use. That's something I'd like to learn."

"So you're here to learn from us?" I asked.

"Learn or burn, isn't that what you say?" He winked as he said this. "And maybe teach you guys a thing or two. We Americans are the ones who came up with the 10 A.M. rule, after all. And we invented smoke jumping and defensible space . . ." Nico stopped suddenly in the street. "Hey, do you want to go play some billiards?"

I declined. I knew the place Nico had in mind, that dive called La Buca. I remembered seeing him there the day of my first assignation with Renato. I knew the crowd there too, or rather I knew what type of mob hung there. Not that I despised the sans-culottes or anything, but those punks were way over the line. Plus it was basically a nursery school for the underworld. My mother had successfully steered me away from that path a long time ago, when I was still a schoolboy. I couldn't see myself at that dive, among that pack, and I wondered what Nico got out of it and how he got along with those guys.

"I think I'm gonna head over there anyway," Nico said. "You don't mind?"

I shook my head. "Of course not," I said. "I'm supposed to meet Renato later on anyway," I fibbed.

We walked a few more blocks together. I was still trying to think of a way to warn him about the riffraff in that billiards place without sounding like a schoolmarm, when Nico stopped to turn toward the pool hall and say good-bye. He clapped me on the shoulder in parting. "When you see Renato," he added ironically, "give him my regards."

As I watched him go, I thought again about what Renato had said to me some time back, about how he'd lost his money the day Nico arrived and that I should keep an eye on him. Renato certainly tried to. But while I was still wary, I didn't necessarily agree with him anymore. I figured Nico just enjoyed playing billiards, that his hanging out at La Buca pool hall was simply his way of experimenting with a rebellious crowd. He could probably take care of himself and stay out of trouble. And as for Renato's continued ill-feelings toward the American, I had to treat that as something personal between the two of them, between Renato and Nico. There wasn't a shred of evidence that it was anything other than that. I swear I had no idea at the time about those other cans of worms, not a clue. About the darker sides of men and what those darker sides could make me do, I was as ignorant as a goat at the teat.

But what will I tell the magistrate, the judges? Before I appear at the inquest of the Tribunale dell'Interno, I must know where I stand on Mount

Maggiore, know where to draw the lines in the diagrams of our disgraces. Perhaps above all, I must learn to paint Nico's portrait, to distinguish between how I saw him and how he really was, and how and where and when the perception and the reality diverged or converged throughout the course of the summer. For to understand this story you must understand this, that his personality was a wild fennel you peeled layer by layer by layer—not realizing until you've peeled the last layer that layers were all there ever were.

Chapter 7

Nico's Italian was curious, full of offbeat rhythms and rubato accents I couldn't quite place. He didn't speak Italian like an American—his pronunciation wasn't soft. His vowels rang out and his "ch" *shshed* like the Florentines' and his r's rolled and he held his double consonants. Yet despite such facility, there rang an odd lilt, a distinct foreignness, in his voice. He frequently inverted his modifiers or employed odd syntax, saying things like, "Give you to me the salt, if you would kind so be," or "I don't speak well with your tongue of Italy," or "So the fire liked you today?" Still, his Italian was very good—so good that I suspected he frequently pretended to understand much less than he actually did.

As I've said, it was thanks to the negotiations of the brigade's district chief, Cavalier Mezzasoma, that fire crews on duty were entitled to take their meals at a restaurant in town called the Trattoria Tramontano. *Vigili del Fuoco* squad members receive next to nothing in terms of salary—less even than cleaning women, I can tell you—and the gratis food was the government's way of getting us to stop grumbling about our pitiful paychecks. As a brigade volunteer, Nico of course joined us often at the Tramontano, and the generous helpings of *suppli,* calamari, *fritto misto,* and other Neapolitan delicacies seemed to animate him, make him talk. I guess the wine he drank loosened him up too, for he liked his wine very much. (I never once remember him drinking plain water; he even poured some powdery substance into his canteen before putting it under the spigot.) And so through his bantering, little by small, he captured the squad's attention at the table. He opened up to us, asked us questions, and joked around and listened to what we had to say.

I was flattered that he sought my opinion on fire matters, for he would frequently ask me what I thought about the latest blaze—fire being, of course, his favorite subject. How he adored discoursing on fire! At each evening meal he would recount the day's fires step by step, making fun of us if we'd let the flames get out of hand, or expressing wonder at the size or speed or character of the latest burn—to describe which, like a physicist naming subatomic particles, he invented his own peculiar vocabulary, a unique poetic jargon. He used words like "supreme" and "spin" and "flowering" and "mesmerizing" and "inspired" to talk about flames and fires. One evening he even compared a small burn we had extinguished that morning to a brioche.

"What do you mean?" one of the squad asked.

"A brioche, that's a soft thing you eat in one bite," Nico said. He waved his hand in a gesture of dismissal. "The fire was a piece of soggy toast, it was boring, too easy. What do you think, Matteo?"

"It's a good thing we got there when we did," I said, "—*early.* It only takes a spark to start a conflagration."

Grinning, he called me Smokey Bear. Then he poked a cigarette between his lips, struck a match, and inclined his head forward to meet the small triangular flame.

"We stopped it before it reached the chaparral," I continued, "and the winds were down."

Nico dragged on the butt and, exhaling, said, "You know what you're talking about." His words came out thick, palpable with smoke. He flipped the match onto his plate. "I'll have to try harder next time," he said—a statement I dismissed at the time as another harmless linguistic error.

Pietro and Massimo encouraged Nico to join the squad's pickup soccer matches. We played—in our large black work boots, because we thought it would be a good way to train—on the ragged field at the far end of the firebase compound, which was still dusty with ashes from when Tonino set fire to the weeds for Nico's *flabello* "training" exercise. Two neon-orange firefighter hats marked the goals at either end. Nico said he'd never kicked a soccer ball in his entire life and we thoroughly believed him. He could neither dribble nor trap the ball, nor could he defend one-on-one. Though he tried hard, it was just too easy to fake him out and dribble past him or, if he had the ball, simply steal it away from his feet. But he did have the knack of anticipating passes—something he said he learned watching someone named Scottie Pippen play basketball—and he could disrupt the opposing team's midfield play. He also had a decent one-touch pass and could whiz by his defenders with a gazelle's speed, which meant that, assisted by the right teammate, someone like Saverio or Cesare, he could help get the ball up the middle into the red zone and maybe take a shot. His shots on goal were competent, more or less on target, if somewhat lacking in power. What more could we expect of an American?

Another day he surprised us by asking to be dealt into a hand of *scopone,* a Neapolitan card game. (One long afternoon, at his request, I had explained the rules to him; he always watched us playing.) We paired him with Massimo and dealt him in against Tonino and Enzo, more for our amusement than anything else—as card partners, Tonino and Enzo were the undisputed masters of the game—and it turned out Nico instinctively understood the risks and odds pretty well. In forty minutes he and Massimo lost only about a pack of cigarettes, the preferred gambling currency in the squad. But Tancredi immediately saw the Americano's potential and, after that initial game, brought his own pack of cards to the firebase and, crouched in the shade under the medlar tree, began coaching Nico on the finer points of the game. Tancredi was a shrewd player, and he'd long been looking for a suitable partner so he could challenge Tonino and Enzo. He'd tried everyone in the squad, but no one could live up to his extravagant expectations. He hoped he could shape Nico into the partner he'd always dreamed of, and he wasn't disappointed. Nico even exceeded Tancredi's expectations.

"The Americano is solid," Tancredi told us, out of the hearing of Tonino and Enzo. "Amazingly, he doesn't make mistakes like all of you losers do. He takes risks, yes, and sometimes he loses because of those risks, but he doesn't make stupid mistakes like you guys. And there's one other thing. He's completely unpredictable, he doesn't discard like a Venetian. I've never seen anyone discard the way he does. At first it really irked me, but now I'm getting to see the shrewd logic to it. He never fails to surprise me. And whenever he surprises me big time, then I know we're gonna win big."

We watched them play and corroborated what Tancredi had said. Nico seemed to throw the strangest cards at the strangest moments—a *due di coppe* when you'd expect a king, an ace when you'd expect a six, the *sette bello* when you couldn't remember anymore who had thrown sevens how many times. At first Tonino and Enzo thought the Americano was making big mistakes, but when they started losing they changed their tune.

"Aw, the Americano's got all the luck!"

Triumphant, Tancredi swept up the cigarettes and tucked them in his pocket.

"What're ya gonna do with those anyway," Enzo whined, "you don't even smoke."

"No, I don't," Tancredi answered, "but *you* do." He slapped Nico on the back. "Bravo, Americano!"

With the notable exception of Renato—who, holding his grudge, found the American undisciplined and frowned on his excessive diary keeping—almost everyone in the brigade got along with Nico. Of course Renato had told the squad about losing his money, but they all just mocked him for trying to blame it on the Americano. Massimo took Nico for spins through the winding hill roads on his Suzuki 450, Saverio gave him some pointers on fashion, and Cesare brought him magazines—outdated issues of *L'Espresso, Car Mechanic, Chi, Playboy,* and *National Geographic* that Cesare took from his father's barber shop. Luchetto and he exchanged CDs of Alanis Morissette and Francesco De Gregori. Pietro explained the gambling tickets to Nico, and whenever we went into town, those two would stop off at the *tabacchaio* to purchase SuperLotto or TotalSoccer forms. Though they'd spend hours at the firebase devising strategies, poring over the forms like high school students memorizing the periodic table, they never won enough lire to buy even a broomstick.

And then there was he and Tonino. I wouldn't call it a friendship exactly, but ever since Tonino had taught Nico how to *flabellare* by setting fire to the weeds in the far field, he seemed to take a genuine liking to the Americano, and the two had established a kind of rapport. They were both loners, both mavericks of a sort, and perhaps recognizing this in one another they came to some mutual understanding between themselves, the kind of understanding that exists only between two people who see themselves mirrored in the character of the other.

Not far from Casabasso, for instance, there's a joint Italian-American military base that regularly conducts training exercises in Campanian airspace. From the firebase we could often hear the jets as they blasted across the sky on their boisterous flights up and down the coast, and Nico, I remember, had a special ability: besides Tonino, the Americano was the only one of us who could visually track the flight path of the jets as they streaked across the sky. The thing was, these state-of-the-art jets—U.S.-built F-series Tomcats flying joint American and Italian colors—moved much faster than the speed of sound, so that by the time most of us heard them coming they had already passed us by, and we'd gaze, in the direction from which the sound had come, at a stark blue sky empty of all but our expectation. Most of the time you couldn't even tell where the sound was coming from, north or south, east or west—there would only be a diffuse roaring, and where your eyes would expect the plane to appear in the sky floated nothing but some ephemeral, vague wisps of cirrus as insubstantial as cigarette smoke.

But Nico and Tonino, they had a special knack, they could always point out to the rest of us (if we were quick enough) the jet that was nothing more than a metal speck glinting in the sunshine high, high overhead—"Look how it's diving!" Or while the rest of us remained absorbed in a game of *scopone,* Nico and Tonino would lift their eyes surreptitiously and exchange a word or a glance between themselves, and only then would the sound of the jet—flying low this time, hugging the peaks and troughs of the mountains—reach our otiose ears.

"You're dull," Tonino would say to us, "the Americano is quick. If it came to a snap decision at a burn, I'd rather have Nico by my side."

So we came to trust him. Despite his eccentricities, he could partner up at any blaze with any of us, and with me especially. It must have been my English—not that it was excellent—which made him feel most comfortable around me. I guess it gets tiring after a while to fish constantly for foreign words, to try to arrange a strange syntax to express even the most basic sentiments—I'm on the hungry side, my stomach feels queasy, I miss my home and family. So it was language that brought us closer together, that

Survival

59

oiled the gears of our friendship. And it put me on a better footing with the rest of the brigade as well—I was always being asked by the squad *how do you say this* or *could you translate that* or *what did that Americano just say?*

Enzo was especially annoying in this regard. He always wanted to be in the center of things, and it irked him to no end whenever he wasn't sure what was being said. He insisted that Nico speak Italian, mostly because Enzo got a kick out of Nico's foreign accent. He said the Americano sounded like a talking G.I. Joe, and when Nico picked up on some of the lingo we used over the shortwave radio (which was so powerful we sometimes picked up transmissions in Arabic and Greek), Enzo coached him and began letting him recite commands into the main transmitter and taught him how to use the two-way radios. That was how Nico learned to use the portable units. We would teach the Polish girls how they worked, too; they would bring one to the palace gardens with them while they restored the statues, and we would call Katja and Lyn every now and then to flirt and shoot the breeze. Our chatter with the Polish volunteers, I realized only later, might have been one reason the portable radios ran out of battery power on the slopes of Mount Maggiore. . . . That idea sticks in my throat like a cumbersome pill that won't go down.

These thoughts remind me of something else, something about Nico that I thought nothing of at the time: he knew an awful lot about circuitry and could dexterously manipulate small electronic devices. I discovered this one day when Enzo, Nico, and I radioed the north watchtower on the old Grundig shortwave housed in the command post. During the transmission I noticed that one of the channels wasn't working properly, and when we'd finished talking I unscrewed the panel of the console and eased off the backing. Dust, wires, resisters from the 1950s. I cleaned it some but didn't see any obvious problems, so I began checking the connections with a circuit meter. Nico, who through his comments proved he knew something about volts and ohms, watched me. His presence there in the radio room slightly unnerved me, though; I still hadn't found his penknife, and I worried that it would suddenly turn up, that he would find it before I had a chance to give it back to him. I almost hoped the thing was lost forever.

After about five tries with the resistance meter I located the broken switch. I unhooked the wires, unscrewed the mooring, and pulled out the faulty part.

"Guess this is bad," I said holding the small switch up with my fingers.

"Let me see it," Nico said.

"I don't have anything that small," I said, looking at the size of the screw on the switch and handing it to him.

"I do."

Nico went to the barracks and came back with a small plastic box labeled MicroTools. The set was full of small instruments designed for fixing telephones, computer motherboards, small circuitry, watches, and the like. Nico chose a tiny Phillips and carefully took the switch apart. One of the contact points was worn down, so he carefully built it up with a miniature soldering iron, snapped the switch back together, and put it back into the console. It worked.

"Bravo," I congratulated him, truly impressed.

"It was nothing, really," he said, as he repacked his tools neatly in their case. I followed him from the command post back into the barracks and watched him put his things in order. Nico was an extremely neat person, almost to the point of compulsion. His luggage was meticulously organized. His large duffel bag seemed to have a hundred pockets secured with zippers or Velcro flaps or sturdy buttons—some even with combination locks. Each compartment held a different type of clothing—his slacks went here, his shirts there, his T-shirts there—and his underwear was rolled up into little balls like Vienna sausages. He owned a lot of gadgets too—a whiskey flask, a classic silver windproof lighter and a set of waterproof matches, a sewing kit, and a sturdy box containing an antique watch collection, coiled wires, and an assortment of electronic parts. Of course I didn't recognize the potential of these objects at the time, how batteries could lie in fields for days or weeks, how watches could be wired into timers, how short circuits could produce tiny electric sparks.

In the compact kangaroo pouch he strapped to his belly and took to fires, Nico kept a pair of binoculars, a Swiss Army knife with a built-in orienteering compass, a "spy" camera smaller than a pack of cigarettes, and a first-aid kit that included some unmarked tube that looked like toothpaste.

"Where's your toothbrush?" I joked as he finished putting away his tools.

"Where's my what?"

I picked up the unmarked tube and opened it. It was more liquidy than I'd thought, and smelled like camphor.

"That's not toothpaste," Nico said. "Don't put that on your tongue, Matteo."

He gently removed the tube from my hands.

"What is it, burn lotion?" I asked.

Nico shook his head no. "It's fire," he said simply.

It took me a few moments, but finally I realized what it was: pyrophoric paste, an incendiary chemical. I'd read in a magazine that forest rangers sometimes used it to light backburns or controlled blazes, but I'd never handled or seen it myself. I guessed it was something American firefighters were trained for, though to me, carrying it around seemed about as smart as strapping a small bomb to your torso. How was I to see the future back then? How was I to know that little tube of unmarked potion would save my life?

"Sometimes," Nico way saying, "you have to fight fire with fire. At least that's what they taught me at school." He paused to tuck the tube back in his bag, then looked up and saw the question on my face. "I studied forestry for a while at Cornell University, before they booted me out . . ." he began to explain.

"Booted?" I asked.

"Kicked. Expelled."

"*Ho capito*, I understand."

"Kicked me out for—" here he paused, looking out the windows toward the mountains, "—let's say, 'for writing obscenities on the windows of the skull.'"

I smiled but didn't know what he meant, so I waited for him to go on. And though it was hot inside the barracks, Nico sat down on his bunk and began talking. I sat on the mattress next to him. At Cornell, he said, he'd been a physics major (which surprised me, since I'd thought he was a shoo-in for literature), and in his junior year he met that Italian girl, Adina, at some political rally. Adina was a foreign exchange student from Firenze, and they became close companions. She was studying chemistry, and the two of them got in trouble for something having to do with one of the chem labs—an experiment gone awry, he said, assuring me it had all been a big misunderstanding. But the university administration wouldn't listen, and what could he do? After he was expelled, he came out to Italy to visit Adina and stayed with her for some months in Tuscany, though their relationship eventually turned sour.

"The in-laws?" I inquired, thinking that the family might have had something to do with it.

"No, nothing like that," Nico replied. "I never even met her family. It was just that Adina was too . . . political. She put politics in front of beauty, and I put beauty in front of politics." He paused, fiddling with a zipper on his bag. "Have you ever heard of GILT?" he asked.

"What's that?"

"Gruppo Internazionale per la Liberazione della Terra."

I'd never heard of the organization.

Nico said, "They're some radical fringe group. Environmentalists, based in Firenze. They want to free the earth from capitalist development. Remember that big hotel that was knocked down in Tuscany a few years back? They fought for that."

"Is that what your girlfriend Adina was a part of?"

He nodded yes. "Too extreme, so leftist they were fascist."

"So how did you end up with our brigade?"

"Life is part intention, part fate, part accident."

The words seemed to hang in the stifling air of the empty barracks. I guessed they were true. I nodded and glanced around the barracks and out the window. "It's boiling hot in here," I commented. But still neither of us moved. It was as though we had attained a spell of some kind, as if the heated barracks were a sort of Indian sweathouse, a sauna we willingly suffered. We sat silently on the bunks for a long time. You could hear voices outside but not what they were saying—the squad going about their usual stuff. Some sparrows chirped in a nearby tree. Finally, in a quiet voice, Nico turned to me and said, "Hey, Matteo, I want to ask you something."

"What is it?" I asked.

Nico rubbed his palm over some stubble on his chin and cheeks and said, "Why did you look in my duffel bag that day?"

Taken aback, I tried to smile, but I could feel my face turning red. "What?" I stammered.

"Like two or three weeks ago, the day of the fire at the marina, the seaside. That evening, when you guys came back and I went to take a walk. What did you find in my duffel bag?"

I could feel sweat in my armpits now, and I moved my shoulders uncomfortably. I said as flatly as I could, "I don't know what you're talking about, Nico."

"C'mon, Matteo." He punched my shoulder lightly. "Absolute truth is, I'm not mad about it at all. I know you guys were just curious."

Though he was smiling, I wasn't sure if he meant what he said or whether it was some kind of a rhetorical trap. How could anybody not care if someone went through their bags? I continued to deny any involvement.

Nico sighed and said, "Luckily, all I keep in the outer pockets are socks and underwear. But I know you Italians: locks are nothing but puzzles for you to solve. I lost a penknife on the train coming down here—stolen right out from under my nose somehow. Look, I'm not holding it against you. Someone put you up to it. Renato maybe? Or maybe it wasn't even you. But when one of you opened my bag, what did you guys learn about me?"

At the mention of the penknife, a cramp shot through my stomach. I'd rifled a dozen times through the radio room where I'd stashed the damn thing but hadn't managed to find it. I'd thought Nico hadn't even noticed it was missing, but now I felt like my pants were on backwards, and I shifted my body nervously. I've never been a good liar. He saw I was uncomfortable.

"Let's drop it," he said. "Okay, I'll drop it." He slapped his hands on his knees. "But I want you to know, I think we all have things to hide, every last person on the planet. And my secrets may not be half as interesting as yours—I mean you Italians." He took his shirt off. "Let's go outside," he said. "I have to work on my tan lines."

Though it must have been thirty-two degrees out in the sun, when I stepped out of the barracks into the open air, I felt like I had happened into a cool river washing me of my sin. I was wrong again. A few days later the penknife got its revenge.

Chapter 8

Unlike most Americans, who wrap themselves up like Bedouins or smear white lotion on their faces and forearms at the tiniest beam of sunlight, Nico was not shy of the intense Mediterranean heat. While the rest of us sweated it out in the terrace shade trying not to move, Nico would drag a chair out into the sunlight and strip off his shirt, his uptilted face following the course of the rays like a sunflower. Beads of perspiration would trickle down his brow and his skin would turn ash-black. Yet when he moved back into the shade (with an exaggerated look of relief, as if he had just stepped into an air-conditioned room) his skin would bounce back to a cool almond color, his teeth moon-white behind ruddy smiling lips. Sometimes, reclining in the full sunlight, he'd sport a pair of dark-green aviator sunglasses for reading and writing, and for a few hours afterward his eyes would be circled by two pale areas, pallid halos that accentuated the darker bags which nagged him beneath his eyes, those haggard eyes of the tortured insomniac or onanist. I was amazed at his wiry physique—he was thin as a bread stick, bony as a fish, with no more meat or muscle than a lizard. When you clapped him on the shoulder of his shirt, it was like grabbing at sticks and marbles in a cloth bag. But it was his chest that was most alarming, even wretched: the chest cavity was sunken in so profoundly his lungs resembled hollowed-out soap dishes. The defect was so pronounced, I often wondered where nature had put his heart.

Despite all that, Nico was seized by unusual bursts of physical energy, pulses of pure dynamism that inexplicably propelled him into bodily motion. At times he would suddenly look up from his books as though he had just remembered something important, or as if some internal biological alarm were sounding in his head. Hearing that bell that only he could hear, Nico would drop his arms, abruptly straighten himself, and disappear around back behind the command post.

Curious one day, I stole around to have a peek—to find that he was doing push-ups! *Uno, due, tre, quattro. . . .* I had counted up to thirty-something when he noticed I was watching.

"Why do you do it?" I asked.

"It's the caffeine," he said breathlessly, going up and down like half of a seesaw. "Italian coffee is something else."

Well, I told the guys about it and they didn't believe me, so one time when Nico went around back, Luchetto and Renato and I snuck into the radio room and watched him through the screen window. Sure enough, there was Nico on the shaded concrete slab out back, touching his toes, stretching this and stretching that, leaning here and there, cocking his neck forward and back and all the rest. And then without so much as a breath the Americano dove to the ground all in a piece, like a tree falling, and began doing push-ups. The thing was, you wouldn't think a guy with the body of Nico could do ten push-ups, much less one hundred.

Luchetto was smiling at Nico in wonder, but Renato was glaring as though another dark suspicion had just taken root in his mind. What was it that so perturbed him about the American? Aside from the stolen money issue, I thought perhaps it was merely that they were so different as men— Renato so military and set in his ways, Nico so relaxed and creative. It was only later that I discovered the common current running through them both, the dark energy that kept them fixated on their obsessions, that motivated them, cranked their gears. They were mutual shadows of one another, unacknowledged doubles. So maybe Renato felt threatened by Nico's presence, maybe there was envy in his hatred. Renato saw the push-ups as a personal affront or challenge.

When Nico finished his exercises and came back out front, Renato and Luchetto and I were waiting for him. Nico's example had inspired us to get up off our butts and do something, and we were taking turns Indian wrestling one another on the dirt clearing. In Indian wrestling you plant your feet firmly on the ground with your legs apart, as if you were straddling a horse, then grab your opponent by the wrist and try to throw him off balance. Pietro, Saverio, Tancredi and Massimo saw what we were doing and came over, and Nico joined us too. When some squabbles erupted over whether or not so-and-so lifted his heel or about who had shifted his foot when, we propped a wooden board across two cement blocks so no one could cheat. Whoever fell off the board first was out. We organized a mini best-of-five competition, and when Nico went up against Renato it was a close match. Hooked arm to arm, they looked like two dogs tugging on the same bone—rabid dogs. You could tell they were taking this seriously. Each of them won twice—first Renato, then Nico twice, then Renato again—and the deciding round was tense. Watching them, I pressed my palms together so tightly they turned white and rubbery. I had to shake the blood back into them.

"You can't win, Americano," Renato said between grit teeth during the final fight, "you won't win." And he forcefully jerked Nico's arm backward by the wrist.

Nico's arm seemed made of hard rubber. "Whatever you say, Renato," Nico replied, bending his knees further and keeping his balance.

Renato swept Nico's arm in the other direction but Nico was ready and used the momentum to almost unglue Renato's stance. Renato staggered, dug down his heels, then regathered his strength and pulled and twisted Nico's forearm like he was turning a spit. Nico was dizzied. He gave a yelp of pain, leaned backward and lost his balance. And though it was obvious that Nico was already falling, Renato gave the arm one more vicious twist, throwing the American off the board and into the dust with such brutal force we thought Nico's shoulder would come out of its socket. Next thing, he was sprawled on the ground like so much laundry.

"Americano," Luchetto asked, "are you okay?"

After a long moment of silence, Nico said, "I'm fine." He sat up on his knees and rubbed his shoulder. He forced a smile to show us he was okay. "*Sto bene,*" he repeated.

Renato was standing over him. "I told you, Americano," he gloated, "you can't win." He walked in a circle, puffing out his chest, then decided on one of the plastic chairs. He sat down, took a knife out of his pocket, and began cleaning his fingernails.

Nico stood up, got a drink of water at the spigot behind the command post, and came back. When he noticed Renato cleaning his nails, he walked over to him and said, "Where did you get that?"

"Get what?" Renato said, not looking up from his fingers.

"That's mine," Nico said, pointing at the hands in Renato's lap. "That penknife, it's mine."

I recognized it immediately. It was the knife I'd taken from Nico's bag a few weeks earlier. Renato must have found it in the radio room or somewhere.

Renato looked up at Nico. The sun was behind the American, and Renato had to squint. "What are you talking about, Americano? This little pocketknife?" He twirled it between his fingers. "I've had it for years."

"Let me see that," Nico said, holding out his palm.

Instead of handing it to him, Renato held up the knife with the blade still open. The metal glinted in the sunlight. When Nico stretched his arm out to take the knife, Renato pulled it back out of reach. "You see?"

"That's it, that's mine!" Nico exclaimed more excitedly. "Where did you find it?"

"Let me be, Americano," Renato said with a wave of his hand.

Nico saw that Renato wasn't giving it up. He stood there awhile motionless, glowering over him, his eyes narrowed, his shoulders tense. We all thought he was going to pounce without a moment's notice. But then, luckily, Saverio came over and touched the Americano on the arm and whispered something to him, and Nico seemed suddenly to think better of the whole situation. Without another word, he turned and walked away, walked right off the firebase and out toward the hills.

When Nico was out of sight, Renato snapped the knife closed and turned to me and said, "What did I tell you, Matteo? The guy is nuts."

I said, "I think you might have hurt him, throwing him down like that."

"Yeah, so what. It was a fair wrestle. But what about this knife? Can you believe. . . ."

"It's his," I blurted out.

"What?" Renato turned his head sharply and glared at me with menace. But then he slipped the knife into his pocket and sat back, and his mouth eased into a mischievous grin. "And may I inquire as to the source of this latest information?" he said sardonically.

"I just know," I said.

"What are you, defending the guy?" Renato huffed. "This crummy penknife isn't worth one one-thousandth of what he took from me. You've gone on too many walks with him, that's what I think. He's infecting your brain. And I'll tell you something else, Matteo," he said pointing his finger at me, "you trust him and you'll regret it. God knows where he's going now with his cigarettes and a pack of matches." He made a gesture with his hand toward the hills, and I glanced at the faraway trees, which loomed brown in the distance. I didn't then understand what Renato said as insinuation, and I wish I could say that hindsight is always twenty-twenty. It is not. Whether Renato just loathed the American for personal reasons, or whether he was convinced Nico had stolen money from him, or whether he even then suspected Nico of something else, I just couldn't say. Now Renato is dead and he can't say either.

Chapter 9

If I look back carefully on the summer, the first fire that raised my suspicion was the burning of the chicken coop—a hutch for fighting cocks, really. The firestarter could have used electronic circuitry to rig up a detonator of some kind; it might have been the guys at La Buca, the billiards hall in town, who put him up to it. They were nothing but local delinquents— poor, unemployed, bored. Some of them were involved in a small cock-fighting ring that intermittently held fights out in the poorer boroughs, and there must have been money troubles of some kind.

The fire flared up in a scrub field bordering Casabasso's old town walls to the east. A fast fire, it fed on the cheat grass and low shrubs, on patches of myrtle bush and oleander and great swaths of spindly weeds, and by the time we pulled up in the squad jeep, the blaze had already blackened more than half the hillside. The flames stretched clear across the slope in a jagged front that was moving uphill like a line of soldiers, devouring everything in its path. Each time the flames reached a bush they seemed to slow a moment, encircling and gathering strength. Then the bush would go up in one quick bright flash, a spot of light more dazzling than day. Then ashes. A thick black plume of smoke like that from an old coal-fed locomotive.

The fire had begun at the foot of the five-hundred-year-old town ramparts. We figured that someone had tossed a cigarette down from the top of the walls into the field. Wind fanned a small flame to life in the dry reeds, and the fire took hold and began spreading out, seeking fuel. It suckled greedily on the dry grasses and leaves, gathered strength, and moved up the incline. I saw that it was now making its way toward the makeshift hutch, which served as a chicken coop and rabbitry, at the top of the field. The hutch was constructed of old weathered planks and wire and didn't stand a chance against the flames.

We split up, Nico following Tonino, Enzo and Cesare. They were going to try to work their way around to the unburned side of the field to meet the fire head-on. The rest of us—Pietro, Saverio, Luchetto, Tancredi and myself—raced up to the fire from its rear, clambering through the field of smoldering ashes it had left in its wake. This was not typically the best way to approach a blaze—from behind—but we thought we could punch a hole through the flames, pass through it, and clear a break around the wooden hutch.

We couldn't. Glutting itself on the weeds and grasses, the fire swept upward at a jogging pace toward the top of the field. This particular fire wasn't very tall, but it was pretty feisty and rambunctious, creating its own gusts and throwing a good deal of fumes and smoke. The weeds were thigh-high, full of fast-burning thistles that snapped in the intense heat, and it was difficult for us to get close enough to the flames to snuff them out with our *flabelli* and handheld tools. We'd left the portable water pumps—tanks of water resembling scuba equipment that we strapped to our backs—in the jeep. Because the tanks were heavy, we hardly ever bothered to carry them. The pumps, besides, sprayed only the weakest streams of water—only enough to douse live embers once the main fire was out—and they wouldn't have been effective in the burning grasses.

Instead we grappled bodily with the flames, trying to wrestle them to the ground by brute force. It was like trying to tackle a crew of gladiators. At one point, as I leaned in toward the flames to strike them with my *flabello,* the fire suddenly reached out a hot hand and slapped me on the cheek, hard. It was a warning, a stern reminder not to play with dangerous things. Fire does that to you once in a while, sends you terse messages, reminders that it wants to be left alone, that it has its own will to survive just as you yourself have. I staggered back—stunned, unbalanced. To my left and right, Pietro, Saverio, Luchetto and Tancredi were also having trouble controlling the flames. The fire's front was several meters thick and so intense with heat I could feel my eyebrows being singed. There was no way to cut through the blaze from our current position. We pulled back.

We heard shouts from beyond the hutch at the top of the field, and through whorls of smoke and black-edged flames I could make out a figure, an elderly man in a white undershirt, positioned at the field's northern edge. He was flailing his arms and trying to douse the hutch with water from a garden hose, but even at this distance I could see the tragic look on the man's face. The lime-green hose, connected to one of the nearby buildings and pulled so taut it was raised off the ground, was too short to reach the flames.

Just then Tonino, Enzo and Cesare rushed past the man and reached the hutch and began furiously shoveling dirt onto the flames. The fire, however, was already eating away at the planks, and the squad's efforts were useless. Our equipment—*flabelli,* Pulaskis and shovels—is designed to fight brushfires, not structural ones. We could clear shrub and bury burning embers on remote mountainsides, but were powerless in the building-crowded suburbs.

Nico didn't realize this. He caught up with Tonino and Enzo, ran up to the hutch, and began slapping at it with his *flabello.* He looked like a frantic maid cleaning cobwebs from the corner of a ceiling.

Then something happened that we'd never seen before. It was actually very funny: the Americano's *flabello* caught fire. One minute he was slapping at the flames trying to put them out and the next thing we knew he was swinging fire back and forth over his shoulder as though he were signaling with a torch or waving a flag made of flames.

It took several seconds for Nico to notice what was happening, and when he finally saw that his *flabello* was on fire, his body froze and he stared at the burning tool in bewilderment. Enzo ran up to him, snatched the *flabello* from his hands and tossed it to the ground.

As the hutch was engulfed in flames, Tonino tore at the cage wire with his Pulaski and managed to knock off a section of the corrugated tin roof. Several of the cocks escaped and began fluttering wildly throughout the field, but most of the animals remained trapped inside and there was an incredible cacophony of cackling and caterwauling amid the thick roiling smoke. Stray feathers and tufts of fur swirled in the heat. And mixed in with the smell of burnt grass and shrub (which we were used to and had even grown to love at times) was the pungent smell of scorched bone and feather—a rank odor that in the present context suggested to us not victual but burning human flesh.

I noticed that Nico had now slunk off to the bottom of the field and was trying to snuff out some tiny flames with the head of a shovel. He seemed to have forgotten everything we had taught him about fighting fire.

Because this was an urban area and there were buildings nearby, the city fire department had also been dispatched to the emergency. Two of their trucks belatedly arrived at the scene and began setting up hoses, although the hutch had already been reduced to a black skeleton and the rest of the fire was clearly under control. In fact, having been surrounded on three sides by cement or brick, and on the fourth by a low stone wall bordering a cornfield, the fire would probably have died out by itself without our intervention. A fast, high-temperature fire that gorged on grass and scrub, it would have been unlikely to jump buffers of cement or stone.

To be on the safe side, Saverio ordered our squad to position itself on the far flank of the field, along the stone wall that bordered the cornfield, where the spray from the city fire department hoses wouldn't be able to reach. We sat on the stones, which were warm from the sun and the flames, and watched the firemen wet down the field. When we saw that the embers had been soaked and there was nothing more to be done, we moved into the shaded rows of corn, passed around a pack of cigarettes, and had ourselves a little tobacco smoke.

As Pietro took the cigarettes, he pointed his chin at Nico, who was wandering around the edges of the burnt field, and whispered, "Did you see what happened to the American, how his *flabello* caught fire?"

We all laughed.

"I didn't think such a thing was possible," Luchetto said. "Aren't those things *fireproof*?"

"It was like a circus act," Pietro said. He leaned his head forward to light a cigarette and came up with a guffaw full of smoke. "I've never seen anything like it."

"He still doesn't quite seem to have got the hang of it," Tancredi said.

"Understatement of the week," Cesare countered.

"Maybe he needs more training," I replied.

"We did that already," Luchetto added.

"We can tell the American what to do," Pietro observed, "but we can't swing his own *flabello* for him, for God's sake."

There was a general grunt of agreement.

"He'll learn how to handle the flames," Saverio said quietly from the next row of corn. "He'll learn just like we all learned: through experience. He'll *have* to learn."

"Learn or burn," Pietro said, dragging on his smoke, "learn or burn."

When we'd finished our cigarettes, we walked back to the edge of the charred field to survey the scene. Tonino was over by the fire trucks, hobnobbing with the city firemen. Wisps of white smoke were still rising from the ground and a thin gray haze suffused the air. I saw Nico off to one side, kicking at something or other in the ashes. At the upper end of the field was the elderly man whom I'd noticed earlier, the one who'd been trying to spray the fire with the garden hose. He was now fumbling around the burned-out remains of the hutch. In his hands he cradled a limp black carcass that looked like a rabbit. He kept wandering back and forth in front of the hutch, or what was left of it, mumbling to himself and raising the carcass up and down.

"Poor guy," I said, pointing my chin at the old man.

"He's lost all his fighting cocks," Saverio said. "Probably used to make a pretty penny on them too."

"Yeah."

"At least the old fogy doesn't have to cook his dinner tonight," Luchetto tried to joke. None of us laughed. Luchetto shrugged his shoulders.

Just then, as if sensing that we were talking about him, the man turned and walked toward us, stopping only when he was close enough to look us in the eye. He held a dead rabbit in one hand, a dead rooster in the other. I thought he was going to thank us for trying to save his stock.

"Look what you've done!" he suddenly cried out in a pitiful whine. His face winced in pain. "Look what you've done!"

I didn't know what to answer.

"What are talking about, old man?" Enzo said, stepping forward.

"Look what you've done to my animals," the man repeated, raising the carcasses up in each hand. The dead animals looked like melted shoes.

Enzo made a motion as though he couldn't believe his own ears. "Are you crazy?" he said to the man. "We tried to save that worthless shack of yours!"

"What good are you if you can't put out a little fire?" the man said. "I've lost them all, I've lost them all."

"I saw a rooster and some others go into the cornfield," Saverio said.

"I've lost everything," the man repeated.

"Get out of here, old man," Enzo said with a wave of his hand.

But the man kept going on about how he'd lost everything, about how we were worthless and delinquent and corrupt. He said he knew about how things worked around here, he railed about "accidents" and kickbacks, he mentioned Cavalier Mezzasoma by name and said he knew about the liquor and the *contadini* and the helicopters and all the rest.

Enzo was furious, his face flared red as a poppy bloom. He kept pacing back and forth like he was going to lunge at the man at any moment, so Saverio and Luchetto each took one of his arms to calm him down. But the old man had had his say. He turned his back on us and trudged up the field. We bowed our heads and kicked at pebbles on the ground. The man had clearly been ranting, but some of what he'd said had truth in it and the truth made us feel dejected.

I wandered off into the devastated field, pretending to snuff out some embers but really wanting to see what Nico had been looking at. Poking around in the ashes with my shovel, I knocked against something hard and metal: a watch. I picked it up. The back of the watch had fallen off, and two long wires—wires that, judging by their large gauges, had nothing to do with horology—were stuck into the gears. When I turned the watch over, I thought it was missing a hand but then noticed that both hands had melted precisely at the hour of twelve. I looked at my own watch—it was eleven eighteen in the morning—and was about to chuck the thing back into the dust when I remembered Nico's watch collection. I walked over to him and, handing him the watch, said, "I thought you might be interested in this."

Nico looked it over doubtfully. "I've never seen it before," he said.

"So you can add it to your collection," I suggested. "I know it's broken—it's barely a watch anymore, huh?—but I thought you might keep it as a kind of souvenir."

Nico turned the watch over and said, "It's junk." He ripped out the wires from the back and threw the timepiece into the field. I watched it sail then skid on the burnt earth. To this day, I wish I had gone back into the field to retrieve it—not so much as evidence of any kind, but as I had suggested to Nico, as a kind of souvenir of our time together.

Our attention turned to some shouts coming from above us. Looking up, we saw a group of fellows perched on the ramparts of the town walls overlooking the field. I knew at least one of them, a guy named Franco who I heard had served in the joint for petty larceny. There were some five other guys, many of them punks I recognized by sight. Local delinquents, petty criminals, if I had to characterize them. Jobless, poor, futureless— they were what we in the squad might have become if it weren't for our involvement in the brigade. Their brazen grins flashed between the medieval archer's notches cut into the rampart's stone crenellation. From up there they could survey the entire fire scene.

"Hey, *vigili*," one of them yelled down brashly, "GREAT FUCKING JOB!"

Enzo was annoyed but tried to ignore the taunts. He made some obscene gestures at the punks and turned his back.

"Hey, *vigili*," another of the guys yelled, "have a smoke!" And with this he puffed on a cigarette and filliped the burning butt down into the scorched field.

Enzo grit his teeth but said nothing. He bent over, picked up a stone, and turned and flung it toward the top of the rampart. The stone fell well short.

"Is that the best you can do, *vigile*?"

"Don't let me catch you in town!" Enzo yelled.

He was answered with guffaws.

Nico, meanwhile, had gone over—unnecessarily, since there was nothing left to burn—to snub out the thrown cigarette. I saw Franco staring at him and thought I saw him nod to the American, but maybe he was just pointing his chin at Nico's hat. The hat was truly bizarre, something like a cowboy hat but with flaps that snapped up on both sides and in the back. I'd stared at that hat when I first saw it too. We didn't usually cover our heads around here; except during the most severe fires, there was no reason to, and besides, it was horrendously out of style.

Just then Tonino swaggered down the hill and joined us. He looked up at the guys perched on the ramparts and made a motion with his chin as if to ask *What's up with those losers?* and then answer his own question. He got in the jeep and started the engine.

Enzo sent the guys several final insulting gestures and climbed into the jeep after Tonino. Up on the ramparts, Franco and his boys were still cackling.

"*Vieni*, come on, Nico," I called over to the American, and I noticed that before getting into the jeep, and in such a way that he thought no one could see him, Nico looked up and—I'm almost sure of this—gave a curt wave toward the ramparts. Maybe Nico didn't fully understand what was going on between us and them, but I felt his gesture was an insult to our brigade.

As the jeep lurched forward, I turned to Nico and asked, "What did you do that for?"

Nico grabbed for a hand strap to steady himself. "What did you say?"

"Why did you wave to them," I asked, "after they insulted us?"

"What?" Nico said again, his eyes alert as a deer's. "Who?"

"Those guys on the ramparts," I said.

"*Non gli ho fatto salutare,*" Nico said, "I didn't wave to them."

"*Certo di no,* Americano, of course you didn't," Tancredi seconded. "Those bastards. I bet it was them who set the fire in the first place."

"Maybe not that fire, anyway," Tonino added from the driver's seat. We all turned to look at him, and by the smug look on Tonino's face we could tell he'd gleaned some juicy gossip from the city firemen who'd been at the scene.

"What do you know about it?" Saverio asked seriously.

But Tonino was tight-lipped. He had to be prodded, and we let Saverio take care of that since he was the most respected of our bunch. Even so, by the time we'd reached headquarters to fill out the postfire report forms, Tonino hadn't divulged much.

"The old man who owns the cocks," Tonino finally admitted, "owes someone some money."

"I thought I smelled some kind of chemicals toward the bottom of the field," Cesare said.

"There was a lot of garbage in the weeds, too," Enzo added. "Someone had been dumping their spent gas canisters."

"I came across a mattress in the field," Luchetto said.

"*La gente è ignoranta,*" Saverio observed. "People are ignorant."

"Did someone set the fire?" Nico asked bluntly. That remark surprised me, because it seemed as though he hadn't been paying attention to what we'd been saying. Plus we'd been talking fast, using plenty of slang and colloquialisms, and it was a wonder the American could follow the conversation at all. It was neither the first nor the last time I suspected he understood the Italian language better than he sometimes pretended.

"We don't know," I answered him.

"*Chi ne sa,*" Pietro echoed. "*Boh.*"

"I knew that crazy old man was a crook," Enzo said.

"That's one factor in the equation—right, Matteo?" Tonino said, peering at me through the rearview mirror.

Everybody turned their eyes on me. I could feel the blood rushing to my face, but I just shrugged my shoulders. "I guess so," I said, not sure what Tonino was getting at or why he'd singled me out. Was he speaking only in a general way, or was he winking at my involvement in the assignations? Or did he, like Renato, suspect Nico of something I was completely failing to comprehend?

When I didn't elaborate on my comment, everyone turned back to Tonino. He seemed to know more—a lot more—but no one could get anything else out of him.

Chapter 10

I stalk the early September backstreets of Casabasso all the warm day, wondering why I didn't see it sooner, how I couldn't have connected the lines between A, B, and C and spied the constellation. I don't mean only Nico, either; I mean the entire web of links operating around me and through me. This was before what happened at Pelle Marone, of course. Though by June and into July I was regularly accompanying Renato on assignations, I fooled myself into thinking of them as legitimate administrative meetings where we coordinated logistics with other brigades—and some of them were just that, in fact. Certainly there were other transactions that were lower under the table, but those I thought of as nothing but petty payoffs, barters, favors. If I got paid—which honestly didn't happen often—the amount was modest, a mere trifle, as much as you'd pay a messenger boy for hand-delivering a telegram.

How much of this will I be expected to narrate at the tribunal inquest about the fire on Mount Maggiore two weeks from now? I loathe the day. I tell you, it all looks different in retrospect, every last detail. Hindsight is nothing but a process of selecting memories, of revision. Who was it that said you can't step into the same river twice? Grant him some great honor.

I walk the town until the soles of my feet sting with heat. I wander to the city's east train station—a stale, sprawling place of crowded local lines, antiquated locomotives and freights. I find myself coming here a lot in the afternoon. I like the tangle of tracks and switches out back of the station. I am strangely comforted by the smell of tar and rough wooden ties baking in the sun, the crunch of gravel underfoot. Tall red poppies and spiky weeds with tough yellow flowers grow in-between the track ties and alongside the rocky track beds, somehow managing a life. I trail my hands along the floating blooms, carrying pollen from pistil to stamen on my callused fingertips.

I am drawn, too, by the shade and anonymity of the station building itself, the haunted space of its architecture. The main hall, with its domed atrium and wooden waiting pews, has the soft light and muted air of a church. I've grown accustomed to the voice that sounds over the loudspeakers, a woman's voice made vacuous and indifferent by the echoes. A certain smell, a stubborn odor of burnt electricity, lingers in the rooms. I wander through the cavernous halls and past the ticket counters, back and forth along the tunnels and train platforms, up and down the grimy cement staircases. Every once in a while, tugging on a cigarette as I shamble along the corridors and ramps, I find myself overtaken by amorphous packs of commuters disembarking from the trains. At the end of the business day their faces seem hollow, they look alien and haunting, like people who can't figure out how their past lives led them to where they are now, vaguely shuffling along a train platform mumbling stories to themselves to make up for some lost past—or like myself, fumbling with narrative threads and character motivations and hesitant, even fearful, ultimately, to navigate the barbs of self-implication.

At the end of the train platform, I squint as I jump from the shade into the glaring sunlight and cut across the train tracks. The sun is a huge spotlight aimed at southern Italy. The afternoon is acutely bright, hot, dry. Fire weather.

To return to my apartment I must cross the main boulevard and pass Palazzo Sangiusto, Casabasso's famous baroque palace. Fugitive, I keep on the lookout for any brigade jeeps; if I see one, I will have to turn my back and hide.

As I approach the palace, I find that I am retracing the route taken by the funeral procession for the perished squad members a month earlier, and my heart seems to trip on loose stones. We buried the bodies on a day like this, glaring with grievous sunlight.

But where last month the funeral procession turned toward the cemetery gates, I now veer off, cutting through a derelict construction site—common in this part of Italy—and heading across the wide lawn leading up to the front of Palazzo Sangiusto. The last time I visited the palace, I realize, was with the Polish volunteer Lyn, that afternoon I took her to see the room of statues. Lyn was wearing a black silk blouse suspended from her shoulders by nothing but two spaghetti straps like two lines of ink drawn on her skin. She was clearly moved by the work of the great artist Il Carpiglio. She whispered to the statues in soft Polish, and when she looked up to study some of the larger busts, I noticed she had a small brown beauty mark on the underside of her chin.

Though it is now September, tourist season is still thriving, and today there are many visitors milling about in front of the palace. I pass the tourists often on my perambulations, and each time the same question rears up in head: When they visit the stately grounds of the military cemetery, do they notice the freshly covered graves? The tourists' presence fills me with a mix of emotions that pool up in some private reservoir hidden deep inside me—shame at my provinciality, envy of their worldliness, disgust at their insouciance, pride in the treasures of my country. The palace, filled floor to ceiling with rare pre-Renaissance objets d'art, is truly magnificent. Yet I recognize that Casabasso must be a low point on their itinerary, nothing but a pit stop to use the toilets, take a snapshot, stroll indifferently through the palace, and loll afterward in the shade licking a *grattachecca* while they anticipate reaching the tombs at Cerveteri, the fountains in Rome, the spectacular ruins of Pompeii. . . . There are many Americans among the tourists today.

My father went to America once. I must have been about eight at the time. I try to imagine him there in the States, in New York City or Pittsburgh, but I find I have no clear idea what America is actually like. I've seen pictures, of course, images of steel towers rising up into the sky, epic panoramas of rugged nature and endless forests and fields, photographs of oppressive urban decay and of gaudy consumer delights. Really, those don't tell me anything. All I know of the world, all my experience has prepared me for, it seems, are the crooked streets and vaguely neoclassic buildings of

Casabasso. I've been to Napoli a few times, yet have seen there but a larger and slightly more regal version of Casabasso, nothing that comes close to resembling America.

In the same vein, I realize that when I met Nicolas Fowler, I had nothing against which to compare his character, no yardstick with which to measure the American's worth or depth. He was a cipher to me, a tortuous enigma, and it was only later, through our conversations, that I recognized the profound sorrow at the heart of him. He'd watched his father light matches so many times, he told me, and he'd inhaled the secondhand smoke from his father's cigarettes on so many countless nights it was as if he were smoking himself at the age of seven. They lived in a hundred-year-old Victorian with a limestone stoop and feeble turret towers facing the stolid urban street front in Shadyside, Pittsburgh. His father worked as a foreman in the steel mills—this was before Pittsburgh turned to computers and military information systems—and he smoked like the smokestacks spewing fumes above the U.S. Steel factory. Air was too thin for the man. His lungs swam with the heavy chemicals, the tangible cloud of filterless Lucky Strikes. Crumpled packs were strewn about the house like the ocean's detritus.

But it wasn't the cigarettes Nico was drawn to so much as the packs of blood red-tipped matches that, like cockroaches, seemed to turn up everywhere. He especially loved the neat clean look of a new pack of matches. So crisp, tidy. The matches were soldiers with red felt hats, all ready to surrender their lives. There were many opportunities. His mother smoked too, though less frequently than his father, and when the father was out at the mill working, Nico's mother would sometimes let little Nico light her cigarettes for her. One afternoon a strange man came to the house to fix the roof and Nico's mother told her son to go outside and play. Nico reluctantly obeyed. He fooled around in the junk at the edges of the yard, grew bored, wandered back inside. He could hear his mother's laughter upstairs and the floorboards of the old house creaking. The roofer's ladder lay on its side in the hallway corridor. Nico could smell whiskey in the afternoon. On the table next to his father's worn recliner lay a pack of Luckies, a matchbook tucked into the plastic wrapping. Nico took the cigarettes and crept into the basement. He smoked two, one after the other, and felt nauseous. But there were seventeen matches (he counted them carefully), and he lit them one by one. Through the pipes and vents he could hear his mother crying; each sulfur-noxious match strike was a curse and a kiss at once. Women, he told me, were heartless and deceitful. Yet still he thrilled with hidden excitement when later that evening his mother leaned forward, her nightgown billowing out from her breasts, and brought her enthralling lips to his cheek as she tucked him into bed.

As Renato so often urged, I tried to keep my eye on Nico—even as, or perhaps because, he gained my interest, sympathy and friendship. At the numerous burns that flared up around the summer solstice, Nico eventually proved himself (despite that anomalous gaffe at the hutch fire, when his *flabello* caught fire) more or less competent as a firefighter. Yet though he'd learned how to wield a *flabello* effectively in the field, we still tried to steer him clear of the worst parts of the burns, typically keeping him in the rear burying embers or "sweeping up the ashes," as we called it.

He wasn't terribly compliant, however, and there was a certain unpredictability to his behavior that made him difficult to keep track of. With his light frame and agile motions, he was a lot quicker and more nimble on the slopes than I was. He would bound back and forth from spot to spot like a buck eluding the hunt; he brimmed over with a wild energy that was difficult to tame. During downtime at the firebase I patiently explained fire patterns and squad formations to him, I told him we had certain procedures we were expected to follow, a methodology that had proven itself in the field. He listened politely, and I think he understood, but he would respond with some cryptic axiom or another—"Fire follows no procedure," "The worst gamblers have their set patterns, too," "Nature is unpredictable"—assertions that, the more I thought about them, the more I found them difficult to disagree with.

So I not infrequently lost him at burns. One minute he'd be behind me, shoveling dirt onto embers or widening the firebreak, the next minute he'd have disappeared behind plumes of smoke, and a few minutes later I'd spot him up front with the point of the squad.

Another time, out in the verdant hills near Sopravia, Nico really surprised me. The squad had just snuffed out a burn on some farmland, and Massimo, Pietro and Cesare and I were waiting for Tonino and Saverio to finish up their final inspection of the perimeter. I was leaning up against the jeep taking a swig from my canteen when I spotted Nico about a hundred meters off in one of the blackened fields. When I noticed that Nico didn't seem to be moving, I got worried and went out to check on him.

The field had been wheat of some kind, but the stalks had been razed to the ground. The earth lay furrowed and black, still smoking beneath the cloudless sky. Nico was at the far end of the field standing beside a wood and wire fence. Beyond the fence was a dirt road that we'd used as a firebreak, and beyond the road was a clump of sycamore and pine that marked the edge of the forest we'd just saved from destruction.

As I strode closer, I saw that Nico was kneeling in the dirt. I thought he'd twisted his ankle or something and sped up my paces, but when I reached him he turned to me and smiled, revealing a face smeared black with soot.

Puzzled, I stopped a few paces off from him. Was he praying in the ashes? I cleared my throat and asked him if he was okay.

"Never better, Matteo," he said. He stood up. He was covered head to boots with soot and ash. It was on his chest and thighs and in his hair, and his face and neck were smeared charcoal-dark.

"You're filthy, Nico," I said, not knowing what else to say. Looking at him unsettled me a bit. What on earth had he been up to? What had he been thinking?

"Actually," he answered, rubbing one hand on the back of another as if to rub the ashes into his skin, "ashes are the cleanest element on earth."

I shrugged my shoulders. I thought it was the observation of a lunatic.

"Look at this landscape, Matteo," he said, waving his arm generously. "See how pure it is."

I saw a burned field, ruined crop.

Nico said, "Nietzsche—the German philosopher—once asked why we value truth over falsity. 'What if truth were a woman?' he asked, then where would we be?"

I wasn't following him.

But he continued, "Why do we have a preference for green, for green and brown and yellow, for crops like wheat and corn? I know this field has been destroyed—that's bad, I admit—but as I said, look how *pure* it is now. This charred land is ready for life, it has been prepared. Ashes nourish the ground, renew the soil—who knows, maybe the crops were too much for it, more than it could support."

"And from ashes rises the phoenix," I said, half ironically.

"Exactly. Ashes are actually full of life, they are purged of pollutants, and smoke is nothing but God's incense. I love the smell of burnt earth."

"It's invigorating, strangely enough," I had to agree.

Nico then did something I'll never forget. He leaned over, scooped up two fistfuls of ash and with a quick but gentle movement ran his hands along the sides of my face, smearing my cheeks black. I recoiled, but not fast enough.

"Nico," I started to say, "what the hell. . . ."

"Fire," he interrupted, stepping back with a strange smile, "is desire for life in its purest form."

I wiped my cheeks with the back of my hand. "What are you talking about?" I said. "What in God's name are you doing out here?" I was uneasy now. I tried cleaning my face with the sleeve of my shirt.

"Take it easy, Matteo," Nico said in a light tone. "I'm just screwing around."

When I heard the levity in his voice I was relieved. Nico was on the edge of crazy, but I guess that's one thing I liked about him. Still, I'd had enough for the day.

"We'd better get back," I said, just as the sound of the jeep's horn came from the far road. "See?—the others are calling for us." I knocked some of the ashes off Nico's clothes and we trudged back through the field, kicking up a gray trail in our wake.

"What the fuck happened to you guys?" Massimo said when we'd reached the jeep.

"I tripped in the field," Nico answered casually.

"Looks like some priest went crazy at Lent," Pietro said.

"Something like that," I said.

The others just shook their heads in disbelief, and soon Tonino and Saverio returned from their inspection of the perimeter and we all clambered into the jeep.

On the drive back to the firebase, my cheeks itched with the ashes Nico had smeared on them. I understood the gesture as a curious proclamation of friendship, but I was also unnerved by it. And the more I thought about it the more I felt that the American was reading me in a way I had not intended to be read. He seemed to be luring me into a cave I didn't want explore. Could it be that Nico sensed this in me, my hesitation, that he glimpsed my uncertainty and decided to do something to force my hand, to compel me to make up my mind either way? In retrospect and only in retrospect, only from my perspective here three months after the fact can I entertain the possibility that what happened next between us—the episode in which we walked together through fire and survived—might have been orchestrated by Nico himself. Not that I believe it was a matter of careful planning. It was more that he *saw*—saw and seized an opportunity. Certainly it irrevocably sealed our friendship. Yet passing through fire was also a religious event for me—an awakening, for want of a better word. I was christened by fire, initiated into its cryptic priesthood. Chances are I could have walked through fire with anyone, but as it turned out, it happened with an American named Nicolas Fowler.

Chapter 11

That June night I was awoken by an annoying whine that sounded like the late-night racket of my neighbor's television set, and it took me a minute or two to realize I wasn't home in my apartment. I was pulling the night shift at the firebase and the whine was issuing from the radio unit in the adjacent control room. Without putting on my pants or turning on the lights, I swung myself out of bed and stumbled to the console.

"What's the matter with you guys?" the dispatcher's voice crackled when I finally got on the air. "We've got a major flare-up in Sector Four. Vallemaio. Squads from Paolino and Marzano are already on the way."

"What time is it?" I asked groggily.

"Past oh-three-hundred," the dispatcher said irritably. He read me the coordinates of the blaze. "Get your butts out there," he said, signing off.

I roused the others and we groped ourselves into our uniforms, climbed in the jeep and held on as Tonino barreled through the city streets, the jeep siren blaring. The night was pitch black, the streets were empty and Tonino was pulling out all the stops. Sitting in the rear compartment, jostled by the bumps and turns, we fiddled with our equipment and tried to forget about sleep. The siren rang pitilessly in our ears. It's one of those old-fashioned sirens, run by an antiquated gyro mechanism, and it sounded like an incredibly long, primitive howl. It seemed to come straight out of nothingness—like one of those classic air-raid sirens from the First World War. There was something unsettlingly human and terrifying about the sound, the fear and adrenaline it summoned forth. It was a cry of violence, a warning, a challenge.

We passed through town and headed northwest over the hills, skirting Città Vecchia and taking what is called the sea road, a long flat highway that runs along the base of the Apennines, north toward Pisa, south to Napoli and beyond. The air was cool with a hint of brine, and every now and then through the trees I caught a glimpse of a huge flat mass of blackness that was the Mediterranean Sea. Opposite, the Fasini mountains were tall dark shadows looming. Everyone was silent, lost in the cavern of the siren's sound, powerless against the noise. I watched Nico light a cigarette with his windproof silver lighter.

After several kilometers Tonino turned off the siren and branched off inland from the sea road to begin our ascent into the hills. The mountain road curved steeply among the trees and cliffs, and as we rounded one of the hairpin turns we caught our first sight of the fire.

"Holy mother of God," Pietro said.

Tonino stopped the jeep. Looking north we could see the ragged vein of orange light that streaked up the distant ridge. Several kilometers long, it stretched over more than a few of the smaller peaks and vales of the Fasini range.

"Take the south fork," Saverio advised, snapping the point of his finger on a map.

Tonino nodded and skid the jeep into motion. A few kilometers up the mountain we turned off the main road onto a dirt and gravel track that wound up into the wilderness. Every now and then we caught another glimpse of the fire, and each time it was like a diamond shard nicking an artery in our hearts.

We parked at the side of the dirt road several hundred meters south of the blaze and clambered out the rear door burdened with our gear. Though the fire was beyond the next rise, the sky was glowing pink and we could make out massive, ghostly plumes of smoke rolling up the mountainside. A distant churning reached our ears, like a pounding surf at night—that was the sound of the forest burning—and the air was acrid with burning wood. Large white ashes floated down from above like stray feathers.

The equipment was divvied up: *flabelli,* shovels, Pulaskis, machetes, a chainsaw and two portable water pumps.

Bushwhacking through the thick foliage with Tonino in the lead, we moved laterally across the incline, hoping to cut the fire off at least three-quarters' of the way up its trajectory. The terrain was steep and dense, and navigating it in the darkness of the moonless night was like walking blindfolded through a jungle. There was no path. Branches lashed at our faces and eyes. We stumbled over roots and rocks, grabbed blindly at thorns, snagged our gear on tangles of vines. As we got closer, the churning sound of the fire increased to a steady roar.

Breathless, we reached the top of the first rise and regrouped. The edge of the fire was about 150 meters in front of us, stretching up and down the mountainside as far as we could see, and we realized immediately that we had mispositioned ourselves. By now the front edge of the burn was well above us; we'd be lucky to catch up with it before it reached the next crest. Enzo cursed and spit. He glared at Tonino and was about to complain but changed his mind.

Tonino grabbed the two-way radio from my belt pouch and contacted the other brigades to coordinate our attack. Then he did something that made us wince. Though Paolino Squad—approaching from the north—had a huge head start on us, Tonino wagered that we'd reach the summit of Fasini before them.

"You shouldn't have made that challenge," Enzo opined.

"We'll make it," Tonino said, tugging on his belt and puffing out his chest. "Right, Americano?"

"Right!" Nico agreed.

"Who's number one!"

"We are, Tonino!"

Squatting down in the dirt, Tonino described the plan. We would split up into three teams. Enzo, Luchetto and Cesare, carrying the water pumps, would turn downhill, tackling the westerly spread of the fire and making contact with the fire crews at the sea road. Once they did so, they were to double back up, checking for rekindled flames and spot fires. Tonino and

Saverio would take the point and head north, skirting the blaze for a stretch and approaching it a couple hundred meters further up the slope. The rest of us—Massimo, Tancredi and Pietro, and Nico and I—would be responsible for the intermediate stretch.

It was a decent stratagem. It would allow us to control the momentum of the blaze as well as hasten our ascent to the mountain summit and beat the Paolino Squad. And knowing that Enzo, Cesare and Luchetto would be doubling back up and retracing our route, the rest of us would be able to spread our forces out wide, working at a fast pace and not having to worry about extinguishing every last spark.

The steep slopes of Fasini were thick with vine-twisted trees and covered with a highly flammable matting of dead leaves and dry branches. A bush-and-tree fire, this burn moved a bit slower than your average blaze in maquis, but it was also more persistent and obstinate. Controlling it meant cutting down trees, digging trenches, clearing foliage, burying ashes . . . and with the thick undergrowth and poor visibility, it was extremely difficult and confusing work. Frequently, after clearing some stretch of ground, we'd watch as the fire reached it, rocked back and forth, and stepped over the breach as though it were nothing but a line we had sketched in the dust. The situation was frustrating and wearisome, and in our haste to reach the summit of the mountain before the fire crowned, we stretched ourselves too thin. The blaze began sending out huge probing tentacles of fire that ate large swaths of timber in-between our overextended deployments.

I stuck close to Nico. During one long stretch, as I was intent on clearing a firebreak through a particularly thick stretch of forest, Nico put his hand on my shoulder and yelled something. He was waving his arms wildly. I stopped digging and looked up. We were in a small grassy clearing that was almost completely surrounded by flames. We had let the fire get behind us and box us in. Immediately we began a southerly retreat across the slope, but found ourselves funneled into a briar patch thick with thorns and vines. I whipped out my machete and began hacking desperately at the vines while Nico chopped at the bushes with his axe. We threw our bodies into the thorns and tried to tear our way through. Then I noticed the orange glow on the far side of the briar patch, and it was like someone had dropped an anvil onto my chest. The fire had already encircled us.

I think that death must be something akin to accidentally locking yourself out of your own apartment. One minute you poke your head out the door for a breath of fresh air, the next moment the door is swinging shut behind you and you're reaching for it and checking your pockets for the keys at the same time—they aren't there of course—and the door clicks shut with a certain firm finality. You find yourself in the hallway in your socks, locked out of your own life, suddenly helpless, foolish, embarrassed.

Nico tugged hard on my sleeve. I turned and faced him. His eyes were turbulent above the blue bandanna that covered his mouth and nose. He was yelling in English, making big motions, a *flabello* loosely held in his hands. I wondered why he had dropped his Pulaski. He kept motioning to the wall of fire behind us, but I didn't understand what he was saying. I was suddenly overcome by great sadness and regret, thinking that I had killed him.

To my surprise, he spoke in a tone of high excitement.

"We can't get through that briar patch!"

There was little fear in his voice. It was more like . . . exhilaration.

"I know, Americano!" I said. "I am sorry," I added stupidly, barely audible. I marched back and forth along the perimeter of the clearing. Gnawed at by the fire, the clearing kept growing smaller and smaller. It was like being trapped inside a garbage compactor.

Nico yelled, "This way, Matteo!" He motioned again toward the wall of flames.

It took me a while to figure out that he wanted us to cut backward through the blaze—something known by firefighters as "making for the black." I thought it was the stupidest thing I had ever heard. Ordinarily, in order to make your way into an already burned-out area, you weren't supposed to have to pass first through a wall of fire! But after a few moments I realized that it was probably our only viable option.

I said, "I understand, Nico."

He nodded, wild-eyed and agitated, then reached over to me and began buttoning my buttons and tucking in my sleeves and collar, covering every last inch of skin possible. I did the same for him. Finally we emptied the canteens over our havelocks, sleeves and gloves, and turned to face the blaze.

The wall of flames was higher than a house. At first it appeared completely formidable, just a solid block of fire composed of smaller shoots of fire, alive and always moving, shifting, blasting with heat. Yet if I trained my attention on it, I noticed there were certain spots that flickered somewhat less menacingly than others, like doorways that seemed to promise dull ashes on the other side.

"Right there!" I yelled, pointing with the tip of the machete.

"Yes!" came the answer. Though he was speaking at the top of his voice, his words were small in the roar of the blaze. "Out of the frying pan and into the fire!" he yelled.

We regarded one another, and a broad smile appeared on Nico's face. Then he pulled his bandanna up so that only his eyes were showing. I could see flames reflected in them.

He said, "*Andiamo!* Let's do it!"

"Together!" I screamed.

Side by side, bracing one another, we moved as close to the flames as we dared. I smelled the noxious stench of burning human hair. With a rocking motion we gathered momentum and, timing ourselves with the waves of flame, flung ourselves forward.

Fear stopped me at the last second.

I watched Nico disappear through the wall of flames. The fire flared up fiercely for an instant, lashing out at me, swallowing him up.

The moment he was gone I found myself missing him desperately. I had never felt so alone. I paced frenetically to and fro, frantically glancing around for another alternative. Suddenly realizing what I really wanted was to stay as close to Nico as possible—I felt that only he knew *that something* about fire that could keep me alive—I took a tremendous breath and launched myself into the great orange light.

The fire offers no resistance: penetrating it is like passing from shadow into a shaft of sunlight, and for the first moments it not nearly as hot or as difficult as I imagined it would be. It is like entering a sauna fully clothed: a bit ridiculous, somewhat uncomfortable and heavy, but not unbearable. The flames are wings brushing against my body, caressing me. It is as though I have walked into a flock of birds. I am a sparrow fluttering through a puff of chimney smoke.

There is some kind of tunnel that appears and disappears, is revealed to and hidden from me by whorls of smoke and flickering flames. I stumble on at a precarious pace, carried dumbly forward by my legs.

A great flame lurches in front of me, blocking my path then swerving aside maliciously like the red cape of matador. I think I hear people laughing, the malicious cheer of a bloodthirsty crowd. It has suddenly grown unbearably blistering hot.

I reach a space of ground, a little clear patch, and think I have made it through. But the heat is still intense and it grows more intense every second. Looking about, I find myself stilled hemmed in by a circle of flames. And yet I want to remain in this coffin-sized clearing, this pocket of burnt ground. I fall to the earth, where there's more oxygen, and press my lips to the dirt, taking a few breaths, loving the hot air even as it scorches my throat and enters hotly into my lungs. I want desperately to sleep. . . . Suddenly it is as though some crazed mob were striking at me with heated irons. I jump to my feet, raising my arms to shield my face, and am struck on the ribs and legs. Spun hither and thither by hot bursts of pure fire, I am no longer sure from which direction I have arrived. I feel as though my lungs are melting.

Over what seems a great distance I hear Nico calling my name. Tossed over the hot gusty blasts, his shouts reach me ragged and frayed, torn into shreds by the conflagration. It is my mother calling to me at the seashore, chastising me for playing too long in the surf. It is the April caterwaul of alley cats, car tires screeching just before the accident, the wails at my father's funeral.

Then, just once, my name rings out clearly through the thunderous roaring and I blindly, instinctively toss my panicked body toward it.

There is no tunnel, no air, only a horrific clamor, a cacophonous din and babble in my ears. I lose track of Nico's call. The fire is playing tricks on me.

I am running, running. My chest is afire.

I break wildly into darkness.

Nico latches onto me with both arms as I pass him. My momentum carries us forward until we bump against the hot, charred trunk of a tree and tumble to the ground. My mouth is full of ashes. I have made it to the black, I have made it through.

We found ourselves on the other side of the fire. It was a landscape of ash, blacker than night, ghostly, hellish. The air was rancid, almost unbreathable. As we stumbled away from the heat, away from the roaring, our eyes slowly adjusted to the darkness. The ashes were ankle-deep, the ground hot as stovepipes. We passed the charred remains of tree after tree after tree, we navigated smoldering bushes and branches, still burning stumps, huge piles of amber-glowing wood coal. Red embers floated down from the sky like remnants of Moses' burning hail.

Then Nico stopped and clutched my arm. I followed his gaze. In front of us, like a great monument to nature, stood a perfectly intact magnolia tree, seemingly untouched by the blaze. We stood just above it on the slope, stamping our boots on the hot ground, speechless as though we had come across Troy. You could see the carroty light of the fire reflected on each shiny green magnolia leaf. It looked as though electric volts were flowing through each waxy vein.

Behind the tree lay the sea, the thinnest crescent of moon setting in the west above it, and we could see the lights of some vessels out on the water, and down below, parked at the edge of the sea road, the wandering aster-blue siren lights of a fire brigade. Behind us, rimming the upper horizon of the mountain, the main blaze was still raging onward. It had just crowned the far summit.

I asked, "Are you all right?"

My lips were parched and my voice cracked, but Nico's answer rang out like a matins bell.

"Like a god," he said, craning his neck to gaze up at the stars. The starlight fell as cool as chips of ice onto our upturned faces.

We made our way downhill, first west toward the sea then south, reaching the edge of the black area about 250 meters below our last fighting position. Before stepping from the ashes onto the cleared dirt firebreak and forward into the living foliage, we paused for a moment and regarded one another. We didn't speak. Indeed, though it was perhaps the most thrilling and somehow most meaningful episode of my entire life, I've never spoken with anyone about it, ever.

Chapter 12

I first met the American almost six full months ago. So much has happened since then it seems I am inhabiting a completely different life. As I've admitted, I was wrong about Nico. Not only did we become friends, we became stepbrothers of sorts; our fathers had died the same death. Every day we fought burns side by side; all summer long, flames soldered a bond between us. And on the slopes of Fasini overlooking the sea, we quite literally passed through a wall of fire together.

Later on, he saved my life. He lit the backfire on Mount Maggiore and helped me to lie down in its ashes. Even though the role that backblaze may have played in the deaths of Enzo, Saverio, Renato or the others remains unclear, there's no doubt in my mind that it saved Tancredi and me. Of course it would be a gross understatement to say that I feel sorry for those who perished. I'm devastated that they failed to stop and listen to the American. But—someone saving your life? You just don't forget something like that, no matter what other crimes a person may commit. It would be like cursing your own mother.

Still, I want to be clear about this now: I never questioned Nico's motives—not, anyway, until much later. If there were any small signs that might have given him away, I didn't see them. I was too busy befriending him. And besides, the trajectory of my life was propelling me in a completely different direction, toward routine burns that seemed insignificant at the time but were actually insidious, toward fires like the one at Pelle Marone and the hard truths they taught me about my own brigade.

Even now it makes me sick to my stomach, like opening the cupboard where you forgot the meatloaf and finding it squirm with maggots. It all had to do with an assignation Renato took me to in a town called Pelle Marone. As I've admitted, I'd been accompanying Renato to such transactions all summer long, so I wasn't surprised when one July morning, after returning to the firebase from a routine burn, Renato told me to get in the jeep and come along with him.

"Where are we going?" I asked.

"For a drive," he said. "Cavalier Mezzasoma's orders."

Renato turned out of town, catching the *autostrada* and heading south beyond the city limits. We drove by the caves of Anilone, which the Partisans had used as hideouts during the Second World War, and passed the sprawling, sulfur-smelling factories in the industrial zone that runs southwest of the valley, following the Turno River. Renato drove without speaking. Past the factories he took a two-lane road that wound its way along the bottom of some low hills thick with aspen and birch. Beyond the hills the land quickly flattened out; the trees grew scarce, and small farms appeared. Many of the farms looked rundown. Decrepit tractors rusted by the roadside. Although there were some bright patches of olive and a few fruit orchards, more often than not the fields looked dry and shabby.

After about half an hour we reached a cluster of stone buildings in the commune of Pelle Marone. Renato parked the jeep in front of a place called the Bar Tre Stelle. Several old men lounged on benches outside in the shade; inside the bar some youths were playing video soccer. Renato got out, told me to wait, and disappeared into the bar. I sat in the jeep for a while, then got out to stretch my legs. I stood in the shade of a medlar tree near the group of elderly men. They were talking about goats.

Within Bar Tre Stelle, past the video games and gambling machines, Renato was talking with two men. One was tall and dressed in waiter's garb. The other man was short; he was wearing a blue jumpsuit like that issued to municipal laborers, street cleaners and the like, but he was most likely a *contadino* who worked one of these provincial farms. As I looked at the man, he pointed toward the sky and said something to Renato. Renato seemed reluctant, then nodded his head yes.

After they'd shaken hands, Renato called me over, and we stood at the bar for an espresso. As I sipped the coffee, I noticed the bartender standing off to one side flicking a silver lighter over and over again. I had the distinct feeling he was studying me. I looked him in the eye and said *Buon giorno,* and he nodded back at me.

Renato and I finished our coffees without exchanging a word and went outside. As we climbed back into the jeep, all Renato said was, "They always want a Canadair."

I looked at him quizzically. The Canadair is a plane used to fight forest fires. It scoops water off the top of a lake, carries it to the fire scene, and sprays it over the flames. I had no idea how a Canadair fit into the scheme of today's transaction.

"The Canadair," Renato repeated, starting the jeep. "I guess it impresses them."

"It can hold thousands of liters of water," I said, just to say something.

"But there's nowhere to fill her around here," Renato said. He pulled onto the roadway and shifted gears. "What are you supposed to do, scrape her belly in these shitty shallow backwater streams? The closest place is Lago di Raviscania, above the dam. They want us to fly from Raviscania?"

"It's within range," I observed.

Renato said, "My point is, we don't need this shit. We don't need to be given demands."

I didn't know what exactly he meant. I thought he was just in one of his crappy moods. I suppose I should have known better.

Renato lit a cigarette, looked at his watch and at the speedometer, and increased our speed. In twenty minutes we were back at the edge of Casabasso. We passed the field where the animal hutch had taken fire several weeks earlier. Some of the weeds were already growing back, and I noticed that people had started dumping junk into the lot again—blue bags spilling kitchen refuse, a big scattered pile of green plastic bottles, large chunks of concrete and tiles, a dishwasher. The hutch where that old man had housed his fighting cocks had been completely leveled.

I thought of the wristwatch I had found in the field after the blaze, the one Nico had chucked away, and remembered the way that guy Franco and his cronies, mocking our squad from the castle ramparts, had seemed to recognize the American. It got me wondering.

"You ever hear anything about the origin of that burn?" I asked Renato as we passed the burned field.

"In case you don't recall," Renato said in his dry way, "I wasn't present that day."

"I know, but have you heard anything?"

"Nothing worth repeating."

"C'mon, Renato," I pleaded.

Renato sighed. "They say the guy set his own cocks on fire."

"What?"

"You heard me. Just what I said."

"But why?"

"Why does anybody do anything around here? He wanted to make a buck on it."

"Insurance?"

"On a henhouse?"

"Then what?"

"I don't know myself," Renato admitted. "Ask me next month." He suddenly downshifted into second gear and veered onto a side street into the business district. He made a few more quick turns, then pulled the jeep over in front of some liquor warehouse—it looked like a wholesale distribution center for wines and sodas—and beeped the horn. I'd never been here before, but when I looked over at Renato for an explanation he avoided my gaze.

A few moments later Tonino came out of the warehouse and got into the jeep. He made me climb into the back seat, and Renato drove off. We made a few other stops—to pick up some smokes for Tonino, to get a couple slices of pizza—and by the time we pulled the jeep into its reserved parking space in front of brigade headquarters—not our local firebase, but the central office of the brigade's commander-in-chief—it was late afternoon. I guessed we'd come to headquarters to check in with Cavalier Mezzasoma and complete some paperwork, as was periodically required of us.

Just as we were going in the front door, two pilots came out of the building. They were wearing the smart blue uniforms of the Airborne Fire

Protection Squad. They nodded, said *Buona sera,* climbed into their vehicle, and drove off.

It wasn't often that pilots visited headquarters—really, there was no administrative need for them to do so—and I said, almost to myself, "What were those pilots doing here?"

"How should I know?" Renato answered in an annoyed way, like I was an idiot.

I shrugged, more irritated by Renato's insulting tone than at my own ignorance. Looking back at that moment now, I understand that I should have been more concerned with my own ignorance. I should have torn my own hair out. It was all there in front of me to see, but I still didn't see it. It was like one of those 3-D posters you find in cheesy art shops; sometimes you can stare at the swirling patterns for weeks before perceiving the three-dimensional figure hidden there.

Renato, Tonino and I went inside headquarters. The front reception room was empty, as was the adjacent map and communications office, but in the hallway I noticed something strange: the corridor leading to Cavalier Mezzasoma's office was crowded with boxes. They were cartons of wine and liquor, I realized, maybe eighteen dozen bottles' worth.

"What's all this?" I asked. I peeked inside one of the cartons and saw the slender, clear neck of a grappa bottle. "What's this?" I repeated, mostly to myself.

"Liquor, you dope," Renato said. "What does it look like?"

"But. . . ."

"For the restaurant," Tonino said, squeezing past me. He meant the Trattoria Tramontano, where the brigade ate its meals—that deal Mezzasoma had managed to work out. The Cavalier always made sure the *Vigili del Fuoco* brigade had everything it needed, from steel-toed military-issue boots to tools and equipment and jeeps. He'd done incredible things with the brigade during his tenure. Half a decade ago our firebase didn't even exist; back then, we worked out of a converted garage and had only two dilapidated jeeps and minimal equipment. But recognizing that the *Vigili del Fuoco* needed to find more funds for itself, Mezzasoma came up with the idea of expanding our forest fire fighting unit into an international organization—an environmental conservation group that hosted volunteers, to be exact. Changing our status in this way meant that we would be able to apply for extra governmental funds. We established ties with a nonprofit group called the International Youth Volunteer Network and began hosting volunteers from throughout Europe and the world—hence the Polish girls, and Nico himself, and many others. Due in part to our new status as an international environmental conservation group, the government gave us the new firebase, as well as a generous budget for our firefighting vehicles and materiel.

Most recently, Cavalier Mezzasoma had negotiated for our provisions at the Trattoria Tramontano. It took almost a year of intense bargaining, but he finally succeeded in setting up an arrangement between Federico (the proprietor of the restaurant) and some minister or other in the government. It occurred to me now for the first time just how expensive such accommodations must be. We in the brigade routinely glutted ourselves on the food set before us, much as the Goths must have feasted on conquered Rome.

Renato took my elbow and steered me down the hallway past the boxes and toward Mezzasoma's office. "Even after all we show you," he commented, "you don't understand much."

I guess that was true. I still wince at how true it was. Even now, regarding the liquor, I can't say exactly how that panned out. I think the liquor people were just piggybacking on the fortunes of the Trattoria Tramontano. After all, feeding a brigade of hungry firefighters twice a day seven days a week translates into quite a bonanza. The restaurant was treated to a tax exemption for assisting the state, and the considerable food and drink tabs were sent to the government and reimbursed. I suspect, as well, that the tabs reflected that we ate and drank more than we actually did. Finally—and once again I'm speculating here—the restaurant owed several local constituencies for its privilege of feeding the brigade. This must have been paid out in cash and fine liquor. The liquor that we didn't consume (we crew members stuck to wine and beer) was funneled through the Trattoria Tramontano and ended up in the homes of the likes of Cavalier Mezzasoma and his cronies. Yet despite all this, I recognize that the Cavalier was just looking out for our interests, for the welfare of the brigade, and I'm convinced that he had a strong distaste for the backroom deals he found it necessary to engage in. Sometimes habits and relationships are difficult to break. Even at that time, I considered Mezzasoma an honest man. I didn't see how a couple of bottles of grappa could end up killing six able men scrambling up a remote mountainside.

Chapter 13

Renato, Tonino and I made our way past the cartons of liquor and down the corridor. District Commander-in-Chief Cavalier Mezzasoma waited for us in his office, sitting behind his large mahogany desk smoking a pipe and examining a display of dragonflies with a magnifying glass. The desk was clear, the blotter spotless. The Persian blinds were completely closed. Three lamps with green glass shades shed a shadowy light. Beside the desk stood a tray with a decanter of brandy and four snifters. Mezzasoma offered us drinks, and we each took a glass and sat down. Renato spoke formally, yet I was taciturn and felt ill at ease. I wasn't accustomed to strong alcohol, especially before dinner, and I feared that I might say something I wasn't supposed to say about the assignations or that I'd be asked a question about the transactions I couldn't answer. I was also nervous about being made an offer I didn't feel comfortable refusing—or maybe getting rebuked for something. Cavalier Mezzasoma himself seemed less affable than usual. He didn't shake my hand.

The only one of us who acted completely at ease was Tonino. He installed himself in a red leather armchair with his feet propped up on a file cabinet and related some ribald tale to the Cavalier using the personal "tu" form. Mezzasoma laughed at the appropriate moments. I was waiting for him to tell us why he'd called us in, but he finished his brandy and poured another round, and I thought that no official business was going to take place at all.

It wasn't until Mezzasoma had finished his second drink that he finally brought the conversation around to the actual subject of the meeting: next month, a neighboring fire brigade was planning to execute a controlled burn in the Parco Regionale d'Abruzzo, and the commander of their fire sector had requested assistance from our brigade. This was not as simple as it sounded. Due to some arcane laws, the various firefighting agencies—the Corpo Forestale, *Vigili del Fuoco,* Protezione Civile, and the like—are required to seek written permission from the proper commune before they can enter any regional parkland that lies outside their fire sector. Each local commune, however, can grant permission only in the case of an existing emergency—that is, only after a fire has started to get out of control. Obviously, in the profession of firefighting, where a quick response is of the utmost importance, such bureaucratic tangles can lead to disaster.

In short, the Cavalier had worked out some kind of special agreement with the other district commander that would allow our brigade to be present at the controlled burn. As we discussed the arrangements, I was struck not by the red tape of regional politics but by the fundamental conflicts I noticed in my own brigade, the differences between the firefighting methods of our two main squad commanders, Renato and Tonino.

With burns Tonino was forthright. His firefighting philosophy, if you can call it that, was based on his machismo nature. He regarded firefighting as a kind of fistfight with nature, and Tonino never backed down from a fight. He met fires head-on without hesitation and couldn't be bothered with fancy control methods or fire theory, which he regarded as "mental masturbation for fags." Tonino was gutsy, instinctual. When faced with fire he slavered heavily and wanted nothing but for the flames to be extinguished by his own hand and spit. This attitude in a squad commander was both good and bad for the crew: bad because it was exhausting to attack fire with the aggression Tonino demanded, and good because in the field his commands were straightforward and unequivocal—*you take the point, you take that section, you two over there, you're on mop-up operations,* or whatever. We instinctively understood Tonino's approach and never had to stop and scratch our heads in the middle of some dangerously chaotic inferno wondering just what it was the squad commander wanted of us.

Someone like Renato, on the other hand, was distant, cold, untouchable. He harbored a stark military vein that either gave him the air of a calculating fascist or else erupted in sadistic bouts in which he would issue a series of peremptory commands—*roll up the hoses, mop out the barracks, do five laps and fifty push-ups, wash the uniforms, refill the water tanks*—that made life at the firebase miserable. More important, his commands in the field sometimes verged on the absurd. He'd order us, inexplicably, to climb some ridge opposite the main fire for "flame behavior observation" or to clear a firebreak a full three kilometers from the blaze—a distance we found outrageous. For some reason that he never made clear to us, he would also prevent us from burying burning embers of deadwood in the black, or burned-out, area; he called it a waste of time, while for us it was a common procedure that had been taught to us in basic training.

I guess it was that, as a married man with children—the only one of us so—Renato had to be more cautious than the rest of us when it came to putting out a blaze. Yet he defended his "prophylactic approach," as he called it, with a fully documented academic rationale that few of us had the least inkling of. Renato was the only one of us with a university degree. His dissertation (University of Napoli, 1989) was on prescribed burns, and he kept up-to-date with fire theory. He was a firm believer in On-Fire Management, a laissez-faire, or Let-It-Burn, approach that holds that wildfires should be allowed to burn themselves out unless they threaten human life or man-made physical structures. "Fire suppression" (here Renato quoted someone named Robichand) "only serves to delay the inevitable conflagration, and to make forest fires more intense and destructive because of accumulated debris. Several low-severity burns will cause less destruction than a single high-intensity blaze." Renato openly scoffed at Tonino's approach. Decades of hard-line fire management, he claimed, were the main reason Italy now faced tinderbox conditions in so many of its Fire Management Sectors, ours included.

Cavalier Mezzasoma, who was a specialist in what is called Urban-Rural Interface Fire Management, concurred with Renato but took a less extreme position. He agreed that wildfires were an integral part of nature, but countered that the current high-fuel conditions of the forest preempted the Let-It-Burn approach. Because high levels of pyrogenic debris had already accumulated in state forests and national parks over recent decades, low-severity burns were now virtually an impossibility. Given the current amount of fuel in the forests, any fires larger than ten hectares were going to be severe, and it was highly unlikely that we would be able to achieve the 10 A.M. rule (have all fires under control by 10 A.M. the morning after they are reported) or to contain all fires to ten hectares or less. To make matters worse, tourism in national parks was up 62 percent in the last twelve years and housing construction in rural areas was continuing unabated—both trends that aggravated the occurrence of wildfire.

Mezzasoma stressed education of the public—teaching campers to be safe with campfires and not to set off fireworks or to throw burning cigarette butts from car windows. He was also sponsoring fire regulations to ensure what is now being called "defensible space"—preventive firebreaks—around housing in rural areas, in order to avoid conflagrations like the one that swept through Oakland, California, a few years ago. Eighty percent of such fires, he argued, could be avoided through defensible space—areas with proper fire-resistant foliage, wide roads, plenty of fire hydrants, and an intelligent and well-publicized fire plan.

After going over the details of the controlled blaze planned for the Parco Regionale d'Abruzzo, Mezzasoma announced a final bit of news. The Cavalier had just received a letter from Sgna. Ewa Cholanaski, coordinator for volunteer affairs in Warsaw. The letter stated that travel and visa arrangements had been made, and that we were to expect a dozen volunteers to arrive in Casabasso by train on July 31 at ten in the morning, final confirmation to follow. The project was a result of our organizational ties with the International Youth Volunteer Network that Mezzasoma had established several years back.

"What's it all about?" Renato asked.

"Restoration," Mezzasoma answered. "They want to clean up some statues in the Palazzo Sangiusto gardens."

"Art students," Tonino said, grinning cheek to cheek. "Art students are always chicks."

"You keep your paws in your pockets," Mezzasoma said in a mock-fatherly way, not really meaning it. He stood up to end the meeting. Tonino disappeared down the hallway, and Renato turned into the map room to begin surveying topographical maps on the Parco Regionale d'Abruzzo. But as I made for the door, Mezzasoma put a hand on my shoulder and said my name.

Chapter 14

I turned to Mezzasoma and for the first time that day found myself staring right into his blind eye—his stray eye, to be more exact. Perhaps because of the shaded lamplight or the angle at which I'd been sitting, I hadn't paid it more than passing attention throughout the meeting.

The eye was blue, suffused over with a gray milky film, and the Cavalier seemed to have no control over it. The eyeball roved in its socket, the iris spinning around and around like a comet out of control. Once in a while the eye would stop and seem to look at you, but after a moment you'd realize its stopping was as random as its orbital movements. Sometimes the iris trembled violently in the eyeball socket. I wondered if he'd been born with the eye like that or whether it was the result of some accident.

Mezzasoma looked at me and said, "Matteo."

"Sir."

"Relax, Matteo. This isn't the army, you know." He shifted his body so that he was leaning against the desk, and asked, "How'd it go earlier?"

"Okay, I guess," I answered. "Renato and I arrived in Pelle Marone at about thirteen hundred hours and . . . completed . . . the transaction. Then we picked up Tonino at the warehouse and. . . ."

Mezzasoma lifted his hand to interrupt me. "I meant this morning's call, Matteo—the fire." He picked up a glass paperweight and toyed with it absentmindedly. "It is better not to talk about those other things," he said. "Besides, I don't know of any town called Pelle Marone."

I nodded, somewhat embarrassed. Then I proceeded to describe the small blaze the squad had been called to that morning. It had really been nothing: some grasses serving as a buffer between a country road and a *contadino's* tobacco field had caught fire.

"Sounds like a misplaced match," Mezzasoma said.

"Somebody probably threw a cigarette out the window of their car," I agreed.

"Do you want to write it down?"

"Sure," I said eagerly. Lately the Cavalier had been letting me fill out the postfire report forms, which recorded the date, time and place of the fire, weather conditions and other such data, and included a general description of the burn and an explanation of probable cause. "Misplaced matchstick" was our informal way of saying "human error."

"Well," Mezzasoma said, tugging on his belt, "I'm going to get some air." He briefly put a hand on my shoulder and smiled, then left me to fill out the report.

I was conscientious about it, maybe that's why the Cavalier liked me. I guessed he liked me. That's why he'd been looking out for me since my father died and why he was getting me involved with the inner workings of the brigade, letting me in on the assignations. The idea crossed my mind that maybe, in the future, he wouldn't be opposed to establishing a paid position for me as brigade communications officer. I could already picture the insignia on my firefighter's uniform.

I considered it an honor to complete the postfire report form. For probable cause I wrote, "Human error, non-premeditated."

The fire in the hills near Pelle Marone occurred a few days later. Along with a squad from the neighboring town of Torona, one squad from our brigade was called to the burn. As we drove along the *autostrada* and past the Anilone Caves, through the industrial sector and along the rural road that led across the foothills and out into the countryside—exactly the same route I'd taken with Renato a few days earlier for the assignation—the oddness of the coincidence did cross my mind. But I thought it was only that, an odd coincidence. Nothing seemed out of the ordinary. I fought the fire as I would any other fire.

The flames had ensnared themselves in some low knobs choking with weeds and thickets, and the burn would have been difficult to handle had it not been for the red-striped Canadair that came racing out of the north with its twin propellers and a belly full of river water. Something in my mind clicked there: the airplane. *They always want a Canadair,* Renato had said. I stopped on a ledge, and the ground seemed to tilt and whirl. I dropped my *flabello* and Pulaski on the rocks and squatted down.

At first I couldn't believe it, I wouldn't. I stood and watched the rest of the squad move along the slopes, following the paths of the burn as if they really meant it, as if we weren't all actors.

My stomach lurched, and I could feel bile pushing at the bottom of my throat. The Canadair whined overhead, coming and going. In repeated passes at intervals of about twenty minutes, the plane took the edge off the worst areas of the blaze and dampened the vegetation in the fire's path, slowing the flames down considerably. Each time it reappeared I felt I was witnessing the explosion of the Hindenburg. Finally I leaned over and vomited my lunch on some rocks. The rocks were hot with the fire, and the regurgitation sizzled.

After the plane had made several passes and was no longer needed, Renato signaled the pilot for a "baptism"—that's when the aircraft sprays a load of water right on top of the firefighters themselves. Usually baptisms are reserved for emergencies, situations where there's real danger to the squad members, but once in a while the pilots will indulge in a frivolous drop. That really did it for me, the fact that Renato, who prided himself on operating by the book, had requested one. I knew he thought of it as some kind of compensation for the trouble he'd gone through to set this all up.

I jumped up and tore through the understory, forcing my way through a thicket of thorns that lashed at my cheeks, drew blood. I ran over to Renato and gripped his sleeve hard and yelled, "It's not supposed to be like this!"

Renato knocked my hand off his arm so violently I staggered back and fell to the ground. He understood me immediately. "What did I tell you, Matteo?" he said. "You're blind as a blind fish." He glared at me as he straightened his sleeve. "And don't touch me like that ever again." We heard the Canadair returning, its propellers whining over the hills. The plane circled the site once, high, taking the bearings of the squad, then came in for a straight low pass. As Renato removed his hat to receive the water, he nodded up at the plane. "Always the Canadair, didn't I tell you?" He raised his face up to the sky. "But after all," he said, directing his voice upwards, "she holds more water than a pregnant bitch, eh, Matteo?" He said something else, but the words were lost in the roaring buzz of the airplane as it raked over us. The water plunged down in a hail of drops as hard as BBs.

I swear to God and on my father's grave, that was the first time I put it all together.

Chapter 15

Though I had long suspected that the brigade was involved in questionable business deals, I'd never been privy to the details until this summer. Even through July, as I was accompanying Renato on all those assignations, I never suspected what I realized the day the plane raked us over with water near Pelle Marone.

It was complicated, but in the end it could be distilled down to one thing: money. The fire brigade needed money, we were short of funds, the government was stingy. In order to finance ourselves, we needed to justify our existence—our materiel, our firefighting equipment, our buildings and ground vehicles, our manpower, our air-support systems and all the rest. Local farmers, particularly in the degraded agricultural areas surrounding Casabasso, were looking for extra cash too, and local businesses like the liquor manufacturers and the Trattoria Tramontano needed more business. Nobody was in this to get rich; we were simply trying to survive in a depressed economy. I guess that's not the best justification, but it's one that was used to rationalize what was going on. So we had *contadini*, or farmers, set innocuous fires in the countryside. Sometimes we put them out ourselves, sometimes we called in the 402s—those are the big helicopters—or the Canadair planes to help us out. This way, even during the off-season, the brigade could demonstrate that it was needed—and worthy of regional and federal funding.

One thing that confused me about all this was the fact that the assignations didn't seem to abate during the high-fire season; in the first two weeks of July alone, I realized in retrospect, we had arranged burns or made payments in at least four different communes. Later on, after I'd gotten over Pelle Marone, I asked Renato why they didn't slow things down in the high season, but he wouldn't explain it, just gave me a stern look and said, "Who? Slow down what?"

Firemen starting fires for profit: I couldn't imagine anything more despicable. So why didn't I quit? I guess it was a mixture of shame and capitulation, a surrender to fate. To resign would amount to an admission of guilt. I was already well into it and decided to give myself over to the entire scheme the way you do when you think nothing can be done about the larger picture. I'm only human, I told myself. I'm limited, fallible. Besides, no one would believe I hadn't known about the whole thing from the very beginning, so what was the use of protesting, of claiming innocence? I was guilty by association—even more than that—and with each passing day I was guiltier than the day before, until I was just plain guilty.

Sure, I played around with the idea of blowing the whistle, but luckily I came to my senses. I didn't fool myself into thinking I could be a star stool pigeon or anything like that. In Italy, the life of an informer is no life at all.

After Pelle Marone I took several days off. I was mad, I was vehement, righteous. But I didn't take my righteousness too far—I never acted on it. Of course in the back of my mind I was scared too, there was that. I was scared of Mezzasoma, fearful of a jail term, frightened to stand up to people. The more I thought about it, the more I realized how many people were involved in one way or another—the squad, the brigade, various *contadini* and commune politicians, the liquor people, restaurateurs, pilots. . . . I didn't know where it stopped. It was like staring into a chasm.

And maybe I convinced myself I could do some good, keep an eye that things didn't get out of hand, minimize the damage. Because I really, honestly love the forest, trees, nature, wildlife. It hurts me to see a destroyed landscape. Even if fires are part of the natural cycle, it is just as natural for men to fight against them, to protect the land. Though to some extent, as I can now admit, I'd grown addicted to fire myself, though I thrived on the theatrical quality of pines geysering into flame and thirsted for the heady adrenaline rush—what really motivated me, convinced me to stay with the brigade, was simply the fact that, whatever our peccadilloes, the fire brigade was doing more good than bad in the world. It was an organization essential to the protection of the environment, of houses and buildings and of human lives.

Someone once asked me why firefighters don't just spray water on the burning forest and get it over with—and it still amazes me that some people don't realize how wild and volatile forest fires can actually be. Dropping several thousand liters of water (which is your typical helicopter load) on a Class C fire (ten to ninety-nine hectares) is about as effective as attacking a battleship with a pellet gun.

That's why firefighters clear firebreaks. You see, a fire is a triangle built of fuel, air and heat; control any one of these elements, and you control fire. But how do you tie up the wind? How do you cool down temperatures that melt glass? How do you run water hoses out into the wilderness? And most crucially, how do you restrain the hearts of men? If you want to stop a forest fire, your only choice is to take away its wood; if a fire has nothing left to burn, it goes out. That's what a firebreak does— cuts off the fire's fuel resources by clearing trees and bushes in a fire's path, creating a buffer zone free of combustible material.

The notion of fighting fire with fire was born from this method of strangling a fire's fuel resources. The theory boils down to the common adage that tells the peasant he can't burn a faggot of sticks twice. So why not burn the forest before it burns itself? Why not clear a firebreak using fire? It's a thorough and efficient and quick way of clearing any area of potential fuel. And perhaps that was what Nico was thinking when, in the great uproar of the retreat up the slopes of Mount Maggiore, he pulled that tube of pyrophoric paste from his breast pocket and bent down to light the mountain grasses afire.

Yes, the question of Nico, of the imminent tribunal inquest. I may have time to rethink some of these other matters, but Maggiore looms. Was it Nico's fault that the others misunderstood or didn't listen, that they refused to enter his fire and instead took their chances racing the wind?

Did the wind take the escape fire off-route and force the others beneath the impassible bluff? Was it the backfire that killed Enzo, Saverio, Pietro, Massimo, Renato? How will I answer when the magistrate asks me, as ask me he must?

I return to my vigil—my prayer, I'd like to call it—in front of the map of Mount Maggiore tacked to the wall of my apartment. I study the mapped terrain as though trying to read wrinkles on a palm. I'm sure I wouldn't have made it up that mountainside had it not been for Nico. But today I see in my mind's eye what I didn't see before, what I have failed to see, what I refused to see. I see Nico's fire cutting off the trajectory of the other crew members, forcing them east toward the impassible bluff, pushing them toward death.

But it is my fault. Renato's fault and Mezzasoma's. Everybody who tasted a slice of the cake. For doesn't it come back to all of us who hired the *contadino* who, in an absurdly businesslike and casual way, on a resplendent morning decorated with birch and heralded by robins, hiked up into the forested hills, spat on the ground, and lit a match at the feet of the gods, at the foot of Maggiore?

Part Two
Torching the Letter

Chapter 16

I know what the others suffered, what Enzo, Saverio, Pietro, Massimo, Renato suffered. I myself was burned—not on Mount Maggiore but several years ago, on the day we found the children's corpses out near the Grotte di Pastena. We were deployed out in some dense knobs due west of the caves. Beautiful terrain but dry, drought-thirsty that year. The wood of the trees was as brittle as a kid's wooden building blocks, the parched leaves flammable and fragile as papier mâché.

The stench of bodies hit us as we were working our way up a long rocky ravine. We recognized the odor immediately—something like putrid meat grilled over wood coals. Pietro pushed his way among the burnt reeds and found the two corpses, charred and shriveled, twisted together in the dry streambed. The flesh was still smoking. The bodies were small—a girl and a boy, we found out later, of eleven and twelve. Obviously they'd been looking for the creek, but it was late summer and the water had long ago dried up. Who knows what had brought them out there into those desolate hills? Maybe they had started the fire themselves—a melted lighter had been found in the boy's pocket—or perhaps they had simply been taking a stroll and had grown curious about a column of smoke they'd noticed in the distance.

Fires can run faster than men. They can spread across a field like an angry mob, charge like a rank of mounted Cossacks. When I saw the small corpses, I remembered the story of Bambi and the fire that spread through the forest, how the animals jumped into the river to escape the flames. The children's bodies were like large fetuses aborted in the gully, two corpses left behind in some utterly useless and violent rush of war. I fought back a gag of vomit.

We left Pietro to stand watch over the bodies and wait for the paramedic team. The rest of us, following the destructive trail of the blaze, entered the wooded stands higher up the hills.

The fire had moved up into the highland forest, mostly pine and aspen with an understory of scattered rhododendron and brambles. Still in shock from the discovery of the bodies, we stumbled along the slopes pursuing the edge of the burn. After several hours of backbreaking effort we managed to establish a firebreak along an old mountain trail, but the fire kept reaching over our heads, sending out huge tentacles of flame that jumped the break and ignited trees on the other side. These trees we were forced to cut down with a chainsaw or with the axe head of our Pulaskis. Once the burning trees were on the ground, we knocked out the flames with *flabelli* and shoveled dirt onto the hot embers.

I remember I had been working on a young aspen, trying to chop it down but having trouble cutting through the tough fibrous wood at the heart of the trunk, which was still green with youth. The blade on my Pulaski was dulling, and I paused to inspect it for a moment and catch my breath. I wasn't thinking about the burned children but trying to decide whether it would be worth my while to spend a few minutes hand-sharpening the blade when I heard a sound that I thought at first, absurdly, was a shipwreck. It sounded like high winds had just snap-filled the canvases of a dozen sails and the mast couldn't withstand the pressure. A gust of wind tugged hard at my shirt, I heard the wooden mast cracking and looked up to see a neighboring cedar, thoroughly aflame, the branches as splendid and bright as giant torches, crashing down upon me.

The tree caught me in midair, halfway through my desperate lunge to clear the branches. It threw me onto the earth like a child tossing down her doll in a fit of anger, and pinned me to the ground. The last breath I'd taken was punched from my diaphragm, I tasted dirt and ashes and saw stars of sorts, which I stupidly thought were gnats or mosquitoes swimming around my head. I could smell hair burning, and cloth and something else, and then a wild pain was shooting down the back of my neck as though someone were pressing a hot iron to my skin.

Trapped beneath the tree, I wrestled crazily, deliriously in the dirt. I thought for a second that a car had fallen on top of me while I'd been sleeping. There seemed to be someone on my buttocks and thighs pinning me to the ground and pouring boiling water on my neck and arms while I squirmed in the seething understory.

What kept me alive, strangely enough, was precisely the pain of that boiling water on my skin. Pain that was fast and expert and that instructed my body to ignore my raving mind and to save itself instantly and at all costs, and with one incredibly supple and violent twist I was on my feet careening away from the blaze—fearful, angry, blind, screaming, my left arm putting out the fire on my right arm.

Tonino took chase, caught hold of me, stopped me, smothered me, calmed me down. I was guided to safety. The paramedics, who had just loaded the children's bodies into the ambulance, cut off my shirt with a pair of surgical scissors and tossed it on the ground. I thought the shirt looked like a kite that had flown too close to the sun.

Though I cannot equate my own experience with the inhuman corporeal agony the burn victims suffered on Mount Maggiore, I am familiar with the smell of my own scorched flesh and with the inhuman stench of the burn ward—that fermenting, gangrenous odor of moribund bodies. When I was hospitalized for the injuries I'd received at the Grotte di Pastena, I became intimate with that horrid smell, intimate with the smell and with the pain attached to that smell. I came to know pain in a way that I'd never thought possible.

I guess I'd grown accustomed, as most of us naturally have, to imagining my body as a vessel whose main purpose is to register physical pleasure—gastronomic, tactile, sexual. Before my sentence in the burn ward, I'd never entertained the notion that pain might serve its own purpose, that it might even be illuminating and intelligent in its own right. But lying in the hospital bed staring at a corner of the sky or at the ceiling or television, I recalled how pain had saved my life up on the mountainside. I remembered how pain, like an instinct or a voice of consciousness ringing in my head, one that I had never before heeded, spoke up and pointed to corners of the universe I rarely acknowledged. The worst bodily discomforts I had previously experienced were temporary hunger, a cracked shin, a tooth rotting over the weekend until the nerve was dead. One time my eardrum burst in the middle of the night, staining my pillow with blood. But in the burn ward I became intimate with pain in its purest form.

I had received second-degree burns along my right arm and shoulder and on the back of my neck. The doctors had me bandaged up like a mummy, and the bandages had to be removed each morning so that the nurse could clean the wounds. That process involved what burn victims call "scraping the slough": removing the curdled white pus that oozes from the entire surface of the burn wound like some noxious fungal mold.

For the burn patient, scraping the slough is the most arduous, the most excruciating, the most primitive process ever devised in the history of medicine. My entire body would stiffen and break into a sweat the moment the nurse entered the ward with her Amazonian step, pushing before her a stainless steel cart laden with medical supplies. The moment was made surreal by the fact of the nurse's astounding beauty. A glorious *ragazza* from the town of Tivoli, her name was Dolores, and she was tall and full-bodied, with dark lips and big eyes and long strands of brunette hair wrapped at the back of her head in a loose knot.

Dolores would approach me with her tray piled with scissors and creams and meters of gauze, and with not much more than a *Buon giorno* she would begin unwinding and peeling off the bandages. Her movements were careful yet casual, as if she were hand-laundering fine lace, and her expression didn't change when the bandage came off nor when she took the metal "sponge" and began scraping off the white pus. It felt like she was using a cheese slicer to rasp off my flesh. There was no skin to speak of. The skin had been burned and sloughed off, the way you can slip off the peel of a pepper or an eggplant after baking it in the oven. Tears in my eyes, I'd stare at Dolores' neck, at the delicate cords there moving provocatively beneath her skin until I couldn't stand it any longer, then I'd close my eyes and try to pretend I was already dead. If I was lucky, I could smell Dolores's perfume—crushed hyacinth, a transporting fragrance I now irrevocably associate, through some mysterious psychic shortcut, with pure, unadulterated sadness.

Then a voice would rise from beyond the white bed curtains, a man's voice singing the national anthem or the "Internazionale" or the dark "Torna Caserio" or perhaps some old pop standard like "Maramao" or "When I Was in Rome." It was the voice of my roommate, Leonardo.

Some months previous, Leo, a devoted aviator, had been the victim of a Cessna accident. When the plane hit the ground, his head had been doused with fuel oil and ignited into a ball of flame—a "halo of lost innocence," as Leo himself called it. He had received the most unimaginable burns, and even the doctors spoke of his recovery with the quiet tone of awe reserved for miracles.

Though in medical terms Leo, when I met him, was well past the critical stage, he was forced to wear a special mask made of tough, clear polyurethane. The mask had been molded from his own features (literally molded, set in plaster while Leo breathed through straws inserted into his nostrils) and it was very tight—it was made to be very, very tight. That was to keep his face from falling off, Leo told me. Though to put it more accurately, it was to prevent his face from ballooning out. You see, burn tissue has a way of swelling, of expanding relentlessly for up to two years—hence the tight bandages common in all burn wards. Leo's mask was designed to constrict the flow of blood to the capillaries in his face, thus depriving the scars of oxygen and nutrients and limiting the swelling, or what is referred to medically as scar-tissue expansion.

Behind his mask Leo looked like a man pressed with great force against a pane of glass. He reminded me of one of those pale, gaunt faces exposed to G-forces without protective gear, images captured in bleak black-and-white scientific clips. Other times Leo resembled a partly constructed cyborg, a Frankenstein monster, imperfect and hideous. What made it worse was the sound of Leo's breathing and talking; he could do so only through two tiny apertures drilled through the plastic. His voice was a strangled noise, unsettling as that of a man trying to talk through his own coffin. And when Leo finally removed the mask—to sing, usually—his skin resembled a flank of meat left to bake out in the sun: raw muscles, tendons, ghastly pink.

What struck me most was the fact that Leo's eyes—irises blue as the Adriatic—remained hauntingly clear, even sparkling, like sunlight off sea water. He was constantly moistening his eyes with an eyedropper, and I soon found out why. The scar tissue surrounding his eye sockets was stretching his face in a peculiar and terrible way: Leo found it difficult to keep his eyes shut. Within months or weeks, the doctors would have to operate, slicing away at the scar tissue constricting the muscles that controlled his eyelids.

You would think that such suffering would engender bitterness or despair, but on most days Leo was upbeat, *spiritoso*. He often told jokes or spun yarns about his stint flying guns in the Ethiopian conflict. I admired his positive attitude but suspected his good spirits masked an underlying fear and depression.

Sometimes I could hear Leo shifting around uncomfortably on his mattress at night. I pitied him, the patient on the other side of the bed-curtain, lying on his bunk trying to sleep but literally having trouble keeping his eyes closed.

Now when I think about that time, what I find most ironic is the possibility that I went through all that excruciating pain, all that long-suffered agony, because of something the squad did. Had we ourselves arranged for the fire to be set at the Grotte, just as we had at Pelle Marone and at so many other fires too countless to name? Was I burned so the squad could ensure itself boots and meals, so we could hold on to the very jobs that endangered our lives? Were those bodies at the Grotte di Pastena, the children's dead bodies, our own doing?

Chapter 17

\-

With the tribunal inquest less than two weeks away, I am hard-pressed to tell the truth and nothing but the truth. Cooped up in my small apartment, I throw myself facedown on the bed and don't sleep. My head pounds. I've been hounded by headaches lately, and my limbs are weary. I seem to *feel* gravity. It is as though my blood is laced with lead.

How can I talk about Maggiore without startling the whole school of fish? Can the truth include the *contadino* but not the brigade, not the assignations? Should it include Renato but not Nico, or Nico but not Renato? Which other squad members were in the loop? What about the district commander-in-chief of the brigade, Cavalier Mezzasoma himself? Shouldn't he too be held responsible in some way? And no matter what I decide to reveal or not to reveal, isn't the truth bound to stretch out its tentacles and strangle me, reveal my complicity and negligence, expose my idiocy with the two-way radios? *Truth,* I think, is too small a word for life. It is an idea too tiny, too provincial to correspond to what happens, to what has happened in the world. History provides no access to itself. The past is a *fata mirabilis,* a castle of clouds riding in the sky, clearly visible one moment then gone the next, never to be recovered—even as I am borne back once again toward it, a moth drawn to torchlight.

After the fire at Pelle Marone, when I finally realized the assignations were all really about arson, I went around in a kind of daze. As I've said, I took several days furlough and examined the whole affair from top to bottom. I was deeply distressed by what I had learned, that the brigade itself was responsible for setting at least some fires—or rather, for paying off some-one to set them—though how regularly or irregularly it was still difficult for me to gauge. Knowledge is supposed to free you in some way, open up possibilities, but for me it seemed to close doors and shut windows. To know something and not be able to speak it—my position was caustic. I felt hemmed in, blackmailed. Not that I'm trying to make excuses for myself regarding my decision not to quit the brigade then and there. To be frank, staying on was easier than leaving; it was the path of least resist-ance, a path I've doubtlessly chosen to amble along too many times.

I remember this time as a period of inner adjustment, a resynchroniza-tion of the synapses and electrodes in my brain; like a housecat left to prowl outside at night for the first time, I instinctively adapted my eyes to this strange new realm. I came to see the brigade and all its activities through pupils dilated with adrenaline, witnessed the universe through irises of a different pigment. But my attention was focused not only on the brigade and my place in it; I also began reassessing Nico. He too seemed to be undergoing a metamorphosis of sorts, and about late July and early August, two events occurred that seemed to disturb him deeply: the air-mail letter arrived from Firenze, and Nico was tricked into an encounter with the woman we called the bikini girl. This latter fiasco originated in one of the squad's perennial practical jokes.

When I first began volunteering for the brigade some five or six years ago, our firebase stood alone on a patch of barren ground outside of town. Since then, the boulevard has been widened to four lanes and a new traf-fic tunnel has been constructed under the train tracks near the palace, replacing the traffic-congested two-lane bridge that formerly served as the city's south-central pass. Little by small, businesses cropped up on the boulevard—gas stations, restaurants, nurseries and the like—and a spate of low-income apartment complexes were built on the northern and eastern borders of the firebase clearing. The yellow-brick apartments, which have gated windows and tropical plants on their balconies, are so close, as Enzo used to say, we could make out the brand of underwear the old women hung out to dry on the clotheslines.

An attractive young woman occupied one of the apartments facing the firebase. She seemed to live by herself. We'd notice her every once in a while ascending or descending the stairs to the parking lot, tending to lingerie on the clothesline or having a coffee and a cigarette on her balcony, which we could see quite clearly from one corner of the command post terrace. One day by pure chance Massimo noticed that the woman was standing topless on her balcony. He let out a yelp and ran for the binoculars, and due to the commotion he started—we were jostling one another for a chance with the binoculars—the woman noticed us and, realizing what we were up to, tossed several sharp curses in our direction.

That didn't stop us, of course, from keeping an eye on her. And though the woman proceeded more modestly—we witnessed no further topless forays—she didn't keep her Persian blinds down or stop appearing in various states of undress on her second-story balcony. We, too, made ourselves less conspicuous. After all, the view to her place was mostly blocked by the supply tent, and if you really wanted to see her you had to perch yourself on one corner of the command post terrace—out back, by the water tank— to get a direct view. There, Massimo knocked a hook into the tin siding of the building and hung an old pair of binoculars onto the hook so that if you happened to notice her while you were out back getting a drink at the spigot, the lenses would be handy.

I, too, trained the lenses on her place. She wasn't exactly a beautiful woman—medium height, blonde, early thirties, with sloped shoulders, a soft stomach, firm legs—but there was something attractive and alluring to her movements, which were casual, or graceful in a careless way, and seemed sexy when spied through a pair of strong binoculars.

One day just for the fun of it, Tonino came up with the idea that we should send somebody over to meet this single woman, and he devised some elaborate stratagem that involved eleven stones and a marble in bag. Whoever was left with the marble—Nico Americano, in this case, since the whole thing was fixed—would have to go knock on the woman's door. The lottery worked, and Nico didn't realize he'd been had.

None of us in the crew would have actually followed through with the thing. We would have taken some licks from the others, we would have hung our heads low for being wimps or pretended to go over and then fabricated a story about it all or whatever—but none of us would ever have been audacious enough to walk over there and knock on the woman's door. But for whatever reason—the guys, especially Massimo and Pietro, laid on the banter pretty thick—Nico felt compelled to go. Such naïveté! I felt sorry for Nico and almost said something to him, almost explained that the stones and the marble were in separate compartments . . . but I chickened out, hoping he would change his mind at the last minute. Instead Nico changed into a fresh green polo shirt and combed his hair. He opened his mouth for a blast of Enzo's pocket breath spray, listened to Tancredi's instructions on how to bypass the electronic building entrance, and made his way over to the apartment complex.

Massimo took the binoculars to the edge of the terrace and trained them on the woman's apartment. The woman was on her porch enjoying an afternoon espresso and a newspaper. Massimo swung the sights to the building's entranceway.

"The Americano's got the door open!" he announced.

"I don't believe it," Cesare said when Nico had disappeared into the building.

"He won't do anything," Saverio commented.

We were quiet as several minutes passed. Massimo stood like a statue with the binoculars to his eyes.

"Maybe he can't find the right door," I said. I was expecting Nico to come back out of the building any minute.

"She's getting up!" Massimo announced excitedly. "She's going to the door!"

We kicked the ground with titillation and guilt, crowding around Massimo and grabbing for the binoculars. I now realize (as I did at some gut level even then) how obtuse and sophomoric we were behaving. What were we expecting to see, anyway? Did we think the Americano was going to join the woman out on her terrace in some kind of pornographic exhibition? What strikes me now is the ease with which I ignored my own gut instinct, how I beat down my misgivings and instead gave myself over to the heat and excitement of the moment, how I elbowed for my turn with the binoculars and trained the sights on the woman's empty apartment window even as I knew that what I was doing was ridiculous and false. I felt the same way whenever I fought a blaze that I knew was not accidental, only this time my hypocrisy would be at Nico's expense.

When Nico shuffled back from the apartment complex a few minutes later he looked as though the woman had stabbed him. His head was hung low and it seemed he could barely lift his feet. He wouldn't look us in the eyes and shook off our inquiries. "*Niente succede,*" he said morosely, "nothing happened. She didn't answer the door."

Massimo, who'd seen the woman get up from her chair at about the same time that Nico would have pressed her buzzer, wasn't convinced it was a coincidence. He pressed Nico for the details but Nico wouldn't respond, and when Massimo grabbed him by the shoulders and waved the binoculars in front of his face, Nico began cursing at him in a severe English I couldn't understand. He seemed on the verge of tears, his words wavered as though he were talking through moving fan blades, and the next thing we knew he made a quick movement with his arms and tore the binoculars out of Massimo's hands, snapping the leather strap. It looked like he was about to hurl the binoculars against the tin siding and Massimo made a move to stop him, but Nico twisted his body around and swung his elbow and suddenly Massimo was on the ground holding a hand to the pain in his ear. Enzo went to grab Nico in a sort of bear hug—not out of violence, it was clear, but simply to calm him down—but Nico threw his hands up in the air in anger and knocked Enzo away like a puppet, sending him backward off the terrace steps and into the dirt. Then Nico turned and strode off as he was wont to do at such moments, as we had seen him do many a time before, whenever he felt threatened or offended. He strode at a quick pace away from us, past the barracks and out the firebase gates— not in the direction of town but out toward the hills, toward Ceprano, striding in great gulps of steps, jerkily, wavering like a drunk. He didn't return until after nightfall, and whether out of shock or sympathy or perhaps bewilderment, no one in the brigade ever breathed a word of it.

The letter was delivered a day later, before Nico had a chance to recover from the first blow.

Addressed in flowery handwriting to Nicolas Ryan Fowler, the missive arrived in an airmail envelope—though the Italian stamps, I noticed, were canceled in Firenze—and there was no return address. The handwritten letters were blue and loopy yet clearly practiced, like that of a girl unwillingly taught script by French nuns. I assumed it was from Adina, the ex-girlfriend Nico had told me a little about.

When I handed Nico the letter, his expression didn't change, but seeing the filigreed handwriting, he held the envelope in his fingers like it was made of glass. Then he methodically capped his pen and closed his notebook—he'd been writing again—and disappeared into the barracks even though it was still midafternoon and the temperature inside must have been unbearable. He didn't come out again for a long time. We received a call in the meantime—there was a small blaze out by Ceprano—but he declined to join us, and when we returned he was sitting outside like before, settled in a white plastic armchair, one knee drawn up for a makeshift desk, penning words into his journal. He didn't mention the letter, didn't so much as hint whom it was from or what it was about, but when he spoke to me I found his voice softer than normal, more labored, as if he were recovering from a blow to the solar plexus.

Maybe it was because of the letter or because of the bikini girl incident, or maybe it was something else that I don't know of, but I noticed a distinct change come over Nico, saw it as starkly as an afternoon shadow creeping across a field. He became distant and burdened, like someone who has something extremely crucial and personal to say but for whatever reason does not, or cannot, say it. He stopped shaving—sharp jet stubble sprouted on his cheeks and chin—and over several days he became surly and more taciturn than ever. He spent virtually all of his free time in the solitary business of writing, scratching out God-knows-what—monologues, unsent missives, complaints, verse?—into his black-bound notebook. I was reminded of the first time I'd seen him, the morning Renato had driven him to the firebase to drop off his baggage. Those first days of his stay in Casabasso, how grim and sullen Nico had seemed, how small-souled and impatient! Compared to his spirited moods of the last month, it now seemed his personality had come full circle.

I tried a few times to draw Nico out of his funk and get him to talk to me, but he was adamant and unresponsive, and I soon gave up trying. I had too much going on in my own life, anyway. I was busy rationalizing my own stance toward the assignations, distracted by my attempts to assuage my guilt, sidetracked by self-pity. The fact that I was at bottom a firestarter was still too big a pill for me to swallow. It stuck in my throat, clung to the wall of my esophagus like some poisonous barnacle. Late and deep into my restive nights I tried in vain to digest the acid seeping into my already tainted blood. Unable to calm my own tortured psyche, how could I possibly have helped Nico with his?

Chapter 18

About this time Nico obtained a *motorino*—or moped, as he called it in English—and began spending virtually every afternoon out scouring the city, visiting museums and bookstores, searching the library for clues to the lives of Numa Pompilius and Ezra Pound, or cruising around the country-side and woodlands with his camera and binoculars at the ready to take in Campania's picturesque vistas. At least, at the time, that's what we assumed he was doing, though I can say with some confidence now that Nico was also—how shall I put it?—*looking for opportunities,* doing what people like him do. Sometimes he would take weekends off and travel by train or bus to the surrounding towns and villages, and one day after putting out a small blaze near Montefalco, we bumped into him at a bar in the center of town.

Renato, Enzo, Cesare, me and a few others were standing at the zinc bartop drinking coffee when a voice behind us asked, "Can you give me a lift?"

We turned. "Look who's here," Renato commented without emotion.

"Nico Americano!" Enzo trumpeted. "What are you doing all the way out here in the middle of nowhere?"

"Looking for Numa Pompilius," he replied.

Renato grunted disdainfully; by now we all knew about the Americano's crusade to find the birthplace of the ancient Sabine who'd initiated the vestal virgins and was, to boot, supposedly born of fire, and Renato found the whole thing absurd.

Playing along, Enzo asked, "Did you find him?"

"*Niente,* not a shadow," Nico shrugged.

"How did you find *us?*" Cesare inquired.

"I saw the jeep outside," Nico explained.

Renato said flatly, "What a coincidence."

"Imagine that, Americano!" Enzo said, slapping Nico on the back. "Have an espresso—it's on Renato."

"He's not on duty," Renato scowled. "He can buy his own coffee."

The next day Nico was back on the *motorino.* I remember noticing then how the freedom of the road seemed to have a positive effect on him. He'd leave the firebase sullen and morose yet return from his rides a few hours later excited, energetic, wide-eyed. Back then I thought it was simply the freedom of the roads that lifted his spirits, but now I read that change in his moods with a different emphasis: couldn't it have been the ecstasy of fire that so transported him?

"*Motorini* are bad!" he'd say, grinding to a stop on the firebase gravel, his hair all on end from his most recent ride.

"Where do you go?" I asked one day.

"Up and down across town, out in the hills, over the mountains, along the flat roads toward the sea. . . . Where don't I go?"

"But where did you get the *motorino?*"

"From Franco, at the pool bar."

Red flags waved in my brain. Franco was that punk who hung out at La Buca, that billiards hall in town—the same guy we'd seen a few months ago at the hutch fire, when the chicken coop burned to the ground. Franco had been one of the fellows up on the town ramparts throwing insults down at us. That time seemed like another life to me now.

I said, "That Franco's a bad egg."

"He's not so bad once you get to know him," Nico said. "He lent me his *motorino*, didn't he?"

"I've never heard of an Italian lending out his *motorino*," I said. "It's the same with cars. Your basic Italian wouldn't lend a battered Cinquecento to his own grandmother."

"I pay him," Nico answered. "Twelve thousand lire a day."

I nodded, but Nico wanted enthusiasm.

"Not a bad price, huh?" he prompted me.

"But what if something happens?" I cautioned.

"What could happen?"

"What if it breaks down?" I said.

"Nah."

"If something did happen," I warned him, "I wouldn't put it past a guy like Franco to beat you to a pulp."

But Nico would say *nah* and rev the motor till it whined and then take off again, and one time when he came back he said he'd met a gypsy and become fascinated with gypsy life.

"That can only lead to trouble," Renato observed. We all shook our heads in agreement.

"That's my middle name," Nico replied, flashing a smile before going off to grab his books and pens.

We lost track of him then more than ever before, sometimes for days at a time. It was the middle of the fire season, after all, and we had more than our fair share of burns to attend to. Nico was like a blur at the edge of our field of vision; we couldn't seem to keep him in focus.

Nor could we depend on him to help out at the firebase, for we spent time between calls performing drills and chores—mopping out the barracks or sweeping out the jeeps or picking up the cigarette butts that had accumulated in the dirt and gravel in front of the command post. Renato was vehement against smoking, and he despised the way we dropped our cigarette butts onto the ground as though the firebase were nothing but one big ashtray. When he got mad enough, Renato would make us check the fire hoses—hoses we never actually used in the field but that just sort of lay around camp like piles of dead snakes. Checking the hoses meant a couple of hours of work. We'd pull the hoses out from the storage shed and extend them full-length across the firebase compound. Then we'd hook them to the *naso*, or hydrant, and Tonino would get out the huge wrench— it was as big as his thigh—and grunt open the valve. While two of us wrestled with the live end of the hose, spraying the water into the far field, the others would check for leaks; by the time we'd roll the hoses, the firebase was nothing more than a mud pit.

Nico was often absent for these tasks, a fact about which Renato—more loudly than usual—expressed his disapproval. He had always been peeved that the American seemed to make his own schedule, fighting fires when he felt like fighting fires and taking time off when he felt like taking time off; and now that Nico had the *motorino*, he was out and about almost every afternoon.

"He sleeps here and eats here," Renato would say, shaking his head as Nico left the firebase, "and he should work here too."

"But when he doesn't work, he doesn't join us at the Trattoria Tramontano," Saverio observed.

"So what!" Renato spit, his face growing red. "He still sleeps on the bunk we provide him!"

"Take it easy, Renato," Saverio said. "What do you want to have, a heart attack? Nico's a volunteer. Can you force a volunteer to work?"

"If he wants to stay here, he's got to conform to our rules," Renato said.

"What rules?" Tonino chimed in, effectively ending the discussion.

The next afternoon we received a fire call just as Nico was hopping on the *motorino*.

"Hey, Americano!" Renato called to him. "You're coming on this one."

"I'd prefer not to," Nico replied.

"What?" Renato said, dumbfounded.

"I'd really prefer not to," Nico repeated. "*Ciao, tutti. Buona caccia.*" And he drove off on the *motorino*.

Renato was furious. The words *happy hunting* seemed to scald him. He fumed as he drove us to the fire. His face flushed red with anger and you could see the veins straining to pump blood in his neck. He banged the heel of his palm on the steering wheel and screamed, "Does he think we're running a hotel here, for Christ's sake!"

"Let it go, Renato," Tonino said, casually flicking the ash from his cigarette out the window.

Renato cursed vulgarly.

Saverio leaned forward. "Just forget it and leave him be," he advised Renato. "Can't you see there's something bothering him?"

"Yeah, well, there's something bothering me too," Renato replied.

"And what's that exactly?" Tonino asked.

"He's just pissed because he thinks the Americano doesn't do enough work," Massimo put in, "and maybe he's right too."

"No," Renato said, pausing to make a sharp turn. A couple of us grabbed onto the hand straps that were bolted to the ceiling of the rear cabin. Renato straightened out the jeep and continued, "That's not the whole picture."

"Well, what is?" Saverio inquired.

Renato took the jeep out of fourth gear, remembered it didn't have a fifth, and nudged it back into fourth. He said with a sigh, "I don't know. I just have a bad feeling about him. You guys all know I think he's a thief, you've known that since the beginning. But there's something else about him that gets in my collar. I can't tell you what it is because I don't know myself, but I'll tell you one thing, I'm not happy about Nico hanging around with Franco and those punks over at the billiards dive."

There were grunts of agreement.

"And," Renato went on, "I don't like the way he writes everything down like he's taking notes, and then running off and what have you."

I could see the guys nodding in agreement, so felt like I had to speak up in Nico's defense. I said, "It's not like he's an investigative journalist or something. He's just a poet."

"Yeah, a regular Dante," Massimo said sarcastically, glaring at me. "What are you, his literary agent?"

"No, I was just saying," I answered.

"Does someone smell something burning?" Saverio asked.

Renato ignored him. "I just don't like it," he reiterated. "That American wrinkles my shirt. He. . . ."

We rounded a curve and Renato lost his words. Two cars were burning on the side of the road. Wind hurled the thick black fumes across the asphalt and we went smack into the smoke like we'd driven into an unlit tunnel. Renato hit the brakes hard. The jeep swayed dangerously and we all grasped for hand straps we couldn't see as the vehicle swerved into the lane of oncoming traffic, but Renato managed to pull us over roughly onto the opposite shoulder. When we came to a stop, most of us were on the floor of the rear cabin. Massimo was cursing and Renato told him to shut the fuck up, he couldn't hear the engine. "It stalled," Saverio observed. Tonino grabbed an extinguisher and jumped out of the jeep. "Where there's smoke, there's fire!" he yelled, and ran toward the burning cars.

Chapter 19

Renato couldn't have planned a better opportunity to voice his suspicions about Nico. That very afternoon, when we'd returned from putting out the burn and were taking turns in the showers trying to wash off the memory of the charred body we'd seen in one of those crashed automobiles, an unmarked white sedan pulled onto the firebase. Since we could only use two or three of the showers at a time if we wanted decent water pressure, most of the squad was on the shaded terrace of the command post when the car drove up, and as it came closer Tonino stepped forward off the terrace to meet it. Two men in cheap business suits stepped out of the car.

One of the men was tall and clean-shaven, the other fat and sweaty-looking. The tall one, the driver, announced that they were there for Renato.

Tonino squinted his eyes. "What do you want with him?" he asked. He looked the driver up and down like he was wondering how big his coffin might need to be. Then he did the same to the other man, who still had one foot out, one foot in the passenger-side door.

The driver tugged at his belt. "We want to talk with him is all," he said, raising a hand to shield his eyes from the sunlight.

"Who are you guys anyway?" Pietro asked from behind Tonino.

The second guy piped up. He stepped away from the car and opened his jacket and put his hands on his hips. His armpits were stained with sweat and there was a brown leather strap just visible around one of his shoulders. "We're the guys here to see Renato Chiarini," the man said, grinning as though amused with his own joke. The driver looked over at his partner and chuckled.

Tonino stroked the stubble on his chin. "We're not sure if he's here," he said.

Just then Renato stepped out of the barracks combing his wet hair and wearing a fresh crisp uniform his wife had ironed for him. He brushed past us. "I've got this," he announced, waving his hand dismissively. He walked up to the driver and shook his hand and leaned close and said something we couldn't make out, then called over his shoulder that he'd be back in an hour and climbed into the backseat of the car. Between the back and front seats, we could see, was a wire cage like they have in taxi-cabs and police vehicles. Then the two men got in the car and the doors were shut and the engine started and the car drove off in a cloud of dust.

Massimo said, "Who the fuck did they think they were?"

"Pigs," Enzo said. "Did you see the cage?"

"No markings on the car, though," Luchetto said.

"Nothing obvious," Saverio commented.

"That fat one was packing," Tancredi said.

"Yeah, but Renato seemed to be expecting them," Saverio noted.

"He could've told us something," Pietro complained.

"What the fuck do you think it's about?" Massimo asked.

"Who knows?" Tonino said. "Just go and take your damn showers."

We had to wait all afternoon to find out. Renato didn't get back until the sun was beginning to angle down behind the cedar trees edging the firebase. The white car dropped him off outside the gates, and he walked over to us without saying anything. Someone got up to give him a chair, but Renato didn't take it, he just stood on the terrace with his hands on his hips. His uniform was wrinkled and his brow furrowed. He glared at us as we waited for him to speak.

"If you must know," he started off in a loud voice like he was annoyed already, "it's all about a fucking fish pond." He raised his hand to cut off our exclamations. "Yeah, you heard me right. My granddad owns a fish farm out near Policastro. It's about the size of a goddamned swimming pool, but it's right next to some well-to-do beach club that's giving him hell about it and took him to court."

"Over what?" Saverio inquired.

Renato grinned. He rubbed his mustache for effect. "It smells," he said.

"You're shittin' us," Massimo said incredulously.

Renato nodded that he wasn't.

Massimo said, "They're suing your grandfather because his fish farm smells?"

"The beach club is owned by foreigners—Americans, I think. They say the smell is bad for business. They're fucking out of their minds, but their lawyers are sharp as razors."

"What's the MDA got to do with it?" Saverio asked.

Renato raised his eyebrows at the question. The MDA is Italy's environmental agency. Its federal watchdogs regulate the use of state land and natural resources. They weren't much liked anywhere south of Rome.

Renato stared at Saverio and said, "Why do you think those guys were with the Ministero dell'Agricultura?"

"I noticed the logo of the parking sticker in the car window," Saverio explained.

Pietro groaned, impressed by this instance of detective work, and turned to Saverio and said, "Why didn't you say something to us earlier?"

"Doesn't matter," Saverio answered with a glance at Pietro. Then he turned back to Renato with an expectant look.

Renato took a breath. "As you know," he said, "the Ministero dell'Agricultura handles all matters relating to the environment, obviously including fish farms." He looked us all in the eyes in turn. Then he shifted his feet and hips, pulled out his cell phone, and studied the display. "Look, guys, I'd love to tell you all about it, but I've got to hit the road. I was supposed to meet the Mrs. an hour ago." He clipped the cell phone back on his belt and went into the command post to sign out and grab his things.

The rest of us regarded one another dumbly and shrugged, but as Renato came out I saw him shift his eyes at me, so I walked with him across the firebase to his car. He didn't say anything until we'd gotten a good distance away from the rest of the squad, well out of earshot. Then he turned to me and said flatly, "Your name came up."

"What?" I asked, not immediately understanding.

"Just what I said. Your name came up, they asked about you."

I guessed he was talking about the men in the white sedan. I smiled and said, "What on earth do I have to do with it?" I was still thinking about fish.

Renato smirked. "You didn't believe that crap about the fish farm, did you? I doubt any of the others did. This is about something else, Matteo—you get me? And you sure as hell do have something to do with that."

When I realized he meant the assignations, I could feel the blood rushing out of my head and my ankles got heavy. Renato, taking out the keys to unlock the car, observed me closely.

Though dizzy, I gave my head a quick shake and stamped the blood out of my ankles. "How about the others?" I asked.

"What others?" Renato said.

"I mean, did they ask about anybody else?" I could hear the worry in my own voice. "What about Tonino, Enzo, Saverio, anyone. . . ."

Renato said, "You think Pinco Pallo, John Doe, Joe Schmoe and all their cousins know about this stuff?" He opened the car door.

"Not even Tonino?" I asked.

"I never said that, Matteo. But I'm telling you, it's not many of us. Less than you think, anyhow. Besides, it's arranged so you don't know who else knows. It's better for everyone that way." He started to duck into his car, then changed his mind. He looked at me closely and asked, "Did you say something to someone?"

I hesitated a moment, but only in order to answer honestly. "No," I said firmly.

Renato tapped me hard on the top of my head with two fingers. "Think, Matteo. These MDA fellows didn't just pull your name out of a hat. You might have said something to someone in passing."

I did think about it, and there was no one whom I had spoken with about the assignations. I was sure of it.

Almost in a whisper Renato said, "Not even Nico, the American?"

I shook my head. "No, of course not."

"I noticed you've pretty much buddied up with him," Renato said.

"A little bit, I guess," I said sheepishly.

Renato gave me a look.

"Why? What's going on here?" I said.

"Look," Renato told me, "if what you say is true, then you've got nothing to worry about. These guys from the MDA know diddlysquat. It was a fishing expedition pure and simple." He got into his car and rolled down the window.

I leaned down to speak. "But they must know something," I said, "otherwise they wouldn't have. . . ."

"They know nothing," Renato interrupted.

"How do you know?"

"Jesus Christ, Matteo, did I not just spend three and a half hours bull-shitting with those guys or what?" He started the engine of his car. "Of course they claimed it was a routine investigation, said I'd been selected randomly from some list. They acted bored. But I could tell they were after something. The thing is, even they didn't know what. It's like the fisherman who drops his line into the sea. He might get a tuna, he might get a mackerel, he might get a pike, he might get nothing. They got nothing, they were just fishing." Renato put the car in gear and started to release the clutch. "Just keep your mouth closed and your eye on the American," he said and was gone.

Chapter 20

Just what Renato meant by that advice puzzled me. Did he think Nico was some kind of informant, or did he mean to imply that Nico himself was under suspicion and that I should stay away from him for that reason? Either alternative seemed to me equally ridiculous. Yet the American remained an enigma, an olive I couldn't pit, and I resolved to watch my words more carefully when he was around. Our friendship, in any case, struck me as fitful at best. Sometimes we seemed to understand one another the way twins do, intuitively, without speaking. That's how it was immediately after we'd walked through fire together on the slopes of Monte Fasini. At other times I'd look at Nico and see a complete stranger, a foreigner who had abruptly and inexplicably appeared in the living room of my life. That his moods were volatile didn't help matters. He would swing back and forth from gloom to sudden unexplained zeal like the winds, and it was getting more and more difficult to keep up with him.

During the morning hours, when Nico generally remained in camp, he spent a lot of time on the ground, for he had developed a fascination with insects, reptiles and small animals. He would spend hours observing the black carpenter ants that seethed through our camp in teeming multitudes, getting down on his hands and knees and putting his nose to the ground to watch them, and calling out like a child if he spotted a worker ant carrying a twig twelve times its size or dragging the remains of a cricket or praying mantis to the colony's underground vaults. (Meanwhile funny stares from Pietro, Massimo, Cesare and the others, fingers tracing spirals of air at their temples.) Finding a column of ants, Nico would place stones or sticks in their path to see how they overcame barriers, or he'd divert them with a trickle of melted ice cream and gaze, absorbed, as they swarmed excitedly over some dropped sweet morsel. One day he traced their seemingly interminable files back to the colony and shoved a rotten corncob into the entrance hole; the next day the cob was gone and the ants were laboring on as usual. After playing with them for a while, Nico would stand up and kill a few hundred with the sole of his boot, then, seeing their numbers effortlessly replenish, lose interest.

Not only ants. Images of Nico snipping the wings off a butterfly with the scissors on his army knife (he glued the wings into his journal). Nico catching a wolf spider in a glass and frying it alive with his windproof lighter, the spider jumping up against the glass pitifully. Nico kicking at stray dogs in the street (he said he was afraid of them). Nico delicately balancing a grasshopper on the back of one hand—then suddenly crushing it with his other. He'd catch lizards and flush them down the toilets, propping his chin on the rim as he watched the reptiles struggle to find footing on the smooth porcelain amid the swirling vortex of water.

And then there was the goat, Aristotle. Aristotle was the brigade mascot we kept tethered on a rope in the shade of the medlar tree near the storage tent. Skinny and brown with white spots on his neck, he had two small black horns and beady black eyes and, like most goats, was always slipping out of his rope collar and getting into trouble. That suited us just fine, since Aristotle was simply another of the ways we had devised to pass the time at the firebase during downtime.

More than any of us, Nico seemed to relish teasing the goat. He called it Pan ("Aristotle, defender of logic and reason, is no name for a goat," he said) and liked to make the animal kick and butt. But one day Aristotle got hold of one of Nico's black notebooks and tore it to shreds, and when Nico saw what had happened he dragged the animal out into the sun, tied it to a steel pole, and began lashing it with the end of the rope. The poor goat wrapped the cord around and around the pole until it had almost choked itself.

Nico stomped back to the command post terrace and flung himself into a chair beside me. "If that goat ever comes near my things again," Nico said, "I'll roast him alive." He stooped down to pick up pieces of the shredded notebook and tried jamming them back into the binding, cursing at every page. It was pretty much unsalvageable.

"It's a goat," I replied as lightly as I could. "That's what goats do."

"Shit."

The word fell like a gob of spit onto the ground. I looked up and saw Tancredi over by the pole untying the goat. Tancredi gave it a gentle kick and sent it on its way. When I looked back at Nico, his mouth was twisted into something resembling a resigned grin. I raised my eyebrows and waited for him to speak.

"You're right," he said, sighing. "It's not worth it. It must be fate that I should lose what I considered to be my best poems of the summer. You're right, a goat—*una capra*—is capricious by nature."

"That's the right attitude," I encouraged him.

Nico opened his eyes wide and his gray irises gleamed. "Hey, speaking of goats, that reminds me, Matteo." He sat up straight in his chair and leaned forward toward me. "I learned a new Italian phrase the other day."

"Let's hear it," I said.

"*Capra espiatoria*," he said.

I said, "You mean *capro espiatorio*?"

"I thought 'goat' was feminine," Nico said. "*Capra*."

"That's right," I explained, "goat is *capra*. But *capro espiatorio* is something else."

"I know what it means," Nico said. "'Scapegoat,' or 'fall guy'—right?"

"Fall guy?"

"The guy who takes the fall," Nico said, "who takes the blame for someone else. Usually he's set up. Framed, you know. Someone who's made to look guilty even if he isn't. Or if he's only partially culpable, then you pin the whole deal on him."

I felt hollow in my solar plexus. I guess I was getting a little paranoid, what with the MDA snooping around. "Why that word?" I asked, trying to sound nonchalant.

"Oh, it was in a movie," Nico said, waving his hand in the air as if to shoo away a gnat. "You know, on the television set at La Buca, the billiards hall—*which*," he said, stabbing his finger into the air, "reminds me of something else."

I cocked my head to one side questioningly.

"Franco said he saw you not too long ago."

"Franco?" I repeated.

"Yeah, this guy I know from La Buca. You know, where I hang every now and again."

I raised my eyebrows inquisitively.

"Don't you know him?" Nico asked. "He knows you. I think his full name is Francesco Lupopasini. We play pool together sometimes."

I did know him. We'd attended the same high school, though had never been friends, and our lives had taken very different paths after graduation.

"I know who he is," I told Nico, "but I don't necessarily like what he is."

"Well, it's nothing important," Nico said. "It's just that Franco mentioned he saw you not too long ago. Out in Pelle Marone."

One of the valves in my heart missed a beat. I said, "At the fire you mean?"

"I don't think so," Nico said. "It was in town. A few days before the fire."

A chill surged up my spine. I shrugged my shoulders. "So what did he say?"

"Nothing, really," Nico answered, turning up his palms. But he scrutinized my face. "What's the matter? You look pale."

"I'm fine," I answered in a straight voice.

"Franco just said he saw you," Nico went on. "We were shooting pool, and Franco was kicking our butts at it, and he knows I volunteer for the brigade—I told everyone, it seems to impress people—but anyway, he says out of nowhere, 'I saw this *vigile* out in Pelle Marone getting a cup of coffee.' When I asked who, he said, Matteo Arteli. I figured that was you, though I wasn't sure of your surname."

"Yup, that's it," I said, pausing to gather my thoughts. My first instinct was to protect myself and the squad. Did those guys at La Buca know something about the assignations? How could that be possible? Had they set Nico onto something, put ideas in his head? I said aloud, "What was Franco doing out there in Pelle Marone, anyway?"

"Beats the shit out of me," Nico answered. "I think he has an uncle who sells goats or something."

"Did he say anything else?" I asked.

"Oh, the guy talks his head off," Nico replied.

"About what?"

"I don't know, Matteo. Just stuff. I'm a foreigner here and I don't always see the whole picture. . . ."

"Right," I said as calmly as I could, though Nico's caginess worried me. To have been identified by that guy Franco was unsettling. I realized my hands were shaking and hoped my face wasn't betraying my edginess. I turned my head away and said something irrelevant to change the topic. You couldn't tell anything from Nico's features about what he had in mind. He'd shaven today, his chin and cheeks were smooth and tan, and he looked as innocent and youthful as a ten-year-old boy.

Chapter 21

I told Renato about Franco having seen me in Pelle Marone but Renato just said so the fuck what, it was a coincidence that had nothing whatsoever to do with the MDA investigation. I wasn't immediately convinced, but when a week or two went by and nothing further came of the MDA agents' visit, I agreed with Renato that they'd left the province and I began to relax a bit, thinking we were in the clear. Besides, I figured the Ministero dell'Agricultura had bigger fish to fry, because in late July and early August a string of intense flare-ups along the heavily touristed coast near Firenze catapulted wildfire into the national headlines.

We hungrily followed the developments in the major newspapers. Saverio read *Corriere della Sera* and I read *La Repubblica* and Tonino read *Il Mattino,* and we'd bring the papers to the firebase and leave them lying around for others to read, so we were all pretty up-to-date about the fire situation around the country. Most of the articles were your typical summer fluff, but certain reporters seemed to be on a crusade this season and analyzed several fires in great detail. In the most destructive blaze, 260 hectares of fir and blue spruce in Roma's regal Villa Argento were reduced to grotesque patches of charred trunks. At first, reports indicated that the fire was arson-related: several propane tanks were found near the fire's point of origin, and the Villa's underground sprinkler system had been tampered with, its faucet handles marred by hammers. Other reports claimed the propane tanks were already empty, nothing but the refuse of careless campers, and that the faucet system hadn't been "tampered with" at all—the so-called hammer marks were simply made by gardeners who opened and closed the tight spigots with plumber's pliers.

"That's a good one," Enzo commented, shaking his head in disbelief. We weren't sure if he meant a good lie or an amusing, ironic truth, and none of us asked him.

The journalists were having a field day with this new spate of burns and with the numerous theories of arson that cropped up. It was all rather entertaining at the time. On the one hand were those who thought a single arsonist or pyromaniac was responsible for most of the fires. To support this idea, Diana Piatelli of the newspaper *La Stampa* showed how the fires followed typical patterns, and a psychological profile of the arsonist was composed: it was a man; he was not married; he was of less than normal intelligence; he was ugly, possibly scarred by burns; he had experienced family instability; and he was a native of Tuscany who traveled widely and regularly throughout the region.

"Hey," Pietro observed, "wasn't the Americano in Toscania?"

"Yeah, stupid," Massimo replied—"why, you think he did it?"

"No, dumbass," was Pietro's reply, "I was just saying."

"You guys are real geniuses," Saverio, who was trying to read, said. He glared at them, then snapped the pages of *La Stampa* in his hands like it had bugs on it.

Almost immediately following Piatelli's article, several witnesses came forward claiming they might have seen the man believed responsible for the Villa Argento blaze, and a police composite sketch was plastered on the front pages of the all the major dailies. The government promised a ten-million-lire reward for information leading to the arrest and conviction of the man, and following the American model, a special national toll-free hotline was set up to process clues.

Opponents of Piatelli countered that someone with a low IQ would not have been able to elude the authorities for so long. The arsonist had apparently been setting fires for several years, and if setting blazes was, as Piatelli argued, a way of calling attention to himself, why did he not come forward or leave more clues as to his identity?

Other specialists attacked the single-arsonist theory as nothing short of ludicrous. The current rash of fires was nothing but a highly organized and systematic criminal outbreak. One journalist who thought so, Giovanni Fondo of *La Repubblica,* published an article that ignited a political crisis. Fondo reported that an undisclosed member of the Conservative Party was quietly pushing through the Senate legislation that would overturn the law prohibiting construction on recently burned lands. Fondo argued that most, if not all, of the recent fires were arson plain and simple; anticipating the new law to come into effect, certain construction companies were simply, and literally, preparing the ground. Looked at in another, even more sinister light, the fires were a way of gathering support for the passage of the new legislation: the burned hectares were unsightly blemishes on the fabled Tuscan landscape, and it was known through opinion polls that the public did not want to see Tuscany besmirched by unsightly scars like that in the Villa Argento—whose rare pine grove, by most estimates, would take seventy-five years to regenerate.

Fondo backed up his claims with facts. The fires had all occurred at times and locations certain to maximize the fires' intensity. First, they had been set in the midafternoon, during the hottest part of the day. Second, they had been set on south-facing slopes, which are much hotter and dryer than northern slopes. Third, they had probably been set using some form of fluid incendiary. (Pyromaniacs, Fondo noted, were known to avoid using incendiary fluids to start fires; their preferred method was the simple matchstick.) Fourth, preliminary evidence showed that many of the recent fires had not one but several origin points—which meant premeditated arson, since pyromaniacs usually set a fire in one place, not in several. Fifth, the fires had been set on hills with strong winds that fed the flames, made them unpredictable, and rendered fighting the blazes difficult. Sixth, the fires were increasing as the summer drought continued; thus, fall rains were sure to flood the lands, wash away the topsoil and leave the ground barren, impossible to regenerate without great expense. Last, the fires had been set on beautiful coastal land easily converted to valuable property.

What this all added up to, Fondo concluded, was *not* a single pyromaniac intent on gaining attention or seeking revenge; rather, this was nothing less than a concerted effort of government, business, and organized crime ("the distinctions are indeed breaking down," another reporter editorialized) to use arson in the service of lucrative real estate deals and political machinations. Following Fondo's lead, other reporters linked several members of Parliament, as well as many high executives in the construction business, with the Mafia, and Italy found itself besieged by scandal.

The politics of it all upset Saverio. "I can't even read the paper anymore," he said one day, tossing a newspaper to the ground. "There's nothing but one politician attacking another."

"I bet that guy Fondo is right," Enzo said, picking up the paper.

"He's gotten into the shirt collar of a lot of bigwigs," Tonino observed from behind the spread pages of his *Il Mattino*. "If I were him, I wouldn't stroll alone down any dark alleys."

Renato, who read *Il Messaggero*, glanced at Nico then said to everyone present, "Fondo's a fool. He shouldn't go poking his fingers in other people's pies."

"He's a reporter," Saverio observed. "That's what reporters are supposed to do."

"If you put your foot in traffic," Renato said loudly, "it'll just get run over."

Nico, of course, had his own opinions about the whole affair. The fires, he claimed, were a natural by-product of the unraveling of the social fabric. "Look," he said, "you guys have got an extremely fractious political scene going on here. You don't even have a government, for God's sake."

That was true. About three months ago the most recent alignment of political parties had fallen apart, effectively leaving the nation without a government. All that held the country together was a complex mosaic of semiautonomous government agencies—including the regional Corpo Forestale and local fire brigades like the *Vigili del Fuoco*—that continued going about their day-to-day activities. As for a president, prime minister, and cabinet—there simply were none.

"Fires increase in both number and size during historical upheavals," Nico explained. "War is the obvious example. Look at what happened in Kuwait. What was the one most destructive element of the Gulf War? Not the battles. It was the burning of the oil fields—a real holocaust that lasted for months!"

"But that's different," I argued.

"War is an extreme example, but it doesn't have to be outright war, only any kind of political uncertainty. There is a high correspondence between rates of fire and periods of social turmoil. I bet you people have more fires during election years, for example."

"I don't know," I said.

"You check the stats yourself," Nico challenged. "Fire is a comrade of revolutionary upheaval. Most of the biggest fires that occur today and tomorrow will be in China, America, and especially Russia, the three superpowers, all characterized by social and ecological tensions. You mark my words. Where there's political smoke, there's real fire."

As if to punctuate his sentence, the radio crackled in the next room. Smoke had been spotted near the town of Luparo.

In the fields at Luparo we struck a routine formation, splitting the squad into two at the burn's origin and fanning out to encircle the fire's perimeter. But the earth is imperfect, its terrain refuses to be neatly graphed, and the dry, bushy ridge we found ourselves on that afternoon was messy and complex. On one side of the ridge, a marble quarry the size of several soccer fields had been cut into the mountainside like an industrial bite mark. On the other side of the ridge were large fields of grass leading down to farmland. Above loomed rugged cliffs with a thick smattering of pine, while directly below us lay a deep gorge with a thicket of wild berries and a small stream running through it.

We figured the flames would burn down into the gorge and edge along the quarry toward the pines, but the fire feinted. It drew us out toward the farms and we followed it. Wanting to be sure to protect the agricultural products, we spent some time kicking up dust at the edge of the olive fields, and Renato started up a conversation with some *contadini* who were wetting down the perimeter of their fields with garden hoses. Nico grew impatient. He kept mumbling, "Let's get out of here, we're wasting time," and finally I went ahead with him over the next rise. When we got there we saw that the fire had swept well north of the farms and was racing along a huge grass-covered slope. The wind was sweeping up out of the valley and kicking the fire away from us, and we had to do everything we could to keep it from spreading along the entire plateau.

Nico and I worked our way up the incline, encircling and extinguishing the edge of the blaze. At one turn in the terrain, we became separated. I found myself blocked by a thorn patch and had to circle around the briars some sixty meters. When I found Nico again, I saw that he had his pants unzipped and was urinating onto the flames.

He turned to me with a wild look. I thought he was going to yell at me, but his face relaxed and he smiled and said, "With what serves a man for pissing, he recreates his life!" Then he raised a fist and screamed out some words—they sounded Chinese—that I couldn't make out.

Later on, back at camp, he asked me if I knew of the ancient Chinese emperor who had issued a proclamation banning urination on fire. I shook my head.

"To urinate on burning or smoldering embers," Nico explained, "was an offense whose penalty was crucifixion."

I asked why.

"The emperor recognized that fire is a gift, Matteo, and to refuse a gift is an insult. In the Greek version, fire was given to mankind by Prometheus, the titan who stole the Olympian fire of Zeus and smuggled it to earth in the hollow of a fennel stalk. Can you imagine what life was like for humankind before the boon of fire? Think about the cold, about the darkness of moonless nights, think about raw food and fear and about not eating popcorn at the movie theaters. . . ."

Though we hadn't done so in a while, we both laughed. Nico had a smudge of dirt on his cheek and a twinkle in his eye. We laughed more than the joke was funny.

"Anyway," Nico said, catching his breath, "fire seems to get around faster than VD in these parts. What do you think of all that stuff in the newspapers?"

"Oh," I answered with a wave of my hand, "it's the same thing every year about this time. All the politicians are on vacation and the journalists have nothing else to write about."

"So you don't think it's different this year?"

I thought a moment. "Maybe a little," I admitted.

We sat for a while without talking. Nico wrote a few lines in his journal and looked up at the sky. Then suddenly he slammed his book shut and sat up. "Matteo, you'll never guess who I saw the other night!"

His sudden movement startled me, but I picked up on the newly upbeat mood I heard in his voice. "Cecilia Bartoli?" I teased.

"I wish!" Nico said sitting back again, his eyes gleaming. He folded his hands in his lap and shook his head. "But it was someone else."

"Who?" I asked.

"Renato!"

He said Renato's name rather loudly and some of the guys looked up from their card game and over at us. Nico and I returned their looks with exaggerated smiles, and they turned back to their cards.

"Yeah?" I said more quietly to Nico, my interest piqued.

Nico also lowered his tone. He said in an excited whisper, "If you can believe this, he actually came into La Buca, and when he saw me he said *Ciao, Bello, come stai,* and acted like he was my best friend and whatnot." Nico shook his head and turned his hands palm upward. "Strange, no?"

Renato had never told me about this. I tried to mask the seriousness I felt gathering between my eyebrows. "What did you do?" I asked.

"Well," Nico said, "I just acted friendly, to tell you the truth. I didn't see why I shouldn't."

"I guess," I agreed.

Nico cocked his head. "You're a good friend of his, aren't you?" he asked.

"Who, Renato? Yeah, well, we used to be closer, but we're still pretty tight," I answered. "But I know that Renato doesn't like that La Buca place. I wonder what horses dragged him into that dive."

"I, personally, am drawn to its fine interior decor," Nico said sardonically.

"I didn't mean any offense," I explained.

"None taken, I'm just joking," Nico said with a half-smile. "Renato just talked to that guy Franco for a bit, then he left."

I didn't think Renato knew Franco. As I've said, I knew him from high school, but Renato was older than me and I doubt they had run into each other at school. "Did Renato play pool?" I asked.

Nico shrugged. "He took a shot or two."

"That's it?"

"That's it," Nico assured me.

Over at the card table the guys suddenly roared. Enzo slammed his hand on the tabletop and stood up and cursed. Tancredi scooped up the cards and yelled over to Nico to see if he wanted to play a hand. I, of course, wanted to ask him more about Renato, but Nico smiled and got up to join the others at the card table under the medlar tree, leaving me with a question hanging from my lips like a cigarette I'd toked down to the hot, bitter filter.

Chapter 22

Renato at La Buca: of course I wondered about that, and as soon as I could I talked to Renato about it too. He could see that I didn't quite know how to take it, so he looked at me like I'd scraped my knee. He put his arm around my shoulders and said not to worry. He'd been there to shoot some pool and "check things out"—this he said with a wink—but he wouldn't say much else. He admitted he spoke with Franco but said he couldn't help but talk to people while he was shooting pool, didn't I think? I asked Renato if he'd asked Franco about seeing me in Pelle Marone, but Renato said that would just have made matters worse—why jog Franco's memory? Why not instead bait them with innocent questions and see what kind of fish we might catch?

I agreed, but the discussion left me confused. The way Nico had related the incident, it seemed Renato had gone there expressly to powwow with Franco. But according to Renato himself, he just went to get an idea of what kind of gossip was being bandied around town. As far as that went, at least, Renato assured me we had nothing to lose sleep over.

That conversation didn't quite put me at ease, and I was actually relieved when the August fire season exploded in our sector and I could throw myself into my work. Burns sprouted up like weeds in every corner of our fire management area. One unforgettable blaze at a logging site southeast of Fuga was ignited by gasoline spilled from one of the bulldozers the company used to raze the oak and pine. The fire spread immediately into the huge fields of downed trees, and by the time we got to the scene, the lumber site was a raging inferno. Seeing there was nothing we could do with our handheld equipment, Renato talked several of the loggers into using the company bulldozers to clear a firebreak. We told them where to clear the line, and everyone stood back and watched as the downed area consumed itself like some monstrous bonfire, so hot it melted the protective plastic on much of the logging equipment. The owner of the logging company showed up in his BMW and a flashy Versace suit about halfway through the blaze. He tore at the ring of hair around his half-bald head when he saw all that money going up in smoke. Furious, he fired the company field overseer on the spot, then turned to us and cursed our descendants till olives be harvested in hell.

We were constantly on call, battling burns in valleys, on cliffs and bluffs, at the edge of beautiful farmland, high in the mountains—wherever fire burned, which was everywhere. More and more often we found ourselves trying to protect houses and commercial structures at the rural-urban interface, stripping trees and bushes from private property, rolling cars in neutral gear to widen the fire lanes, reassuring tearful property owners about the chances of their six-bedroom villas surviving the flames. One day we successfully prevented a fire from sweeping through much of a sports complex on the outskirts of Venafro, and afterward the owner let us kick a ball around on one of the fenced-in soccer fields and served us free American beer and potato chips "so the Americano will feel at home." There were several awesome, sublime moments as well. We walked on a cloud of smoke in an olive grove in San Apollinare, we ducked under a flaming canopy in the conifer stands at Sessa Pecasta, we traced the haunting orange glow of a night fire that rung itself around the slopes of the volcanic Monte Roccafina. Even amidst the most ferocious or most stubborn blaze, we could become fascinated with fire for its sudden magnificence— because it stood up and danced before our eyes, or because it lit up the nights with its hypnotic glow, or because it shone brighter and hotter than the brightest and hottest day.

Still, the work was grueling, the romantic moments few and far between, and mostly we complained. About the heat and dust. About the smoke inhaled into our lungs, the equivalent of two packs of cigarettes a day. About swinging *flabelli* for hours at a time while trying to gain a foothold on the mountainside and then about clearing foliage and digging firebreaks until it seemed there was no blood left in our veins. Or about sawing down trees by hand. Or about sifting through hectares and hectares of knee-deep ash, double-checking for live embers.

Despite our grumbling, we recognized that fire rescued us from the boredom that would have ruled our lives without it, for fire rendered unpredictable the hours and the minutes, it gave a sharp edge to what would otherwise have been long, dull days. Every minute of our lives was spent in the anticipation of fire. Whether we were rolling the hoses at the firebase or topping off the water tank or eating free meals at the Trattoria Tramontano or just taking our turn in the toilet, we were on call. Fire took precedence, it had priority over all other activities. Our thoughts and moods, our worries and fears, the very warp and woof of our existence, even our sleeping patterns were governed by fire's caprice. We were never quite in control—that was perhaps the most intimidating, and at the same time one of the most enticing, aspects of firefighting. Fire was more than us, it was always more than us. We couldn't just turn it off or tell it to come back again some other day. And because fire handed us ultimatums, because it challenged us, because it insisted on asserting itself as a force to be reckoned with, so did it raise the hackles on the back of our necks, putting us in touch with the primitive core of our humanity, as though we were dogs fighting for corpse meat on the veld.

The pace was physically and emotionally draining. In fact, the emotional demands of firefighting were probably its most punishing aspects. Think of a prizefighter, a boxer. Think of how his opponent mirrors his own fears and of the awesome investment of spirit the fighter must devote to facing those fears in the ring. And to beat your opponent, to conquer the dangers he symbolizes, you must expose yourself to his blows, you must risk defeat, for there is no way to knock someone out unless you're close enough to hit him, and if you're close enough to hit him, he's close enough to hit you. That's exactly the way fire was for us. We'd have to duck in low and close with the *flabelli* and wrestle the flames to the ground. And despite the danger, we'd jump at the chance every time the radio crackled with a call. It was like this: you're in the jeep racing through the streets with the sirens blaring, you catch sight of smoke on hills, then a glimpse of the blaze, of the neon flames themselves, and a great space seems to open up inside you that you hardly ever get to see and your adrenaline pumps like you're about to face the gorgon.

During the high season we often got no respite for several days at a time. And though we would never admit to it, the long hours of constant firefighting were by early August considerably wearing us down. No one seemed more susceptible to the intense schedule than Nico. Though he had his good days, he remained for the most part restless and troubled, and I noticed that he seemed to be having difficulty writing. When he sat down to write in between calls he would constantly shift his posture, gnawing at or twirling his pen repetitively and making exaggerated motions with his lips as if he were a kindergartner struggling to sound out the letters. Often he stood up, trod a measured circle around his chair, then sat heavily back down, shifting in distress until he discovered a decently comfortable position. I noticed, too, that he acquired the habit, virtually a tic, of hitting the side of his forehead with the end of his pen. While doing so, he would screw up his face in an odd grimace, then take the tip of the pen with his free hand and begin stroking it with his fingers as though he were cleansing it of some imagined debris or trying to milk ink from the ballpoint. Finally, grasping the pen between his teeth, he would wipe the palm of each hand on the thighs of his pants legs then quickly scribble a sentence or two, only to recommence the process from the beginning the moment he seemed at a loss for words, which happened frequently enough.

When the time approached for a meal, Nico grew visibly impatient and irritable, throwing anxious glances in Tonino's direction (since it was Tonino and only Tonino who said, "*Andiamo a mangiare*") and acting as though he were going to faint from hunger. Yet after lunch he would be even worse, visibly suffering through *pomeriggio*, those torpid hours after lunch when the sun beats down on the firebase compound with cruelty. Nico had become accustomed to enjoying a little nap after lunch, and he often disappeared into the barracks in the afternoon with that purpose in mind. The problem was, the barracks sit full in the sun all morning and most of the day, and to spend any time inside them before sunset was simply unthinkable. The American tried, but before long he would stumble outside in a full sweat, looking as though he were suffering from a terrible hangover, as groggy and irritable as ever.

"Why don't you try the shade?" Enzo would suggest.

"I don't like lying on the ground," Nico would answer, petulant, his hair falling down in strings over his sweaty forehead.

Cesare shrugged. "A good espresso, then, will do the trick."

Nico didn't answer. He clutched at his books and pens. Enzo, Cesare, Tonino and the others turned back to their *scopone* cards. Though I pretended to watch the game, I was really studying Nico, watching him out of the corner of my eye as he slumped into a corner and opened his journal. Every once in a while he'd look over toward us, his eyes cocked in thought, and then he'd turn again to the page and write. I guess it made me feel like there was something too private there, something that wasn't part of our friendship. I guess it made me feel left out. When Nico noticed that I was watching him, he ceased writing and rested his hand in his lap. I got up and walked over to join him.

"I must have written her a hundred times in the past week," he said despondently, "but I haven't sent a single one of the letters."

It took a moment, but then it dawned on me whom he was talking about—his ex-girlfriend. "Adina?" I said.

"Yup." He had his feet propped up on one chair, but he took them off and motioned for me to sit.

"You wanna talk about it?" I asked, taking the chair and sitting down.

He shook his head. "Nah. The whole affair pisses me off, but I don't want to get depressed over some girl I left three months ago. *Aqua passata*, right?"

"Water under the bridge," I agreed.

"Still," he said, running his fingers through his hair, "love's a bitch."

I bobbed my head up and down slowly in agreement.

"If you really want to know," Nico said, "Adina's found someone else. I wouldn't care so much," he added before I could say anything, "but does she have to write to me and let me know all the gory details?"

"Is that what's in the letter she sent you?" I asked, incredulous.

"Can you believe—?" Nico began. But his voice broke, and I could see his eyes growing wet and red. He covered his face with one hand and waved me off with the other. "Don't say anything," he pleaded to me in a wavery voice. He stood up abruptly and began to walk away. "Just let me be."

I hung my head and watched him go into the barracks. I felt bad for him, but I didn't follow. I wouldn't have known what to say anyway. That kind of stuff you just have to let go, like a raft you abandon on the river. But knowing what Nico was going through with Adina helped me understand what happened next—or rather, it whet my perspective on the strange events that were about to occur along the Marathon. You might even say Nico had prepped me for the fire. He'd proven how his guts were all twisted up with women. He'd roused my sympathy for him, oiled me up for his next spectacular move.

Chapter 23

Stringing through the pine woods of Pantano dell'Osa valley is via Mara-
tona—the Marathon: a hot, flat, long road along which can be found, even
in the dead heat of the afternoon, prostitutes. The women are mostly old,
fleshy, mascaraed things. There are several transvestites too—full-busted,
tall, muscular black Africans in tight white shorts, their olive-brown hair
straightened with acids and irons.

On lazy afternoons Tonino would sometimes drive the jeep slowly
along the route. Enzo and Massimo would catcall out the jeep window in
the best English they could muster—"I love you, *baby*!"—or ask prices of

the Africans, who would return a haughty stare or a challenging "Come on, then, *ragazzo*, let's see what you got." We'd hoop and holler adolescently.

One afternoon, thinking it might give Nico Americano a kick, Tonino drove us to the Marathon after lunch. We stopped at a fountain midway along the road and were greeted by three or four of the best-looking girls on the route. These women were younger than the others, less ragged, better treated by their pimps, not yet jaded. And despite their compelling circumstances they maintained a rather playful outlook on life. I think they actually enjoyed our stopping by. One of the girls, Sofia, seemed to have a special liking for Tonino. Sofia took her nom de guerre from Sofia Loren, and she bore some vague resemblance to that fine actress. She was tall, with high reddish hair and a full body. We all suspected that Tonino came out here on his own once in a while.

After we'd bantered a bit, Sofia turned to Tonino and, pointing a chin at Nico, said, "Hey, Toni, who's the new one?"

"*Quello é* Nico Americano."

"He's kinda cute, Toni," Sofia said, pursing her lips. "I might even do him for free."

She didn't really mean it, she was just being playful. But hearing the words made us giddy and we all turned to see what Nico would say.

But he was in one of his gruff moods. He had hardly said a thing all afternoon, and since he'd seen the prostitutes he hadn't so much as breathed. When he realized Tonino and Sofia were talking about him he got back into the jeep, shut the door, took a book out of his pocket and wouldn't look up again. Massimo and Pietro kept trying to get him to come out but Nico, without even looking at them, just gave them the finger.

I am certain that sometime during the following week Nico went back to see the prostitutes at least once. Often he'd forgo his nap and hop on his *motorino* instead, disappearing for two or three hours. Usually he'd be back in time to join us for afternoon fire calls, if they came late in the day. But seeing the women apparently didn't relieve Nico of his surly moods; if anything, he was darker, more troubled. His eyebrows knitted together in a dark shadow across both his eyes as he smoked cigarette after cigarette. A sickly yellowish nicotine stain dirtied his upper lip. Often he would barely answer even my *salve*, hi. Utterly morose, he'd mope around the firebase as though plagued by a tremendous, unspeakable hangover. And when he finally did talk, all he could offer was a steady stream of complaints. The earth was a mess, he'd say, the world with its dirty cities full of the unemployed and the destitute, the trees razed, traffic snarling the streets with sickening fumes, the environment ravaged and pillaged, the culture meretricious, the politics unspeakable. . . . It was worse in America, he'd assure me, with those endless highways and chain malls and double-speak about free trade and liberty and democracy and all the rest. Everyone had to have two cars, three television sets and a microwave to thaw out their frozen hamburgers, animals butchered and ground up into a wormy pulp. . . . People were idiots and the world would be better off as a burned-out cinder, he'd tell me, they had the right idea in Chicago in '68 and LA in the '90s—civilization should be burned to the ground, all ash-black and clean. . . .

Then he'd jump onto his *motorino* and vanish, leaving me astonished and oddly wounded.

One afternoon that same week, while Nico was off riding the *motorino,* the radio crackled: smoke had been spotted north of Pantano dell'Osa in the flat, dry forests along the Marathon.

We drove out into a valley hazed in a noxious fog of brownish vapors, and once on the Marathon, Tonino headed straight for the fountain. Not far to the east, plumes of smoke billowed up in huge white columns as from erupting volcanoes. We found some of the girls on the road near the fountain. They were cowered together in a tight-knit, panicky clique, looking around at the forest and smoke with wide eyes.

Saverio told me to radio in for assistance—we saw straight off there was no way we could tackle this conflagration on our own—and leaving the girls at the jeep, we spread out into the woods. It was a deciduous forest and the ground was covered with a layer of dried leaves and compost, stands of rhododendron and lilac, some low blueberry. A yellowish mist of smoke hovered in the air, so thick it was like making our way through a fog. We could hear the crackle of burning leaves ahead of us, and about fifty meters off was a wall of dense brown smoke. The wind had been nothing when we started, maybe one or two knots out of the north, but the fire began generating its own source of oxygen—it was kicking up its own wind and gathering force. We'd hoped to reach the flames while they were still on the ground but the blaze had already spread up into the trees and become a crown fire feeding on live leaves. Pretty soon little whirls of smoke and flames were swirling and gathering in eddies, and leaves and small branches were being hurled through the air, and where they came to rest on the ground spot fires ignited, which in turn grew and gathered strength, merging with one another. We were witnessing the formation of a fire whirl, something like a tight, roving tornado of fire. Many of the flames were burning upside down out of the treetops, and smoke roiled downward out of the canopy as though there were an invisible ceiling above the forest. The fumes smelled poisonous. Even Tonino, who rarely backed down from the most intense blaze, saw the futility of the situation and ordered us back to the road.

Renato had arrived with Cesare, Tancredi, Luchetto and several others. Nico wasn't with them.

"Forget it!" Renato yelled to us, gesturing at the main blaze. "That's a goddamn fire storm! That thing is swirling!" He turned to the woods on the other side of the road. "Let's see if we can take the spot fires in there and at least save half of this godforsaken valley. Enzo! Drive along the line and see what you can see. I want any spark that crosses the road to be crushed immediately. Use the radio, go!" Then he nodded toward the prostitutes. "Luchetto, get these . . . civilians out of here now!"

Renato took out a map and spread it open on the hood of the jeep. The fire was threatening to turn the entire valley into an inferno. "We need more manpower," Renato grumbled, shaking his head. "Where's that goddamned American when you need him?"

Nobody knew so nobody answered, but we had all heard the comment and carried it within us as we geared up and deployed to fight the burn. I imagined Nico tooling around on the *motorino* along the sea roads and thought he wouldn't be back till nightfall, but as it turned out I bumped into him later that afternoon. I was taking a water break by the jeeps when a Corpo Forestale van drove up and Nico climbed out the back doors with some other reinforcements. Exhausted though I already was from the day's exertions, I thought Nico looked depleted. His shoulders were slouched, and he merely shuffled his boots across the ground.

I walked over to him. "What's up, Nico?" I asked. "You look pale." Now that I could see him up close, I was concerned. His cheeks were sunken and pallid, and he hadn't shaved in days. Noticeable black-purple rings, almost bruises, hung below his eyes. He looked stricken.

"Matteo," he said weakly, "I have to talk to you."

I nodded. "What is it?"

"Not here," he said, gesturing at the bustle of people around us. "It's too loud." He tugged on my sleeve and began walking. I thought he was just going to move a few paces off, but he led me out along the road well away from the fire. He was moving quickly and I had a hard time keeping up with him without jogging. I asked where we were going, but he just kept leading me further away. He said he wanted to show me something. We walked a good distance, until you could barely hear the flames.

Finally I took him by the shoulder. "What is it?" I insisted.

He stopped and looked at me and his eyes looked bloodshot and wet. He turned off the road and strode into the forest, and I followed him to a small clearing. "Nico," I kept saying, "Nico, where are you going? What is it?"

He wheeled around so suddenly I bumped right into him. He grabbed me hard with both hands. His face was wrenched horribly to one side. "Matteo," he gasped, "it was me!" He looked like a deer caught in headlights.

"You?" I said, backing up a step. I shrugged my arms from his grip. "What was you?"

Nico swallowed like something was stuck in his throat. "The fire. Today's fire," he said with difficulty. "I started it." A spasm jerked across his face.

I was sleeping, I thought. I was in bed sleeping. The words seeped into me like drops of water squeezing through a dike's ramparts. An entire sea lay shouldered up against the dam and I didn't know if it would hold.

"It was an accident, Mat," Nico continued quickly, pleadingly. "I came here to talk to Giovanna—she's one of the prostitutes. . . ."

"You came here to talk to one of the prostitutes?" I asked, incredulous. I wasn't sleeping. I was suddenly very aware of my not understanding what I was hearing.

"Just to talk, Matteo. I rode by on the *motorino* one day and we started talking. Giovanna, she. . . ." He cut himself off and wiped his forehead with his sleeve. "I mean he. . . ." Nico stopped himself again. He took a deep breath and shook his head. "Anyway," he went on, "what's important is that I came out here this morning to talk to . . . her, but I couldn't find her. I just wanted to chat about that letter I received from Adina, my ex. I told you about that letter, the one where she gives me all those fucking details on her new beau. I know it sounds stupid, but I wanted a woman's opinion on it and I thought of Giovanna. I walked out into the forest to look for her, then took the letter out of my pocket and," he paused and glanced at my face, "I don't know why—without thinking or anything—I lit it on fire." His voice sounded flat and serious.

"Lit the forest?" I asked.

"No!" Nico refuted, flailing his hands through the air as if to stop my words, "the letter, only the letter. Can you imagine what it's like to read about your girlfriend's sexual trysts? The details, Matteo, she gave me all the sordid details! I burned the damn thing. I dropped it on the ground and walked away. I thought it had gone out, I swear. But for some reason as I was riding away I had second thoughts about it and came back, only

I couldn't find the spot. It all looks the same along here, these woods. . . ."
He gestured vaguely. "I got disoriented, and by the time I found the place
the fire had already taken hold. I'd been careless, and it was already too
big for me. I was all alone! I tried to stop it, I took off my shirt and used
it as a *flabello,* but the flames were too much, they were in the trees
already. . . ." Nico broke down, taking his face in his hands like it was
about to fall off.

I could feel the earth tilting on its axis. I leaned back against a tree and
let myself slide down into a sitting position. Nico's legs buckled and he
squatted on the ground in front of me as though begging for mercy.
Though it was quiet where we were in our small private clearing, we could
hear the fire off to the east crackling in the trees. The air was hazy with
light gray smoke, and here and there big black pieces of ash floated down
like large pieces of lint. I thought long and hard for the both of us.

"We've got to tell them," I said finally.

On his hands and knees, Nico crawled over toward me with wide sad
eyes. "No," he said. "We can't. It was an accident."

"That's just it," I said, trying to sound upbeat. "If it was an accident,
then it doesn't matter."

"It was an accident, Matteo," Nico echoed. "But don't you see, it
doesn't look like an accident."

I could see where he was going with that. I nodded my head slowly
like I understood, but I was still noncommittal.

"Matteo," Nico said. "There's something else you should know."

"What." I said the word flatly, as though I didn't care.

He hesitated. "It's Renato."

"Renato what?" I said, sounding annoyed.

"He's setting you up," Nico said firmly.

"What are you talking about?" I blurted.

"I don't know the details. It's just some stuff I heard at the billiards
hall. Rumors. But I'll tell you all I do know—and I realize it's all *he said,
she said* but there might be something to it. You'd know better than me."
He paused for a moment and regarded my face carefully. "Remember that
guy who saw you at Pelle Marone?"

"Franco."

"Yeah. He said a few things about the brigade that I personally didn't
think were true."

"Like what?" I said impatiently.

"Like, you guys start your own fires," he said without hesitation. He
looked me right in the eyes but I kept mine blank and didn't answer. "I

don't know if it's true," Nico went on, "and I don't care one way or the other if it is or not and I honestly don't want to know but"—he took a breath—"it seems as though some people do think it's true and these are the kind of people you don't want to think that."

It took me a few seconds to unwind his syntax. His sentence was like a whip winding through the air, and when the tip cracked I cowered at the gist of it. As convincingly as I could, I shrugged and said, "So, it's not true." I tried to look him in the eyes as I said this but couldn't quite do it.

"Okay, Matteo, I believe you," Nico said. "And like I said, I don't care either way. But listen, think about it. Do you remember those guys who picked up Renato, those guys from the Ministero dell'Agricultura?"

"How do you know who they were?"

"That's what I picked up, is all. I heard they were from the MDA and I heard they talked to Renato."

"So?"

"Don't you see, Matteo? It's the prisoner's dilemma. Whether you're involved in something or not, Renato could have set them on your trail."

I said bitterly, "Have you lost your mind?"

"I'm just repeating what I heard from Franco. His uncle or godfather or someone knows someone in the MDA who knows someone else in the MDA who knew your father and"—

"My father?" I said, my heart jolting. I loathed having him connected in any way to this situation.

"Yeah, this guy apparently knew your father, and he said he didn't believe the accusations laid against you."

"What accusations? I haven't been accused of anything," I said defensively.

"But you might be, maybe, in the future."

I looked at him blankly, trying not to give anything away. It couldn't be true, I thought. I was dizzied. My lips parted, but my shell-shocked brain couldn't find any words to speak.

Some shouts came from afar. I heard my name called across the distance and realized the squad was looking for us.

"We'd better get back," I said, not moving.

Nico said, "Do you understand what I'm telling you?"

I shook my head vigorously and roused myself. I stood up and began striding back to the rendezvous point, at first slowly and then with more hurried paces. Nico followed behind me silently. The noise of the fire increased as we drew closer, until it was louder than a convoy of diesel trucks. Just as we were about to reach the jeeps, Nico tapped me on the shoulder and said, "You won't turn me in?"

I stopped walking and thought for a long second. I thought for the forest, I thought for us all. "I think it's better if we keep this stuff to ourselves," I said, looking up at some flames burning in the treetops to the east.

Nico also looked toward the fire. Seeing the flames and remembering why we were out here in the first place—to protect the forest—seemed to invigorate him, give him courage. He clapped me on the back. "Let's go put this sucker out," he said.

We battled the blaze for two days. The fire covered a swath of land four kilometers long, and other fire crews were working to the south and east of the blaze. Luckily a riverbed served as a natural containment line to the west and south, and so the main fire was channeled east, where the forest was broken by farms and grassland and a crew all the way from Napoli dug a fire trench using commandeered tractors and farm shovels. Our brigade covered the northern front, patrolling back and forth along the Marathon and making forays into the woods whenever a spot fire was identified by one of the helicopters circling the area. Then we would race into the woods like attacking soldiers, stopping the fires while they were still stoppable, on the ground. Another helicopter was dipping water from Lake Quirino, but the lake was twenty minutes flying distance each way.

It was exhausting work. Running back and forth, snuffing out the flames, praying the fire didn't reach the canopy. And then—most time-consuming and enervating of all—mop-up operations. Digging huge pits in the ground, which was knotted with tree roots, then sawing off branches and piling them in the trenches and covering them with dirt. We must have dug enough graves to bury the dead at Isonzo.

Chapter 24

Even as the stubborn remnants of the Marathon blaze were still holding out, Renato found a chance to have a private word with me. I was standing by the jeeps, waiting in line for a turn at one of the water jugs, when he tugged on the sleeve of my uniform and pulled me aside from the crew. He put his arm around my shoulders and said, "Chin up, Matteo."

Of course—after what Nico had said—I tried to look at Renato now with new eyes, but what I saw was the same drooping mustache, the cheeks firm and familiar, the unchanged hard green eyes. I couldn't see him as Nico wanted me to. I was so exhausted from fighting the Marathon fire and dealing with the emotional can of worms that Nico had opened, I felt numb to the world.

"What is it?" I said glumly to Renato.

"Now don't be like that," Renato said, giving me a pat on the back. His mustache wriggled with some kind of grin.

"What do you want?" I asked.

"It's not what I want, it's what you want," Renato answered.

"So tell me," I said.

He leaned in so close I could smell salami on his breath. "Sunday the second of August," he said. "You on?"

"Haven't they had enough?" I said. I looked at him closely—his eyes narrowed for a moment—then I turned my head away.

"You know it's not like that," Renato said. He took his arm off my shoulders and fiddled with his utility belt. "Some things, like this Marathon blaze, just happen. Other things you need to make happen. This is an assignation we set up weeks ago. We're not gonna change the game plan because of a little fire."

"A little fire?" I pressed my fingers to the sides of my forehead. A headache was pounding in my temples.

"Okay, a big sucker," Renato said, "a fucking doozy. Nevertheless, business is business."

I shook my head, exhausted. I wanted to go home and shower. "Can't we talk about this later?"

"My contact is waiting over there," Renato said, discreetly pointing at a firefighter I'd never seen before. He was leaning against one of the jeeps not far from us. His uniform, black with soot, looked Neapolitan. He was smoking a cigarette and didn't look over at me.

"So are you in?" Renato said.

"Do I have a choice?" I asked.

Renato laughed. "Not much," he said.

I shrugged. I felt so depleted I didn't care either way.

"Sunday, twelve noon" Renato said. "We'll meet at the firebase."

"Should I wear my uniform?" I asked.

Renato smiled widely. "You think you're getting pretty good at this, don't you?"

"I guess," I said. "I've done enough of them."

"So you have." He slapped me on the back and pushed me away. I started back toward the water jug. "And Matteo," Renato called to me. I stopped and looked back at him over my shoulder. "The answer is *yes*, you should definitely wear your uniform for this one."

Renato had told me to meet him at the firebase on Sunday at noon, and I was obedient. When I arrived, I found Massimo, Pietro, Cesare, Tancredi and Luchetto lounging on the terrace of the command post, and I pulled up a chair and joined them. The air was still and humid and the sun strong, and we sat around and squinted in the sharp light, wishing we were at the beach drinking iced coffees and checking out the chicks. Nico was busy washing his socks and underwear and hanging them out to dry on the line behind the command post. In the trees around us, cicadas shook their rattles in a rising and falling rhythm that seemed to reverberate menacingly inside our skulls.

This was several days after we'd finally extinguished the Marathon blaze, and in the meantime I'd had some time to sit back and think about everything Nico had told me. The more I thought about it the less I believed what he'd put forward about Renato, that he was cooperating with the Ministero dell'Agricultura. That was nothing but jelly and jam, pure billiards-room gossip. With all that I knew about Renato and his role in the assignations, he had every reason to fear turning me in. Mutual deterrence, the nuclear strategists call it. Also, I'd known Renato for more than fifteen years. We'd struggled up through the ranks in synch, we hung out together after hours, went to the soccer stadium in Napoli to watch games half a dozen times. I had enjoyed dinner with him and his wife on a few occasions, and I couldn't imagine why he'd spoil our friendship or break the trust we'd established. We'd squeezed through some tight fire situations together, after all. Besides, I reminded myself, those fellows from the Ministero dell'Agricultura had driven out of town in their white government sedan weeks ago and hadn't been heard from since.

As for Nico, I was wavering on what to do about him. As I watched him go about washing his laundry, I almost regretted the closeness we'd established, almost regretted our friendship, which was cobbled together from nothing but bits and pieces of adolescent confession, stories of dead fathers and absent mothers, bitter recollections of old girlfriends. I wish he'd never shared his intimate experiences with me. It would've been better if he'd just buried that stuff about the Marathon blaze somewhere deep inside himself. Even though I believed that his starting the fire was an accident—or not exactly an accident, I thought, but an unfortunate incident arising from poor judgment—I felt burdened by my knowledge of Nico's part in it. If it was an accident, I reasoned, then why not tell somebody about it, get it in the official report? Where was the harm in such an action? I knew that a fire inspector would be filing a report on the Marathon blaze—all Class B fires or larger require it by law—and if by some chance the inspector located the origin of the fire, he might be able to piece together some kind of coherent narrative, maybe even point a finger. Then of course it would look bad for Nico, and I might even find myself in the frying pan for withholding information.

Having brooded for several days about everything, I decided that I would try to bring up what happened at the Marathon to Renato in some indirect way. He was fluent with fire brigade regulations and procedures, and I wanted to get his opinion on some of the details without actually telling him about Nico—which would be tricky, I knew, but I felt I had to try. I figured that today would be a good opportunity to pick Renato's brain; we'd have plenty of time to talk on the drive out to Sanviolenza for the assignation.

Renato was late. He finally drove up in his red Peugeot at 12:40. The tinted windows were up to keep out the dust, but I could see his wife, Vittoria, sitting in the passenger seat. She waved curtly at me through the front windshield and I waved back. Renato set the parking brake with a quick pull then stepped out of the car wearing a nice white button-down shirt and beige slacks with a crease ironed neatly down each leg. He looked at his watch and hurried over toward me, leaving the car engine running.

"Hey, Matteo," he said, "sorry I'm late. Vittoria and I went to eleven o'clock mass." He nodded toward his car. Vittoria was peering into a compact mirror checking her eye makeup.

"That's okay," I said.

Renato glanced over at Massimo and Pietro, who had started a game of *scopone* with Cesare and Luchetto. They grunted hello.

"Did you guys sweep out the latrines?" Renato asked them.

"It's Sunday," Pietro said, not looking up from his cards.

"Every day is Sunday to you," Renato replied wearily, shaking his head. Then he turned to me. "Let's go inside," he said, pointing his chin at the command post door, "I've got to pick up something."

I followed Renato into the radio room. He peeked out each of the windows to see if anyone was there, then pulled an envelope from an inner pocket and handed it to me. "Here you go," he said.

Written on the envelope was *Sanviolenza, August 2nd, 3 P.M., Main Stables. (Sgn. Cardo)*.

"Cardo's our contact?" I said stupidly.

"You got it."

"What time will we leave?"

Renato put his hand on my shoulder. "You mean, what time will *you* leave."

"What do you mean?"

Renato pressed his lips together and seemed to frown. "You're going alone on this one."

A look of disbelief and protest began to cross my face but Renato raised a finger and put a stop to it. "I've got to see the in-laws today," he explained. "You know I don't work Sundays."

"But Renato. . . ."

"I can't help it if they arranged something on a Sunday, but I can't go. You're lucky I even had time to drop this off to you." He took a step toward the door.

I said quickly, "Can I take someone with me?"

"Tonino might go with you."

"Where's he?" I asked hopefully.

"Beats the shit out of me," Renato shrugged.

"What about Luchetto?" I asked.

Renato shook his head in the negative. "No good. Tonino or nobody. What's the big deal?"

"I don't know," I said sheepishly, "I've never done this alone before."

"Don't play the virgin on me, Matteo boy," Renato said patronizingly. "You know what to do. It's all written down for you." He snapped his index finger on the envelope in my hand.

"But what if"—I looked at the writing—"what if Sgn. Cardo has questions?"

"There won't be any questions."

"But"—I hesitated, tried to look Renato in the face—"what about the Ministero dell'Agricultura?"

Renato waved his hand dismissively. "Oh, they left town weeks ago, you knew that. I told you that fiasco was nothing but a fishing expedition."

"But you said they mentioned my name!" I whispered urgently.

"Yours and two dozen other people's," he said as if repeating something to a child for the fifth time. "They had a list of everyone in the brigade, and yours was randomly spot-checked."

"That's not what you told me before," I said, trying to sound indignant.

Renato narrowed his eyes at me. "What's got into your head, man?"

"Nothing."

"Then what's the problem, Matteo?"

"I guess nothing."

"Chin up," Renato urged with a smile. He slapped me on the shoulder, glanced at his watch and said, "I'm out of here, *buona caccia*!" and before I knew it I was standing alone in the room with the envelope in my hand. It felt heavy. Out the back window I could hear Nico running the water to rinse his dirty clothes. I squeezed the envelope between my fingers. There was certainly cash inside, and by the weight it seemed like a lot. I opened one of my breast pockets and stuffed it inside with a curse.

"The world is what it is," I once read in one of my father's books. "Men who are nothing, who allow themselves to become nothing, have no place in it."

I remembered this quote that Sunday afternoon after Renato had driven off, experienced it as a kind of mild epiphany. The words gave me courage alloyed with a resigned acceptance of my fate. I would do what I had to do, and to make sure I would be in Sanviolenza by three I prepared to leave the firebase at about one thirty, well ahead of time. I figured I could always stop along the way for a cappuccino or something or, if I needed to, kill some time hiking in the hills.

When Nico saw me buttoning my uniform and preparing to take the jeep, he came over and gave me an inquisitive look. "Where are you headed?" he asked, his brow furrowed.

"I've got some business to take care of," I answered.

"Alone?" Nico cocked his head to one side. "Where's Renato? Don't you usually go with Renato on these things?"

"What things?" I said.

"Whatever you do, I don't know," Nico shrugged. "Fire business, I guess."

"Renato's off today," I said.

"I know, I saw him," he replied. He slowly nodded his head a couple of times as if he was thinking about something but didn't want to come right out and say what it was.

I padded my pockets, looking for my keys.

Nico raised his eyebrows as if suddenly coming up with a pleasant idea. He asked, "Can you give me a lift into town?"

I pressed my lips together, hesitating.

"I want to see a movie," Nico said with a smile.

I checked my wristwatch. It was still very early and his smile disarmed me, so I nodded toward the empty passenger seat in the jeep. What would be the harm in it? Nico ran to gather his things while I turned the jeep around.

When he saw Nico getting into the jeep, Massimo got up from his card game and yelled, "Hey, where are you guys going?"

I was sure I'd told him earlier that I had official business to do for Renato, but this time I said loudly, "We're going to see a movie!" and drove off. It felt like a small good joke to play.

When we got off the dusty shoulder and onto the paved road Nico rolled down his window, stuck his arm out into the wind and asked, "Have you ever seen *Dr. Zhivago?*"

I told him I had.

"It's one of my favorite movies," he said. "They're playing it over at the Imperial. I think you should come with me."

"I told you, I've seen it already," I said.

Nico lit a cigarette and offered me one. I declined.

"Matteo," he said, "I really wish you'd come with me. It'll be good for you, something different. I think they have air-conditioning, too. And I need someone to translate the difficult parts."

"Oh, so now I learn the real reason," I joked.

"Oh, come on." He dragged on his butt. "What do you want me to say, please? Please—there I said it."

"I can't, I have an appointment."

"Since when do people arrive on time in Italy?"

I don't know why I gave in. I guess I was mad at Renato for leaving me in the lurch. I felt like he and Mezzasoma and Cardo were all jerking me around, and it put a kink in my chest. I guess I was also having third thoughts about Renato. Even if he wasn't setting me up in some way, wasn't out to frame me outright, it did look like he was making sure I had my hand stuck well into the pie should the Ministero dell'Agricultura take an interest. Let Cardo wait in the main stables for me, I thought, instead of me waiting for him (as would no doubt be the case). I was going to the movies.

At the ticket counter, Nico was louder and more gregarious than I had ever seen him. He flirted unashamedly with the ticket girl, then got into a friendly conversation with the movie-house manager.

"Do you know how to say *pizza* in English?" Nico asked the drably dressed manager.

"No, signore."

"*Pizza!* Ha, ha."

I shook my head from side to side, slightly ashamed. I'd never seen Nico play the loud American before.

We entered the theater and sat in the back row. The lights dimmed down and the previews began. The opening funeral scene reminded me of my father and made me sad, and I snuggled down into my seat. I was beginning to think I might enjoy the film after all when Nico nudged me with his elbow.

"You can go now," he whispered.

"What?" I said. "I'm getting into this."

"You should go," Nico said, "It's your responsibility. You don't want to get on someone's bad side. Use that door," he said, pointing to the rear emergency exit. "The movie is at least two and a half hours long. Do you think that will be enough time?"

My skin got cold, as if in a draft of air. After some moments' thought I answered. "Yes."

Nico handed me a small wooden chip. "Stuff this in the door so you don't get locked out. If you do, just knock and I'll open up."

I took the chip, got up, and made my way along the side aisle. When I slipped outside the sun was as bright as Christ's ascension.

Don't get me wrong, I was thankful to Nico for having considered me and my situation enough to think that he needed to help me establish an alibi that Sunday afternoon. Yet I also wondered how much he was motivated by concern for himself. That he had helped me out felt almost like a bribe, like he was greasing my palm to ensure that I kept my mouth shut about his role in the Marathon fire. I wasn't comfortable with the *scratch your back if you scratch mine* mentality of the whole affair, though in the coming weeks, distracted by the Polish girls, I pushed it all out of my mind.

Now, however, with the tribunal inquest coming up, I have to wonder—not so much about whether the Marathon blaze was as accidental as Nico made it out to be, but about Nico's remorse, about the sincerity of his remorse. I try to picture him in my mind's eye as he burned the letter in the woods along the Marathon. What stinging words had the woman written to him, what cutting phrases of love or hate? I can see him crouching in the forest holding the missive by one edge, lighting one corner of the paper with his silver lighter. I can see the weak orange flame reflected in his eyes, and though in this imaginary tableau he isn't smiling, I see a strange gleam on his face, an appreciative gaze that makes me finally understand just how much Nico liked fire.

And I ask myself now: did Nico *enjoy* setting the backfire on Mount Maggiore? Did he *intend* it to be an escape fire, or was that just a convenient label he thought up afterward in a flash of genius and fear? Nothing is more crucial for me to know. Nothing. My forgiveness—what I do or do not divulge at the inquest—depends on how such hairs split.

Part Three
Into the Black

Chapter 25

Despite the squad's grueling August workload we had two weeks of heaven during the visit of the Polish girls. They'd come from Warsaw and from towns like Poznán and Bielsk Podlaski, Rzesazów, Kraków, and Gdánsk—a dozen art students bearing backpacks full of lingerie and sketchbooks. Their project was to restore Il Carpiglio's decaying statues in the gardens behind Palazzo Sangiusto, and the International Youth Volunteer Network had arranged with Cavalier Mezzasoma that the visitors be accommodated in the barracks at our firebase.

The presence of the women changed our lives, infused it with a tenderness and fragility we had forgotten. We looked at our dirty uniforms and unkempt barracks and suddenly recognized our own boorishness. And we felt awkward, as though, burdened with our firefighting gear, we had wandered into a museum filled with beautiful ancient figurines. We combed our hair and tried to stop cursing. Firefighting itself, which we had only the day before viewed as pure drudgery, became newly exciting, dangerous and noble.

We watched Nico fall in love. We thought it was the blonde, the one named Yvonne, he was after, and perhaps he thought so too at first. With her full-bodied locks of flaxen hair, her voluptuous torso and heart-stopping pierced navel, she stunned us all. And in the circle of white plastic armchairs that arranged and rearranged itself on the dirt clearing in front of the command post, we watched as Nico tried to engage her in talk. It was a task. Yvonne's English was worse than bad, and he knew not one syllable of Polish, so it was like trying to communicate through a barrage of radio static. With much patience, Nico did manage to gather that she enjoyed literature as much as he, and their broken dialogues often consisted of little more than naming authors they enjoyed. Whenever they thought of another luminary they both admired, they would nod their heads and moan as if melting chocolate-covered raspberries on their tongues—their way of expressing awe at the beauty of Gabriel García Márquez or Milorad Pavić or J. M. Coetzee or Italo Calvino. Yvonne's eyes would blink blue beneath her sexy blond bangs, and Nico would lean close and peer into those azure beams as though he were going to kiss her at any moment. But Yvonne would turn her head away and laugh, change the topic, and I could tell Nico was frustrated only to mention names and murmur moans of literary approval. I knew that he wanted to talk deep book meanings and stylistic subtleties, for I had once mentioned Giovanni Verga to him and was treated to an hour's animated talk about peasant classes and free indirect discourse, stuff I couldn't fathom. As he sat with Yvonne, I watched him attempt desperate pantomimes to illustrate ghost ships, alchemical experiments and ice, or painting with tea or unearthing frozen corpses, or climbing up ladders to the moon as the mysterious satellite swung down close the sea. But it was arduous and unsatisfactory, and in the end the gestures of friendship between him and Yvonne were fated to remain only gestures, only friendship.

Then Nico discovered that the one named Katja could speak English pretty well, and he'd arrange for the three of them to get together, with Katja providing translations forth and back between English and Polish. The ploy was mildly successful in the beginning, but I noticed that Nico grew less and less interested in the translations and more and more interested in the translator herself. He seemed very excited that he had found someone who spoke nearly fluent English, and when, in the midst of their conversations, Yvonne would eventually wander off (she had her eye on Saverio, I noted), Katja and Nico barely seemed to notice.

Katja was a slip of a woman with kiwi-green eyes and smooth, long legs. She was quite tall and slim, on the borderline between awkward and graceful. Her pinecone brown hair was straight and silky, her lips small and soft like those of a child. She seemed shy. Nico confided to me that she was sad about something that had happened to her recently in Poland. He was drawn to that. He seemed to understand that sadness in her and made a special effort to dispel it, to distract her and show her that life constantly renews itself—just as he had done, I realize now, for me and for the squad with his childish enthusiasm and energy. Katja . . . *responded*. Fireflies swam in her eyes when she regarded him; it was obvious she found Nico magnetic. She would faithfully sit beside him while he wrote in the shade of the medlar tree, then he'd read her prose poems he'd drafted in his black-bound notebooks. They took long walks on his afternoons off. They toured the inside of the palace together, sampled one another's linguine during meals at the Trattoria Tramontano, licked pistachio-and-peach ice cream cones on benches in Piazza Il Carpiglio, their thighs grazing. In the evenings they began taking strolls along the firebase perimeter, holding hands and talking softly and kissing in the dark spaces. The kisses were innocent at first, soft brief meetings of the lips that seemed like natural extensions of the words they whispered. When their kisses grew more heated, I'd turn my head away.

We eased into new patterns—it was like slipping on a pair of satin pajamas. After the oppressive swelter of midday and the prolonged afternoons spent battling burns, we welcomed the evenings as they spread cool lilac light over the firebase and turned on the first twinkle of stars and planets in the ebbing sky. We'd drag our chairs into the clearing and sit and talk in the mellowing light, watching the Poles from the corners of our eyes as they emerged from the showers in the dusk, their hair wet or wrapped in colorful towels, their fine bodies trailing scents of perfumes and powders, of moist skin, of the wild thyme growing by the wayside that released its fragrance at every brush of an ankle. The girls would go into the barracks and choose their clothes and reappear wearing blouses with black spaghetti straps, sheer linen skirts, gold drop earrings that caught the last rays of light. And always that velvety whisper, that satin rustling of the Polish language, inflecting endlessly, like someone lolling cherries and wine on the tongue. The foreign words—indistinct, sexy, indecipherable—washed over to us as though we cradled conch shells to our ears.

Little by small, the Polish girls would gravitate toward us. We'd stand to offer them the chairs, then take our turns in the showers. Though there'd be no more hot water, we welcomed the cool spray; we were grateful simply that our limbs grazed the same tiles just caressed by the lovely creatures outside. One evening Enzo found a bar of aromatic soap in the showers and—guiltily, ecstatically—we passed the soap from stall to stall and lathered our bodies. If we were lucky we'd have a clean spare uniform tucked under our bunk, or sometimes we'd don our civilian clothes—a pressed cotton shirt buttoning down the front, snug trousers or jeans ringed by an old leather belt, leather loafers afoot. Then, since we'd just shaved, maybe we'd add a modest dash of cologne on the wrists or a dab in the depression at the base of the neck, right where the shirt opens at the top of the chest.

Our attraction to the girls was nothing but an extension of our intense emotions about firefighting, and there were many fires at this time, big and small, on all peaks and in all valleys of our fire sector. The fires never ceased to amaze us. A burning field that seemed lit up by a network of flickering neon lights dug into the ground. Flower seeds, snug in the heart of the flowers, popping in the searing heat. Fire shooting up over our heads, bounding from treetop to treetop out of reach, rocketing huge bursts of flame fifty meters into the sky. The burning forests roared like marching armies, and even after a blaze had been extinguished, the din would still resound in our ears. One afternoon we walked through a thicket full of birds—a large flock of starlings escaping a nearby fire. The creatures alighted on our shoulders and arms and hats as though we were merely part of the landscape, strange trees providing odd perches. And every now and again, as we fought burns on the mountainsides, a pine tree would explode with heat and sap, a single cannon salute celebrating nothing or everything.

Returning from a blaze, black and messy with soot, reeking like damp fireplaces, we'd immediately seek out the Poles. Our utter exhaustion would dissipate instantly the moment we saw them. They were so clean, so fresh and tan, so delicate and soft as they sat at the Trattoria Tramontano waiting for us. It was the very contrast between our groups, I think, that brought us so close together, that made our interactions so dynamic and intimate. While we reeked of smoke and ashes, while our green uniforms were smeared with sweat and dirt, the Polish girls would be decked out in their evening outfits, summer dresses and halter tops, yellow sandals with straps that wound round and around delicate ankles. Their lips were wet with wine, their eyes sparkled like jewels in the lamplight. They would tease us, calling us brutes and telling us to head for the showers.

"We wanted to save the warm water for you, ladies."

"We already bathed, *cari*. Besides, I'd rather bathe in ice water than eat next to a chimney sweeper."

"What? We are brave heroes! We fight fire!"

"And we fight your stenches!"

"Come, *ragazze*, drink some more vino."

One evening at dinner I found myself sitting next to the Polish girl with straight black hair, darting eyes, and ruddy lips. She was very quiet and would touch a cloth napkin to her mouth after each bite she took. As she did, the small jewels of the bracelet she wore on her thin wrist would flash. She wore a collarless blouse, and when she drank I could see the tendons ripple along her neck. I noticed that she rarely showed her teeth. This was Lyn. I felt like reaching out and running my tongue along the lipstick stain on the rim of her wineglass. She felt my eyes on her.

I said, "So how do you find Casabasso?"

She opened her eyes wide and nodded. "Yes, I do, I like it." She gave me a quick smile and pushed a strand of hair from her brow. "There are many fires here?"

"We get a lot this time of year."

"It is dangerous, no?"

"Not really," I said. "Only if you don't know what you're doing."

She was waiting for me to go on, but when I didn't she said, "Oh, yes, that's like art."

"Art is dangerous?"

"Yes, I mean restoration, like we are doing with the statues. It is easy to ruin art thinking you are improving it. We are meant to clean the statues, you see, but the cleaning process itself can be dangerous for them. Do you understood?"

I nodded *yes*. Her irises were the refreshing brown of juniper bark.

In halting, heavily accented Italian, which I found charming, Lyn told me all about Il Carpiglio's famous statues and explained the restoration project, how she and the other Polish *ragazze* spent their days pressed up against the carved figures, the marble cool in the mornings and warmer than blood in the afternoons. Lyn's fingertips were bleached with the cleaning fluids. She showed me her wrists, how the muscles in her forearms had grown tight and powerful with the work. She said she knew every intimate detail of Il Carpiglio's Prometheus, from the curls in his hair right down to the small ridges cut into the fennel stalk he clutched in his left hand.

Lyn also mentioned that the Palazzo Sangiusto held several more busts by the same artist. These busts were unfinished—Il Carpiglio had been stabbed and killed by a rival while working on them—but held much significance for art historians. Because they were unfinished, the works might reveal some of the artist's secrets, his methods of cutting the marble and that sort of thing. But the rooms in the palace where the busts were stored were currently closed to the public.

I happened to know a guy who worked at the palace, and in the next few days, with his and Cavalier Mezzasoma's help, I managed to arrange a private visit. Much to Lyn's delight, I surprised her one afternoon and took her to see the busts.

She was clearly moved, not only by the statues but by the efforts I had taken to arrange our private viewing. Though I really hadn't had any ulterior motives when I'd set up the viewing, as we left the palace our hands brushed against one another, and I gently took hold of her fingers. Lyn didn't resist, she entwined her fingers in mine.

On our stroll back to the firebase, I led Lyn along a path that ran through some nearby farmland; it was a scenic route I sometimes took on my way back and forth from my apartment to the firebase. A few weeks before, I had noticed a robin poking around in a rosemary bush nearby and had marveled at the soft blue eggs in the nest.

I pulled Lyn off the path. We'd have to cross a cornfield to get to the nest.

"Where are we going?" she asked. Her lips curled open in a smile.

"Would you like to see some robin's eggs?" I asked.

"Yes, okay."

Lightly squeezing her hand—how soft and fragile it seemed!—I led her across the cornfield. Walking through those rows of large green leaves, the stalks taller than ourselves, it seemed as though we were being caressed by a thousand hands. At the far end of the field was the huge old rosemary bush, as big as a car, where I'd seen the nest. I reached in and carefully spread the branches apart.

Three tiny chicks sat in the nest, twittering at the tops of their voices, hungry mouths gulping for food. Lyn gave out a soft cry of wonderment and delight.

When she turned away from the nest, Lyn raised her forearm to her face and smelled her skin.

"*Rozmaryn*," she said in Polish. *Rosmarino*. Rosemary.

The Polish word sounded like it was full of water. Lyn's lips were dry, and she wet them with her tongue. I took her wrist and raised it to my mouth.

Chapter 26

Heat more like August than September seeps into the valley. Fine-grained reddish sand, borne from the Sahara on atmospheric winds, swirls down and dusts the town. The last cicadas of the year croak menacingly in the trees. Casabasso is a lump of yeasty dough set beneath a hot, moist towel. Sirens ring in the parched vales and gulches of the countryside. Italy is a page whose edges curl with flame.

I fritter away hours worrying more than ever about the tribunal inquest—only ten days away—and chasing shade through the hot streets. The women, I think on my long, daily walks—the bikini woman, the prostitutes, Adina in Firenze, the Polish girls Lyn and Katja—are important. What would a man do for a woman in the guise of passion? What would Nico do? Would he quite intentionally set a fire in order to prove or invalidate his love, then call it an accident? And since there was more than one woman, would he set more than one fire?

I stumble back to my apartment at the peak of the sweltering afternoon, when not even sparrows will venture from their nests, and stare at the map of Mount Maggiore tacked to my wall. Night falls. I fill my stomach with stale bread and lie on my bed sweating, grappling with fits of sleep. Thinking of women keeps me tossing most of the night. I imagine Lyn in Warsaw, strolling through a museum or attending art classes, her fingertips stained with paint, the smock clinging to her body. But strangely, the woman who comes most to mind as I lie in bed in the darkness, the woman whose beauty I find myself most adoring—is Katja. I remember her hips, the thin blouses she wore, the neat part she cut in her straight brown hair as she emerged from the shower. And though fire is the usual metaphor for passion, the images that come to me tonight, the scenes that flit across the prism of the night, are filled with water. Katja's a mermaid, my desire the heavy tides. She stands waist-deep in brook water brimming with bass, her rain-drenched shirt clinging to her chest, her skin dripping with seawater. Slowly she swims toward me, ducking underwater to shirk her clothes, but who surfaces is a stranger, some woman I glanced on the street, a dark-haired beautician in a lab coat who bares her breasts and moves toward me with the certainty and grace of an ocean wave.

But when the wave finally breaks, the shorefront is littered with burned corpses. Renato and the others—Enzo, Saverio, Pietro, Massimo—are dead. Their mouths have been sealed. Other lips, too, have been sewn together, some—like those of the *contadino* on Mount Maggiore—soldered shut with flame. Can I simply call it all an accident when favors were exchanged, equipment misused, strategies in the field abused? Can I pin it on a single person, some convenient *capro espiatorio*? No. When I testify at the tribunal inquest, certain itineraries to outlying villages, villages like Pelle Marone and Cavuoti and Ruviano, must be traced; certain afternoon drives, assignations and deliveries, certain radio transmissions and Canadair flights, certain transactions, now unspeakable, must be spoken.

In early August I accompanied Tonino on an assignation near the Monti Acuti. Tonino was excited about this one—so excited he wouldn't let me so much as touch the envelope with the money—and I found out why: he had arranged (without Cavalier Mezzasoma's or Renato's approval) for some of us to ride in one of the Airborne Fire Protection Squad helicopters. He said he wanted the Americano to feel what it was like to sit on a chair in the sky. So on the afternoon of the fire, Tonino, Nico and I drove to the heliport and buckled ourselves into a 306, one of the smaller copters.

The first bucket had been filled at the heliport, and when we reached the scene of the fire, the helicopter circled once before going close to release the water. Then the pilot banked up sharply from the burning hill, dropped the copter's nose, and swung toward a lake to dip the bucket. This was out near Matese, at a large blaze on the slopes of Monte Máio in the volcanic Monti Acuti, and the water lay in a volcanic lake some four kilometers to the south. From above, the countryside looked like a large unfinished jigsaw puzzle. The mountains were khaki, with bald spots of great cracked boulders that flashed white in the sunlight. Farms edged themselves up against the foot of the hills, slicing the earthen grounds of the valley into neat quadrangular fields. The fields, crisscrossed with ribbons of unpaved road, were ocher and furrowless. Then appeared the thick, winding inkline of the main thoroughfare. A dirty white delivery truck labored up the curved mountainside road, flanked on both sides by canopies of trees as thick and green as moss on a crèche.

Tonino was in the navigator's perch up front talking loudly with the pilot. I was in the cramped back passenger seat with Nico beside me. Nico had his forehead pressed to the side window and was looking down at the scene in silence.

Beyond the plains lay a green swath of pine forest, and as we crossed above these woodlands, the earth swooped upward abruptly, hurling itself up at the helicopter until I thought the bucket would catch in the trees. I gripped the edge of my seat and checked my seatbelt, the noise of the rotors resounding loudly in my ears. A small, tight bubble of air rose in my gut and burst, and when I looked outside again, the land had turned bare and rocky like a broken crust of bread. We had reached the rim of the volcano; for several moments the helicopter seemed poised like a fly on the lip of a great, deep bowl. The land plummeted down and away into the crater; we passed over a strip of birch trees and were over the lake. I saw the shadow of the helicopter loom on the surface of the water below, and as the helicopter descended I saw the quick-moving shadows of the rotors going around and around. The lake was battleship gray and placid. Several sloops and sailboats, puny pleasure craft, floated motionless on the surface of the water.

"Matteo," Nico said, suddenly leaning toward me to direct his voice to my ear over the noise of the rotors, "think for a second! This is a volcano!" His face was animated as he swept his palm in a gesture that seemed to encompass the entire scene below us. "Can you imagine? Do you realize that this is a volcano!"

"Yes, Nico," I answered, following his line of thought, following it down below the surface of the lake as one might picture a fishing line dropping into the depths, and followed it further still, down below the water and mud, plummeting below the earth's crust to the orange cauldrons of lava seething underneath. It was suddenly obvious and amazing to me, the simple, fantastic fact that the core of the earth was nothing but a molten brew, a kind of primeval conflagration—part liquid, part solid, part gas—that defied the normal boundaries of nature. The earth had a heart of fire, and the tourists swimming in the lake were idly splashing near a force so powerful it could literally obliterate the top of the entire mountain.

The copter hovered and dropped, the rotation of the blades making irregular circular furrows on the water's surface. Tonino had his head out the window and was motioning to the pilot with his forearm: down, down, down. . . . When the water reached the bucket's lip and flooded the container, we could feel the steel cable tighten and tug, the rotors of the helicopter seemed to skip a beat and the motor groaned, and then we were ascending again, altitude five meters, fifteen meters, fifty meters. . . . The lake dropped away and the helicopter strove upward to clear the crest of the volcano's lip.

When we got back to the burn site, we saw the squad spread out in a jagged line at the edge of the blaze on the eastern mountainside. The flames had cut cragged corrugations in the maquis. As we drew closer, I spotted Saverio down on the slope; he had removed his hat and was motioning to us with it, and at the same time Renato's voice came crackling over the radio. They wanted us to dampen the point of the blaze. The pilot circled once then flew us directly into a plume of black smoke and Tonino yanked the lever. The bucket emptied instantly and the helicopter lifted and shook, tilting in a cross-port gust, and the pilot tacked with the wind and banked us up and out of the smoke.

As we turned back toward the lake, I noticed the others—Enzo, Cesare, Tancredi, Pietro, Massimo and Luchetto—down on the mountainside waving their arms up at us, though whether with joy, or for thanks, or in warning I will never know. This is the way the whole summer looks to me now, a loose series of ambiguous signals impossible to pin down. There were always dangerous currents running below the ordinary yet often beautiful sheen of our days. The utter unknowability of those currents disturbs me; they will never fully be mapped out. Getting a grip on them is like trying to read a book whose pages are stuck together. I wet the tips of my fingers and try to pry the pages apart, but the paper falls to pieces in my hands.

Chapter 27

We spent the next week or so fighting other, less sensational fires, enjoying what time remained with our Polish visitors, and preparing for the Festival of Giovanni Secondo, the patron saint of Casabasso. Gaudy decorations were going up all around town for the celebrations, merchants were setting up booths and stalls in the pedestrian market, and healthy numbers of visitors had come to the city to take part in the festivities. The crown jewel of the festival is an enormous public bonfire that is set on the plaza in front of the palace.

During downtime, the brigade was put on a detail tasked with erecting barricades to block traffic off from the bonfire area and to create fire lanes for the emergency vehicles during the festival. The barricades were kept in a warehouse not far from Palazzo Sangiusto, which meant that we could drop by to say hello to the Polish girls pretty often. We'd find them in some corner of the palace gardens clambering on ladders and scaffolds, caressing the statues, stroking the marble. Sometimes they'd chat and giggle as they worked. Other times, when they were silent with concentration, we simply watched on without interfering.

To be honest, my romance with Lyn didn't roll smoothly along the tracks. Though she was quite sweet with me (so sweet that I'll remember those few moments we had together for the rest of my life), she made her limits clear, so those hellos in the palace grounds were emotionally ambiguous for me, even stressful. I was usually relieved when we would finally wave good-bye to the girls and get on with erecting the barricades.

We'd take the van to the storage loading dock, pack it full, and then try to follow a map marked with red lines that showed where the barricades were to be set up. Every year we used the same map and the same barricades, wooden sawhorses stenciled with orange letters spelling out LINEA POLIZIA and NON ATTRAVERSARE. As Tonino drove the van, Saverio sat in the passenger seat wrestling with the map, which was hopelessly outdated. Most of the streets had been changed to one-way since the map was made, and no one had bothered to make the changes. We winged it best we could. To help pass the time, Enzo and Nico had given the Poles one of our portable two-way radios (walkie-talkies, Nico called them) so we would call the girls every hour or so to flirt and chat, a playful distraction that helped relieve the boredom of setting up the barricades.

Enzo and Cesare were crouched in the van passing the legs and crossbars down to the rest of us. Massimo was counting each barricade we put up.

". . . Three-hundred thirty-two, three-hundred thirty-three. . . ."

"Shut up already, Massimo," Enzo whined, "it's bad enough as it is."

"There's gotta be thousands of these suckers," Pietro said.

"Millions," Tancredi offered.

Massimo droned on, ". . . three hundred and thirty five, three hundred and . . . c'mon pass it down."

"Where's Nico?" Cesare asked.

Nico and Katja were off on one of their rendezvous. They often spent mornings or afternoons together exploring the town, preludes to their romantic after-dinner strolls in the moonlight around the perimeter of camp.

There is a certain urgency to international love, and Nico and Katja quickly grew intimate. Yet though their nighttime kisses waxed passionate, they didn't seek out privacy. I guess they assumed we couldn't see them necking in the nighttime shadows, but often we could. And one late evening when most of the Polish girls were asleep in the barracks, some of us lounging on the command post steps noticed Katja and Nico making out in a corner on the far side of the firebase compound. The truth was we couldn't keep our eyes off them. They were leaning against the fence embracing. They kissed for a long time. We could see Katja's hand moving along Nico's back, pulling at his neck, tugging at his shirt. Nico's kisses circled slowly, achingly downward. He kissed her cheeks, her eyes and ears, her chin. His mouth clung to her neck until Katja's fist opened up like a desert flower blooming before our eyes.

He unbuttoned her shirt, and she leaned forward slightly and offered him her breasts, first one, then the other. Katja ran her hand through his brown head of hair, she looked down on him and lovingly stroked his cheeks, and after a long while she spread her arms out wide and grabbed the hard steel bars of the fence as though she were being flagellated.

"What's he waiting for?" Enzo asked.

"You wouldn't know, would you, Enzo," Pietro said.

"What's that mean, I wouldn't know? What are you trying to say?"

"Go for it!" Tancredi whispered loudly.

"Shut up, you morons, pigs, sons of whores . . ." Pietro started.

"Who's a pig?" Enzo said.

"Just keep it down, everybody," I said. "We shouldn't even be watching this." But I was as powerless to turn away as all the others.

"They're all the way over there, for Christ's sake," Enzo said.

"Just keep quiet."

"Matteo is right, guys. We shouldn't be watching them," Luchetto offered.

Just then a car came through the gate, sweeping its headlights across the compound. It was Saverio's red Cinquecento. The car beeped and Yvonne waved to us from the front seat, and when she got out and tilted the seat forward, out popped Tonino and Vanessa.

We rearranged ourselves and made some room for them in the circle. They had brought several cans of beer and we passed them around. When

I looked back over toward where Nico and Katja had been, I saw that they were already on their way over to us, hand in hand.

As the Americano's friend, I guess I should have said something, given him a heads-up or a hint, but I found myself too embarrassed. Had I done so, he would have figured out that we had been watching him and Katja on previous nights. And besides, the squad never saw them together like that again, so I swallowed my tongue and kept my mouth shut.

I myself, however, did watch them once more. I was alone one night in the radio room when I heard some voices out back that I recognized as Katja's and Nico's. The rest of the squad was out front lounging on the helipad with a boom box, drinking and watching the stars. I switched off the inside light and peeked outside and saw Nico and Katja together in the shadows several meters away. They were leaning against the fence locked in an embrace.

Nico had his hands in her shorts, and Katja tilted her head back and opened her mouth like she was drinking the night air. She leaned down onto Nico's fingers and after a while bit the back of her fist, stifling a cry. They kissed then a while longer, and soon Katja began rubbing the front of Nico's pants. Huddled down in the dark room, I watched as she unbuckled him and bent over to take him into her mouth. Then something strange happened. She stopped and looked up at him and then kissed him some more and stopped again. He gently pulled her up toward his mouth and kissed her, and they hugged for a very long time, whispering to one another.

I heard a sound out front and saw Luchetto coming toward the office, so I quickly stepped outside onto the front porch.

"What's up, Matteo?"

"I was just checking the radio."

"I've gotta take a leak, man," Luchetto said. He pushed past me toward the toilets. I went over and joined the main group out on the helipad. Lyn smiled at me, but it wasn't the kind of smile that led to anything else.

It was the penultimate evening. The next night was the festival, La Festa del Nostro Padrone Giovanni Secondo, and the morning after that the Poles would board a train back to Warsaw. I opened a last beer and breathed in the cool night air.

The next day Nico and Katja seemed estranged, and when the Poles left for the palace for half a day of finishing up, Nico was in a particularly black mood. We spent the day erecting barricades and fighting a few small burns in the area. We called the Poles several times on the portable radio units, but each time we offered Nico the handset, he'd decline.

The festival is actually a bastard of two holidays: the birthday of patron saint Giovanni Secondo and the Late-Summer Fire Festival, a pagan ceremony begun by Goth invaders centuries ago but somehow appropriated by the Catholic church. The culminating bonfire is supposed to banish evil spirits from the town and ensure good fortune.

The bonfire site was cordoned off with rope. Three days before the festival, the people of the city began arriving with their offerings and placing them within the ropes. The stuff was mostly old furniture and clothes, but there was a little bit of everything, from wooden toys and framed photos to an expensive-looking finely veneered antique bureau. The fire is considered to be sacred in some way—it's blessed by a priest when lit—and tradition has it that the offerings are hallowed by God. Other people thought of the whole affair as some kind of potlatch, and the result was that the bonfire accumulated more than a truckload of junk. After not too long the bonfire site was overflowing, the restraining ropes buried beneath broken boards, wicker chairs, desks, tables, a horse's saddle and plow, car seats with busted springs, sequined dresses, books and old bills, flowers and ears of corn, war medals. . . .

By nightfall the streets of our little city were thronging with pedestrians. I was amazed at the masses of people who showed up for the festival. I don't remember it ever being so crowded. Many of those present were visitors—rich bankers from the North, Romans, families from Umbria and Abruzzo out for a holiday, even a surprising number of foreign tourists—but most of the crowd consisted of local residents, either from Casabasso itself or from Città Vecchia or one of the other nearby villages in the province. The scene put me in an outstandingly good mood.

Nico still seemed a bit down—I thought for sure he'd had a spat with Katja—so I convinced him to accompany me to church. There was an important, ceremonial mass before the bonfire, and I thought it might take his mind off whatever was bothering him. Though he said he wasn't religious, I convinced him it would at least be an interesting experience for him, and he reluctantly agreed. So, weaving our way through the happy crowd, Nico and I made our way to the Duomo. And though the air was charged with a merry energy and people were eating ice cream and watermelon and drinking grappa on the streets, I don't think I saw Nico so much as crack half a smile.

After mass, the priest, swinging incense heady with smoke, walked solemnly to the head of the procession that would make its way through town to the Palazzo Sangiusto and the bonfire site. The priest was flanked by a contingent of altar boys bearing candles, chalices, Holy Water, prayer beads, a large gold cross and other paraphernalia. In front of the priest were larger-than-life papier mâché likenesses of the Virgin Mary, St. John the Baptist, and Giovanni Secondo. It took six bearers to carry each of the icons.

The procession was so crowded I soon lost track of Nico. It was difficult to walk among the throng, and the procession kept stopping for some reason only the people in the very front could divine. Finally I got fed up, turned down a side street, and navigated a shortcut through the back alleys. When I reached the others at the bonfire site, the procession was still half a kilometer away. The squad was grouped around one of our jeeps, with most of the Polish girls close by. I saw Lyn and Katja, but no one knew where Nico was. And though the procession took almost an hour to reach the bonfire site in front of Palazzo Sangiusto, the Americano never showed up.

Finally the priest was handed a torch. When he went over and dropped it onto the pile with a prayer, flames immediately shot up, almost exploding in the priest's face.

The crowd was entranced. Katja's green eyes lit up and an orange glow suffused her face and hair. I'd always found her pretty, but now for the first time, seeing her smooth skin illuminated by the fire, a mixed expression of sadness and wonder on her face as though she were asking herself a question that had no definite answer, I understood the angelic beauty Nico must have recognized in her.

The fire call came not long after the fireworks ended. Someone had reported seeing smoke issuing from the palace gardens a kilometer away. I gave one last look around for Nico, but he was still lost in the crowd somewhere so I jumped into the jeep with the rest of the squad and we began clearing a way through the throng. It was an excruciatingly slow crawl. Many people had simply ignored the barricades and were milling around everywhere. It was like trying to drive through a sea of people. The crowd opened up reluctantly in front of us and closed in again immediately behind us, and there were a lot of children running around. Outside the pedestrian zone, traffic was gridlocked, and drivers were so angry and frustrated at being stuck in traffic they didn't bother yielding to our siren. Tonino was navigating centimeters among the cars, surfing the curbs and sidewalks, cutting the wrong way down one-way streets. Several drivers and pedestrians cursed us as we forced our way through.

Finally we made it to a side gate of the palace gardens. The gate was padlocked, but we could see and smell smoke in the dense swath of trees that provided a buffer between the palace grounds and the street. Tonino edged the jeep up beside the iron fence and we tossed our gear down and climbed over. Pietro got his boot caught between the upper spikes, came down head first, and hung there like an uncut prosciutto. We got him off, but he was bruised and his ankle was twisted.

We found ourselves in the well-tended garden-forest perimeter. The fire had so far confined itself to the understory, and we used *flabelli* and two handheld water pumps to extinguish it. Only the smoke was bad. After about twenty minutes, drops of water began falling from the sky. We thought for a second that the wind was blowing the fountain water over, then that it was raining, but we soon realized that the city fire department had sent a truck over and was spraying a cover of water over the fence onto our position, and soon the fire was out.

Though we advised them not to, the Polish girls insisted on seeing the statues before going back to Warsaw, even against the orders of Cavalier Mezzasoma.

They had already packed their suitcases and loaded everything into the transit van, which Renato drove. The rest of us rode in the squad jeep and they followed us to the palace. Tonino easily talked us past the guards at the VIP entrance and slowly cruised through the courtyards to the extensive gardens in the rear. We passed more than one shuttle bus full of gawking tourists; city officials had roped off the burned area of the gardens but hadn't closed down the entire park, and there were an exceptional number of visitors who had come to witness the destruction.

We followed the kilometer-long fountain out toward Il Carpiglio's sculptures and the burned patch came into view on our right. It actually wasn't too bad, relatively speaking. We had contained the fire to less than four acres. But the scorched trees and grasses looked particularly awful when compared to the rest of the magnificent parkland.

"Stop! Stop here!" Ewa, the Polish chaperone, yelled from the van. Renato pulled over, and some of the Polish girls got out of the van. We had stopped next to a tableaux of statues the Poles had just spent the last two weeks straining over, their fingers reaching in to clean each crevice. And now . . . the statues weren't burned, exactly—how do you burn marble?— but they had been inundated with smoke and ruined, scorched black. Some of the Polish girls began crying, Lyn included. The rest of us stood nearby helplessly.

Finally Ewa began coaxing the girls back into the van. Lyn grazed my cheek with her lips and tears, but when Katja turned for Nico, I noticed, he was looking the other direction, and when he turned back, Katja was already stepping into the van. She gave him a small wave of her fingers, but Nico, almost imperceptibly, just nodded. Though they'd obviously had a falling out, I thought he was really acting like an idiot. Say a proper goodbye, I wanted to say to him, this is the last time you'll see her. But she was in the van already, and without fanfare Renato turned the vehicle around and headed off to the train station, leaving us there beside the ruined statues, our hands in our pockets and shoulders slung low, our hearts nothing but half-eaten apples.

Chapter 28

After the fire of the statues I was upset with Nico and I pitied him too. He was like a child who had hurt himself through his own misbehavior. He hadn't acted the gentleman with Katja, and I thought he'd be regretting it now. I wanted to talk to him about the Polish girls, but who was I to say anything? What did I know about treating women right? I let it lie instead. I fell back on one of my habitual strategies for dealing with problems: I tried to avoid him—exactly as I've been avoiding everyone since the funerals, avoiding everyone who's important to me, everything that I must face up to.

Now that September is slipping by, I try to muster up some courage. With the tribunal inquest only a week away, I get my hair cut and check the train schedule for Napoli. Back at my apartment, I am gathering up my dirty clothes to do some laundry when the phone rings. I hesitate for five rings, then pick it up.

I recognize the voice at once. It's the district commander-in-chief of the brigade, Cavalier Mezzasoma himself. I wince with regret that I answered.

"Cavalier, sir," I say.

"I thought you were on vacation, Matteo."

"Yes, sir," I lie, embarrassed that I've been squandering my days like some unemployed bum, which perhaps I am.

"Where did you go?"

"Sperlonga," I answer off the top of my head, giving him the name of a popular vacation spot not far from here. It sounds plausible. I have to tell him something. Can't admit I've been lurking around Casabasso like an insect in the crevice of a wall. I lie again: "I just got back yesterday."

"I'm glad I caught you then," Mezzasoma says. "Matteo, did you receive a summons from the Tribunale dell'Interno?"

"Yes." I walk over to the table where I keep my pile of mail and find the letter. "Judge Ceruta-Levitas," I read, "September 26th in Napoli."

"Yes," the Cavalier says carefully. "Have you spoken with anyone about this inquest yet?"

"No, sir, I was just. . . ."

"Don't talk to anyone."

"I won't, sir."

"Good," Mezzasoma says. "There's something I want to inform you of, but first let me ask, how are you getting along?"

"I'm okay, I guess." I look around at my apartment, at the books, the framed maps, a stray sock. There's nothing I haven't looked at two thousand times already, and it depresses me.

"It's good to have taken time off," Mezzasoma is saying, "to get a fresh perspective on things. I've been to Sperlonga myself. Nice town. Excellent beaches. Clean."

"Yes, sir," I agree.

"But the others—" Mezzasoma is saying—"Tonino and the others are expecting you to come back, to rejoin the squad. At least eventually. I hope you're thinking about doing that. *I'm* expecting you will."

"I have every intention to," I say to Mezzasoma. I look up at the ceiling, at some stains on the ceiling that resemble dour faces. One of the faces has a tongue stuck out at me. It knows that the words I have just uttered are false. The Cavalier says something I don't catch.

"Excuse me, sir?"

"Matteo, it was the American's fault."

"What was?" I ask, trying to get my bearing in the conversation.

"The deaths, of course."

A wave of dizziness shakes me. I drop the summons and put my hand on the edge of the table to steady myself. Now the pattern on my rug swims, it is like reeds and fronds swaying in ocean water.

"Do you hear me, Matteo? The local Fire Review Board has returned its findings. They just came out of session not one hour ago. I was there. It was Nicolas Fowler's fault. His fire killed the others."

My head is reeling. "With all due respect, Cavalier, sir," I blurt out, "Nico's fire may not have. . . ." I say this a little too loudly.

"I'm telling you, Matteo, what happened. The facts. The board has already made their recommendations. They've *concluded*. Do you really think Renato and Saverio and Enzo and the others weren't capable of beating a routine blaze? Do you really think. . . ."

"Routine, sir?"

"A routine blaze. Standard procedures. Workable terrain. No winds."

"But, sir, I didn't get a chance. . . ."

"As I've already repeated," Mezzasoma interrupts, "the local Fire Board has reached its findings. The only thing that remains is to document the facts for presentation at the tribunal inquest in Napoli—which reminds me, there's been an injunction to postpone those proceedings."

"So I won't have to testify?" I ask hopefully.

"Not next week, anyway. It'll take a while to get the legal loose ends of this mess straightened out. But there is one more thing I want you to do."

"What's that, sir?"

"Go back to Maggiore."

The words chill my scalp. I don't answer.

"With me," Mezzasoma continues, "and a fire inspector. As I've said, we're ready to document the impact of Nico's backfire scientifically."

"No," I say. "I can't do it. I can't go back there after what's happened."

"Listen to me, Matteo"—Mezzasoma coughs here. He must take a drag on a cigarette too, because his next words sound palpable with smoke. "You do want to come back to the brigade, don't you? Or do you want to let the others down? Let Tonino down? Let me down?"

"Of course not," I say, not liking the implications of those questions—or are they veiled threats?

"Good, that's very good," Mezzasoma says. "Because I've just received word that the position I've been telling you about for a long while now, the position that I've been working on establishing since your father died, has been approved. There is now an opening for a full-time communications officer—not just for the Casabasso brigade, but for the entire North Campanian Fire Area."

"Thank you, sir."

"Your father would be proud. Did you know that he helped me with the proposal?"

I didn't realize my father had been involved in that, and I say so.

"Well, yes, he was quite involved," Mezzasoma assures me. "He was especially instrumental in the early stages. Got me through a lot of red tape. You know, he had you in mind all along."

"Thank you, sir," I say again, but I am thinking of my father, loving him, wondering why he never said anything to me about it.

"It's not yours yet, Matteo," Mezzasoma reminds me. "You'll have to apply for it."

"Yes, sir."

"Then I'll set something up with the fire inspector for early next week—say, Monday?"

"Cavalier, sir," I say, "I'm still not sure about going back to Maggiore."

"Nonsense. We'll be at your place early—at oh-seven-hundred hours."

"Sir . . . " I begin.

"Oh, stop with this 'sir' thing, Mat," Mezzasoma says casually. "It drives me crazy. Tell me, how is your mother?"

I have not spoken to my mother for almost a month. In fact I've hardly told her anything even about Mount Maggiore. She knows about it in a general way, but I played down my involvement considerably. I lied to her that my brigade showed up long after the dangerous blowup.

"My mother's well," I tell Mezzasoma.

"Please send her my regards."

"I will, sir," I say, and I'm hardly listening to the rest of his pleasantries. Yes, sir, I say, No, sir, not at all, sir, Good-bye, sir, I say, and I hang up.

It's like running into a door that is actually a trompe l'oeil; I stagger. Poor Nico, I think. My poor *capro espiatorio*, poor, darling scapegoat.

After the departure of the Polish volunteers, the fire season, much to our chagrin, continued unabated, and the more fires we had the more Nico tried—

out of lost-love desperation perhaps—to intellectualize them; indeed, he was impossible to stop. Though familiar with the debates on fire management, he viewed them as ultimately insignificant. He seemed to think that fire was a kind of life form following its own evolutionary paradigms, that it was constantly evolving, constantly refining its patterns of movement, its strategies, that it was reacting to man's efforts to stifle it. "Fire is a force," he would say dramatically, "that scoffs at man's petty interventions. And it is something more as well. As the intersection of air and heat and light, fire is a kind of opening, it's a scar in the skin of the universe, a crack in the ether, a crevice leading to another world. It isn't destructive but metamorphic, for what it touches it transforms, transforms into pure potential. It breaks physical objects down into the most basic compound of life, carbon, which then combines with other elements to create new forms. In this way, fire is the basis for life—it's the phoenix, the life force that generates from death. It is creation through destruction. . . ."

Despite the craziness of his theories—and I wasn't sure whether he actually believed what he said—Nico's words did affect me. At burns now, rather than simply attacking the flames, I found myself observing them, watching their movements, trying to *see* what Nico saw, to learn what fire was, to search out its heart. I peered at the flames until I was practically blinded by their brilliance. Mesmerized by the swirling and the crackling, I began to understand why Nico felt the need to invent his own syntax to describe fire. Each burn was unique, had its own personality built of fuel and wind conditions, of humidity and dryness, of terrain and temperatures. Through endlessly inflecting combinations of this alphabet, the book of fire was written.

Fire, I came to discover, is most like the sea god Proteus, the titan who could take and discard any form. It can be a pomegranate opened roughly or a naughty frolicking fairy or a motorcycle in the distance. It can be a slap or a punch in the face, a warm hand on your shoulder, a gnashing of canine teeth. Fire can feint or astound, it can be silent or rush like water or crash like cymbals beside your ear. It can run and jump or stroll leisurely along a perimeter, it can die and come back to life, it can be as impenetrable as brick or as ephemeral as a ghost, it can fly or stand stock still, it often laughs at you with its hands on its hips. . . .

I was drawn to fire's overwhelming power, drawn dangerously close. For though hell is full of flame and the devil steps out of fire in the modern imagination, it was as a flaming bush that God first revealed himself to Moses on Mount Sinai. Every time I was pushed back by the heat, each time I raised my hand to shield my face from flames, I was being dazzled by a power no man can bear. Not even Moses himself could look into the eye of God—yet who can resist the call? Who has not turned on the gas burners at midnight and marveled at the ghostly blue circles of flame, four gaseous jewels floating in an empty kitchen? Who has not watched with fascination the tiny oval match flame as it burns toward the fingertip, or held a lighter till it hurts the palm, or dropped an insect into the fireplace? We huddle around campfires, cuddle up before the mesmerizing glow of a hearth, we are seduced by candlelight reflected in our lover's eyes. Who is not exhilarated by a fire truck's silver and red shining? Who doesn't ease their foot off the accelerator, awed at the sight of a house gutted by flames? Who has not been tempted by the power of fire?

Chapter 29

Without the Polish girls, life at the firebase fell into a desultory stupor. Though we still had fires to fight, we approached them without bravado. They were mere chores that got in the way of our real purpose, which was to brood on lost love. We stopped showering after blazes. Moping like cats, we'd congregate on the command post steps and slouch down, smoking cigarettes or playing cards. Renato tried to snap us out of it with his military sense of things—he'd harangue us in his sergeant's voice, calling us blue-eyed schoolboys too big for our knickers and so forth—but we ignored him as best we could. He was married, we reminded ourselves. He didn't know what it was like to have the ambrosia of Polish lips torn from his mouth. No one talked much about the fire of the statues, except to vaguely express sorrow and regret; it was regarded by all of us as a coincidence of ill-timed, cosmic irony. Even now, despite what I have come to know about Nico, I still tend to view it against all evidence in that tender nostalgic light.

Nico recommenced his *motorino* excursions, disappearing for hours at a time almost every afternoon. Though I understood he wanted to be alone, I missed him during those long hours. I imagined him riding over the hills and taking walks along the rocky seashore. I imagined him healing. But one early evening, after having been gone since lunchtime, Nico came walking back to the firebase looking morose and homeless. He sat down next to me and groaned. The *motorino* he'd borrowed from Franco had been stolen.

Nico said he was sure it had been taken by some gypsies. He'd seen them hanging out by a fountain and eyeing him as he parked the *motorino* outside La Buca, where he'd been playing billiards with Franco and his buddies. Nico had chained the rear wheel of the *motorino* to a lamppost, made sure the handlebars were locked with the key, and disconnected the fuel hose from the engine.

He was inside shooting pool with Franco and some other locals when an argument started in the rear alley. They went out the back door and saw a signora yelling at a gypsy woman and her three kids. The gypsy woman, her face set in an expression of stolid indifference, was leaning against a wall near the signora's car, cradling an infant in her arms. A girl of about eight stood next to her, holding a basket and a cardboard sign begging for money. An adolescent boy sat nearby, holding but not playing an old accordion.

Two of the signora's tires were flat, and the signora was fuming. She strode back and forth among the gypsies, yelling at the girl, the boy and the mother in turn, and when Nico and Franco appeared, she began venting her anger about parking fees and doctor's appointments and vehemently cursing the radical party (presumably for their liberal interpretation of gypsy civil rights). The gypsies didn't move; their faces remained blank, unreadable. Nico and Franco told the signora they were sorry, but what could they do? Frustrated, the signora dug a cellular phone out of her purse and made a call. As she did so, the little girl began following behind her with the basket. With her free hand, the signora was swatting the air above the little girl's head. Finally, the signora took some change out of her purse and threw it on the ground, but instead of picking up the money, the gypsies walked away. Just as they were about to turn the corner, the little girl ran back, picked up the change on the ground, and hurried off again.

An hour later, when Nico went out front to unchain the *motorino*, it was gone.

"What are you going to do?" I asked him.

"Kill them," he said.

"I mean about the *moto*."

Nico sighed, "Franco says I have to get him a new one or else. . . ."

"Or else what?

"I don't know. But I have to do it," Nico said despondently.

"But how?" I asked.

"I don't know," he repeated impatiently, lighting a cigarette. "How much does a *motorino* cost?"

"About three million lire."

Nico rolled his eyes and blew out a stream of smoke from his nostrils. "Maybe I'll just skip town," he said. His grin was half-despairing, half-mischievous.

The fire in the gypsy encampment occurred a few days later. Nico was off somewhere when we received and responded to the call. The camp was out on the edge of the city, on the border of the industrial zone. It was nothing but a squalid clutter of filthy canvas tents, broken-down campers and ramshackle hovels of rotting plywood, plastic and cardboard. We drove up late; the city fire department had already arrived. The gypsies had congregated into the furthest corner of camp and were streaming out of the gates. Dark-skinned women with large eyes and loose breasts, covered in generous muslin throws. The children naked or half-naked. The men in dirty white polyester shirts, dark slacks high on their ankles, and long thin leather belts. Several Mercedes-Benzes, recent models, clean and ivory with impenetrably tinted windows, were parked outside the gates, and a few trailers had been pulled out of the encampment and tucked along the dirt shoulder of the thoroughfare. We left the jeep between two of the trailers—with Pietro and Tancredi standing guard—and walked into the camp. The ground was brown packed deeply pitted dirt. The uneven shapes of the huts were disappearing into dark shadows as the sun set. *Watch your wallets,* Enzo whispered. And Cesare: *they carry razor blades.* Thin, menacing figures loomed in the shadows and smoke. We passed through several alleyways littered with junk, using the light of the fire as our guide. Then the ground opened up again and we felt the heat against our cheeks. Thick brown and gray smoke was pouring up from a garbage heap at the rear of the camp. A huge mass of flames lifted itself out of the heap, burning intensely and reeking of garbage. A fire engine was lazily spraying arcs of water along the fire's edge, creating rainbows with the last of the afternoon light.

We suspected that the newspapers would get hold of this and we were right. The fire made the front pages of local and regional newspapers as far away as Napoli. The political Left was adamant about protecting the rights of gypsies, and an investigation was begun into the origin of the fire. There were a lot of people going around saying the fire was arson plain and simple. Its message was unequivocal: no gypsies in our backyard. Though no one claimed responsibility for the blaze, it was blamed on extreme elements of the conservative Right—local residents dismayed at the numerous sprawling gypsy encampments that had in recent years cropped up and entrenched themselves in the district.

It was perfectly clear to me, however, that Nico had set the fire. I guess I'd been ready for something like this, because the knowledge didn't strike me as any grand illumination; it was more of a tardy acknowledgment of something I'd known but repressed for a long time. I remembered other fires too, I ticked them off in my brain: the Marathon fire, the fire of the statues, maybe even that small burn in Ceprano that came on the heels of the bikini girl incident. Which others? There must have been others. There was always the *motorino*—that provided a quick mobility; it opened up possibilities. And there was Franco and those guys at the pool hall, punks who'd do anything for a price. If Nico had joined up with them. . . . Then I remembered Nico's watch collection, his assortment of wires and batteries—did he have the technical ability to set timed fuses? The more I thought about the whole thing, the more possibilities piled up before me until I had a mountain. Maybe if a reporter had approached me then or if I'd been questioned by the authorities, I might have been compelled into revealing my suspicions or allowed myself to be drawn out. But as things stood, I didn't want to go near that. After all, I'd made a good number of payoffs just in the past several weeks. You understand, the MDA seemed to be ignoring us now, and we didn't want any more federal investigators or reporters sniffing around our wine caskets. I wasn't about to stick my own head in the oven. I kept my tongue on a chain. As a brigade, we did, after all, spend most of our energies on legitimate burns; our sector had more than enough natural fires to keep us busy. The fires we commissioned were superfluous; the deals and assignations were merely something we continued to do out of habit. The system was too pervasive and entrenched and there was too much at stake and too many people involved to throw a monkey wrench into the machinery. I was watching out not only for my own skin and for

Fire on Mount Maggiore

Nico's but for the welfare of the whole brigade and of the countless businesses and individuals implicated in our intricate web.

As for Nico and his tendency—well, maybe I was being too philosophical about it, but I figured that his activities were basically the equivalent of what the brigade was doing—setting innocuous fires and putting them out. And if I was as guilty as he was, how could I turn him in without being a hypocrite? After all, he was my friend—virtually my twin or double, in some ways. Fire had created us of similar molds, and I really meant to talk to him about the whole thing. I wanted to let him know that I was aware of what was going on; I planned to give him a heads-up and encourage him to leave the country, but in the next few days I kept putting it off. I could never find the right moment, and before I knew it, the brigade made its own headlines with the prescribed burn that spilled out of control in the Parco Regionale d'Abruzzo.

Chapter 30

Abruzzo's regional park is a major tourist spot on the slopes of Monte Mora, a beautiful volcanic lake. The area is a mixture of basic European forest and Mediterranean maquis, and in the last decade it has been a major burn area. Despite that, the former chief of the Corpo Forestale in Abruzzo had taken a very effective firefighting approach, and though the area experienced a high number of fire incidents (started by dry-lightning strikes and careless campers, mostly), a full 98 percent of the blazes in the past fourteen years had been contained, held down to a maximum of ten hectares.

Last year the old fire chief retired, and when the new chief took over he looked at the stats. He knew that although 95 percent of wildfires are easily controlled, it is the 5 percent that get away that do all the damage. And though the Corpo Forestale had controlled virtually all of the fires in the park for almost a decade and a half, the new chief decided that luck was running out. In his view the heavy-handed intervention of his predecessor had set nature off-balance. You see, in the long run fire acts as its own suppressant, consuming any excess deadwood through naturally occurring wildfires. But due to the old chief's hard-line approach, the forest debris had accumulated dangerously over the years. Touring the extensive park area, the new chief was alarmed at the large amount of deadwood and snag in the forests, and he decided he wanted to defuel, to set a series of controlled burns in the driest, most fire-prone and heavily touristed areas of his domain. Anticipating a surge of burns late in the season, he wanted to nip the blooms in their buds.

Our brigade was serving as a backup detail. It was a routine, if somewhat exaggerated, operation. The area in question was a one-hundred-hectare triangular chunk of land that stood between the town of Bressia Minore, the southeastern tip of the park, and the *autostrada*. The area was several kilometers west of the Sorrento Cliffs, a series of geographically unique and visually stunning overhangs near the fabulous Maico Falls. Throughout the summer, the sites were chock-full of tourists; many Germans and Austrians came here to kayak in the waters, rock-climb, and go spelunking.

The Abruzzo fire chief had enlisted a small army of Corpo Forestale, *Vigili del Fuoco,* and Protezione Civile to oversee the burn. A great swath of park was cordoned off using hundreds of personnel. The day before the prescribed burn, we had helped clear a firebreak two kilometers long and ten meters wide. Firebreaks are usually about three meters wide, but they weren't taking any chances here. Using chainsaws, bulldozers and shovels, we cleared the trees and brush and scraped the ground down to the dirt. It looked like the moon itself had been dragged across the hills.

The next morning we headed up the north rise and took position on the opposite ridge, a natural firebreak of steep rocks. At ten o'clock—three hours later than planned—we heard the helicopter fly in from Bressia Minore and spread the ignition gel in a stand of trees down by the Nardl River.

It took hold quickly, too quickly. It was like one of those napalm flashes you see in American movies of the Vietnam war, the jets sweeping in low and setting an entire swath of palms up like a torch. The fire started up the slope, moving east as planned, toward the main firebreak. But the wind picked up, or the fire was so intense it began creating its own winds.

They must have used too much gel, or there was more deadwood among the trees than had been estimated. The fire beckoned to the air, and the air began whirling, and the wind must have kicked some sparks over the road.

We were watching the main fire when Tonino spotted smoke on the knolls across the road. I immediately radioed it in. For some absurd bureaucratic reason, some overconfidence or lack of foresight, no squad was posted there. The fire wasn't supposed to jump the road. So we were told to send half our squad down from our current position on the ridge, cross the road, and head up the other hillside to take care of the spot fire. A crew of Corpo Forestale would circle around from the other side of the spot fire and meet up with us.

In the twenty minutes it took us to climb down the mountain and cross the road, the spot fire had come into its own. They already had a copter on it, dropping buckets of fire retardant that gave the smoke an eerie red haze that stung our throats and eyes. The smoke was so thick we couldn't see the top of the crest. We were at the northern edge of the fire, clearing a firebreak as we climbed up. We hoped we could beat the blaze to the summit, where it was easier to fight, or that at the summit the fire would simply burn itself out in the rocks.

The wind hadn't died down, though. It was swirling, not blowing any direction in particular, and there was smoke everywhere, obscuring our view. You couldn't see fifteen meters. My eyes had a bad reaction to the fire retardant, too, and I ended up lagging behind as the others moved up the incline. My boot felt loose and I saw it was untied; one of the laces had trapped a piece of charcoal and been burned through. I dropped my tools, took off my gloves and made a new knot halfway down the boot. I thought about relacing the entire boot but decided against it. I had noticed that the fire was getting louder and I couldn't hear the others. I knew they had gone up ahead of me, but I couldn't see anyone. I peered along the firebreak we'd hastily scraped up the slope and quickly scanned the burned-out area. Something wasn't right. Though the fire looked dead, I could still hear it. I thought we might have missed a crucial section and went back down the slope several dozen meters but didn't see any breach along the line. Then I turned. It was one of those moments when you don't know what comes first, your perception of the event or your realization that it is in fact taking place. I turned. The hillside circled over north to west. I couldn't see beyond the curve, but I saw a plume of white smoke over the horizon and heard a deep, rumbling roar. As I moved toward the sound, the wind kicked up and I glimpsed flames over the horizon—they were the flames of a treetop, and I realized another spot fire had started up on the far slope and was burning in the canopy. There was no way to tell how long it had been burning. I didn't know then that the further slope had already turned into an inferno.

I immediately began racing up the knoll to warn the others. The wind was kicking up, and the smoke was so thick it was like swimming through a noxious cloud. I had gotten maybe halfway up the slope when I heard some yelling and Saverio and Cesare came careening down the mountainside. They were followed by Massimo, Enzo, Pietro and Nico.

"Behind us!" Saverio yelled.

He said something about rendezvousing with Tonino, but at that instant we saw Tonino and Tancredi running across and down the slope toward us. I had rarely seen Tonino running away from fire.

We sprinted down toward the road together but found that, as I had suspected, the first spot fire had jumped the firebreak we'd hastily cleared below us. We were cut off.

"Goddamn idiots started a firestorm," Tonino said, glaring at the rekindled fire below us. He spit on the ground. "Follow me," he ordered.

We turned south and made for the black, cutting across the firebreak into the already burned-out area. The fire behind us roared forward, urged on by winds racing off the river. I looked back once to observe the wall of flames, and that's when I saw the forest ranger. He came out of nowhere, right out of the smoke and flames. He almost raced past me, headed downhill, but I grabbed him by the shirt and yelled, "Fire down below! Stay in the black!"

We hurtled across the blackened hillside toward safety like a platoon of soldiers fleeing a rout through some devastated battlefield. Though we were in the black—the area through which the fire had already passed— many trees and trunks were still ablaze. Our boots sank inches deep into gray and black ashes mixed with live embers, and thick smoke tossed itself on the winds so that at times you suddenly found yourself running at full speed into a bank of smoke thicker than Piedmontese fog and realized you were in danger of impaling yourself on some stray branch or snag. The ground was strewn with rocks and hidden crevices and half-burned fallen branches, and the mountainside seemed to shift beneath your feet. It was like trying to run on one of those rotating cylinders you find at amusement parks. You'd be running next to someone, then enter a coil of smoke like a door to another world, and when you found your way out again, the other person would be gone. There were also patches of unburned forest in the black area, and these were perhaps the most dangerous of all, for fire was always searching for fuel and you could easily find yourself in another mini-inferno. . . .

I almost lost my own bearings because I was trying to keep track of Nico. He was lagging behind for some reason, and I had to keep slowing down, even stopping and turning to yell, "*Sprigati,* Nico Americano! Hurry up!" And then Nico would come along begrudgingly, like a boy who didn't want to leave the playground just yet. He seemed fascinated by the fire that was racing back along the outer edge of the black area.

"Come on, Nico!"

"Matteo, look!"

I turned to where he was pointing and saw the flames in the treetops at the edge of the black about thirty meters away. They were truly spectacular. Like lava or Greek fire, the orange-black flames cascaded downward, burning upside down out of the canopy and spewing deep brown smoke that looked like great plumes of fine coffee grinds poured into the atmosphere.

"Listen!"

"What's that sound?"

There was a hissing noise, then something like a factory whistle and an explosion some fifty meters off. It sounded like fireworks in the treetops. There was another explosion slightly farther by, and flaming chips came hurtling out of the sky. Then for some reason the fire moved away from us, up the mountainside. We were basically out of danger.

I took Nico by the sleeve. "Let's get out of here."

The Americano seemed hypnotized. His wide eyes shone like coins.

"Isn't it beautiful, Matteo?" he said. "Isn't it the most beautiful thing you've seen in your entire life?"

We made our way down the knoll to the main road. It was crowded with emergency vehicles and fire personnel.

Everyone in our squad was accounted for—Enzo, Tonino, Saverio, Pietro, Massimo, Luchetto, Tancredi, Cesare, Nico and myself—but three members of the Corpo Forestale hadn't yet made contact at any checkpoint. A ranger was radioing the far post to see whether they'd rounded the western knob. The forester who I'd seen emerge from the flames was brought to paramedics and attended to; he would shortly be transferred to a hospital with minor wounds.

Tonino, meanwhile, was chewing me out for having taken so long to reach the road. I tried to explain what I'd seen with Nico, and that there'd been no danger, but Tonino gave me an earful.

"Where is the Americano, anyway?" Enzo asked.

I glanced around but didn't see him. "He was here just a second ago," I said.

I searched among the emergency vehicles parked along the shoulders, then noticed a figure across the road, down a gulch in the woods. It was Nico. I thought he'd gone to take a piss, but when he didn't return after several minutes, I crossed the road and climbed down a meter or two to check on him. What I saw I still do not know how to put into words. There was a bank of fire far up above, but the American was down in a shady gully leaning against a great flat rock. Legs spread-eagle, shirt untucked over his torso and groin, head perched in some angle of intensity and concentration, Nico was touching himself.

I should have moved, I should have fled before he craned his neck in an attitude of pain and release, I should have flown like a piece of white ash borne by the heat and winds that created it. But I couldn't move; I turned into a pillar of salt. The trees around me cackled, and the alarms and sirens whining along the road were impatient spirits calling to me, daring me to some unspeakable fate.

Chapter 31

A car alarm in the street below blares loudly. It has been going on and off all morning and given me a headache. The alarm is too sensitive, for the car is merely being nudged by the *ponente* wind that in recent days has been carrying in cool air from the northeast mountains.

I move to the far end of my apartment and stand in front of the map thumbtacked to the wall. Mount Maggiore: 1,313 meters. For the thousandth time I retrace that day's itinerary, following in my mind the path we took from the jeep and down along the mountainside until the valley exploded open and swallowed five of us in its hot breath. The topographical loops waver before my eyes. Tomorrow I am supposed to visit the site with Cavalier Mezzasoma and the fire inspector. Tomorrow I will go back and face it.

Nico spent his last days at base camp taking stock. Though he didn't mention anything about leaving, it was obvious that he was preparing himself. He spent one afternoon looking through what he'd written in his set of black-bound journals (not seeming terribly pleased or rapt, I noticed, but skimming the pages with a frown and a shrug of the shoulders) and once again he flipped through his worn copy of Conrad's *Heart of Darkness*. He washed his clothes in a wooden bucket and hung them out on the wire behind the barracks, and when they were dry he folded them into small tight bundles and tucked the items neatly into his duffel bag. He rummaged through his things and gave away several items—a compass for Enzo, a knife for Saverio, the set of MicroTools for me, three bottles of Chinese beer for Tonino. It seemed that he wasn't so much preparing to travel as to start a new life, purging himself of his belongings.

On August 6, exactly ten days before the fire on Mount Maggiore, I accompanied Renato on an assignation out by Ruviano, in the foothills near Maggiore itself. Renato acted as he usually did with me, like an old grumpy buddy. He wasn't the type of guy to talk things out. About the drop I'd completed by myself in Sanviolenza the other week Renato only mentioned that our contact, Sgn. Cardo, had been satisfied. Though I'd scared myself with visions of the police knocking down my apartment door in the middle of the night, nothing even remotely out of the ordinary occurred; apparently it was true that the Ministero dell'Agricultura had lost interest in our brigade. And since I'd seen that Nico was getting ready to leave Casabasso in the near future, I let that sleeping dog lie. With just a little time, I figured, the American and all the difficult questions that revolved around him would blow away like so much chaff in the wind.

Renato and I met our contact at a dingy bar on the outskirts of Ruviano. The *contadino* wore faded blue peasant overalls and had hands scarred with dirt. He and Renato talked for a long time, longer than was usual for this type of transaction. I distracted myself by playing a game of video soccer and couldn't hear what they were saying; I scored four goals to my opponent's three, and the crowd went wild. When Renato and I finally emerged from the bar, he seemed like he'd had too much caffeine. He rubbed his hands together and grinned and said, "This one's gonna be something, Mat." I simply nodded. I thought it involved another Canadair, and I didn't really care to know the details. This type of thing already seemed routine to me. As we drove off, we were treated to a glorious panoramic view of the valley and surrounding mountains. Up above us, the slopes where five of us would meet deaths of our own making—and where Nico would set a fire and tackle me down in fire so that I could be saved from fire—loomed indifferent and motionless, a sea of pacific green pointing up to the empty sky.

"Everything go okay?" Nico asked me when Renato and I arrived back at the firebase that afternoon.

"What do you mean?" I said.

"You and Renato just got back, right?" Nico said. "All I asked was, Did everything go smoothly?"

I wasn't sure if he was trying to get at something or not. I said, "Smooth as ice."

"So everything's okay between you and Renato now?" Nico inquired.

"Sure," I answered.

"Just checking," Nico said innocently. He kicked lazily at some dust on the ground. "You know, you're a curious bird, Matteo."

"Ditto," I answered.

Nico nodded and smiled, then his face grew serious. "You know I'm leaving in a week or so, right?"

"I figured as much," I said. I almost told him I'd miss him, but I felt a wad of emotion in my throat and the words wouldn't come out. I hoped he knew anyway, I figured he understood that much. I said, "You've been here quite a while—you must miss home."

"Yeah, well, there's that," Nico answered. "And I figure I'd better quit while I'm ahead."

"There's that too," I said.

Nico gave me a long regard, then shook his head as if to dispel some unwanted thoughts. He said, "Actually, I was thinking of heading back up north."

"To see Adina?"

"Either that," Nico frowned, "or catch a train to Warsaw."

I thought of how Katja and he had parted badly. I said, "I think that's a great idea."

"Oh, I'm full of ideas," Nico said more brightly now. "They're like a bunch of little candle flames in my head. I've got so many I don't know where to put 'em."

"Just make sure you don't light *too* many of them," I said.

"I'll try to remember that," Nico said, "but I can't make any promises."

The dreaded day—the day that I have spent the last week pretending would never arrive—arrives: it is time for me to return to Maggiore. Cavalier Mezzasoma and the fire inspector pick me up in a white sedan bearing the markings of the Ministero dell'Agricultura. I dislike the inspector immediately. He is small and bald and doesn't shake my hand, and when he talks to Mezzasoma about me he uses the third person, as if I weren't sitting in the backseat of the car. Judging from a few comments he makes, I can tell that his mind is already made up about what happened on the slopes of Mount Maggiore.

We head out of town and bear northeast off the *autostrada,* skirting a sports center and an abandoned mining complex, and begin ascending into the hills of the countryside. Great fields of sunflowers and tobacco stretch off on both sides of the road. Long rows of grapevines, trained in neat columns, line a river in the valley. In the distance, groves of olive trees hover like silver-green mists, and hay has been combed into great swirling patterns resembling calligraphy on the hillsides. The road climbs up out of the valley and courses along the upper ridge of Monte Giubileo. This stretch of road used to be a piece of the Appian Way, and it is lined with umbrella pines more than 150 years old. Though the terrain undulates up and down, ramparts and excavations keep the road straight and level as a board, and the vista is spectacular. In one of the valleys a few kilometers off, I can see rain dropping from a thunderhead; it looks like a few pencil strokes smudged with a wet finger on the low horizon. The beauty of the land stings my eyes, and a tightness in the back of my throat reminds me of the emotions that enlivened me throughout my first years of fighting forest fires. I doubt I will ever experience those thrilling moments again.

We slow down at a fork in the main thoroughfare and turn onto a smaller road that hugs the mountainside. Cavalier Mezzasoma, who's sitting beside the fire inspector in the front seat, turns to me and says, "We're almost there." The road snakes back and forth and up and flat and up again, and we cross a stone bridge, originally constructed by ancient Romans, laid across a deep ravine. I wonder how the Romans dealt with forest fires. . . .

I smell the slopes before I see them. The odor is faint at first, hardly noticeable, a mere trace of something in the air that wasn't there a moment before. And then my brain is sending signals: it is an ashtray I smell, a damp fireplace, a campfire doused with beer, the spit after smoke inhalation. It is the pungent odor of soot that I brought back with me from each and every fire I ever fought, entangled in the threads of my clothes, clinging to my hair, lodged in every pore of my body.

Into the Black   **213**

Suddenly the trees on one side of the road are gone: there's nothing but a wasteland of blackened trunks, bushes that are charred skeletons, raven stones, sable earth. Only the thorny stems of some wild blackberries bear any semblance of color. On the other side of the road the land is green, the knobs choked with foliage. The contrast between one side of the road and the other is the difference of a single matchstick.

We slow down, happen upon the dirt entry road, and turn onto it. The lane is gravelly, and the inspector, having a hard time with the gears, curses the Blessed Virgin. We lurch forward until Mezzasoma raises his hand and the inspector stops the car.

The squad jeep we'd driven to the Maggiore blaze a month ago lies demolished in a ditch at the side of the road. The vehicle is completely burned out. The windows are all broken and the tires are gone. When I get out and go over to it, I see that the steering wheel and radio are melted down to the steel parts. I pick up a small piece of glass that has hardened into a perfectly smooth flat oval.

"We found the jeep lying on its side," Mezzasoma says to me. "The fire must have knocked it over."

The inspector has taken out a sharp pencil and a little notepad with a textured faux-leather flip-cover. "Did you park near the ditch?" he asks me.

"I don't know," I say. "I don't think so. Tonino was driving."

"Yes, I know that, but you did exit the vehicle here, did you not?"

"I don't know," I repeat. I scan the ruined landscape, trying to get my bearings. "I'm not sure, it all looks so different."

"Try to remember," the inspector says.

"I am remembering—I do remember," I say, my voice rising. "Do you think I could forget what happened?"

The fire inspector gives me a dubious and unsympathetic look. Mezzasoma takes him by the arm and nudges him away from me. "Let's move on," he suggests.

It all looks strange to me. It is like returning to the house of your childhood after a very long absence. Distances are shortened or lengthened, perspectives don't fit, everything looks too small or too large, alien. I realize that my own memories are being distorted and reworked by this encounter with reality, and I am suddenly uncertain about my ability to remain accurate and truthful. But my face doesn't falter. I don't want this inspector to get the best of me.

Step by step we review the main stages of the squad's August 16 deployment, following a map and schedule the inspector has extrapolated from our accounts. Bright orange surveyors' flags have been planted at key points on the slopes. Point A: squad leaves the jeep. Point B: squad pauses to survey the flames. Point C: Tonino and Saverio cross to the south side of the ravine with one of the radios. Point D: the squad begins a fire containment line. Point E: furthest point west reached by Tonino and Saverio. Point F: Tonino and Saverio recross the ravine, back over to the north side. Point G: Renato doubles back east. Point H: squad begins its retreat. Point I: heavy tools ordered dropped; one radio found. Point J: Tonino turns back into the blaze. Point K: point-of-origin of Nico's backfire. Point L: Enzo's body found. Point M: Saverio's body found. Point N: Massimo's body found. Point O: site where Luchetto and Cesare crossed through a key in the bluff. Point P: Pietro's body found. Point Q: *contadino*'s body found.

It is a grim alphabet, and I find the inspector's businesslike tone annoying. We descend back to Point K. This rough spot of blackened earth is where Nico and I survived. From here I can see another flag, this one neon green, that is supposed to mark the main fire's point of origin low on the far southwestern slope. Though the inspector doesn't know it, that is where the *contadino* dropped the match on the ground and set our lives aflame.

Chapter 32

Like many catastrophes, the fire on Mount Maggiore began as a routine operation and escalated into something out of control. Perhaps it was precisely the illusion of control that enabled the catastrophe to come into its own, but it was aided by several happenstances, all seemingly trivial in themselves, that harmonized together with inexorable and tragic logic.

The *contadino* had chosen a bad place to set the fire, though when we in the squad first saw the blaze from a neighboring summit, it didn't look like much. Though there was a lot of smoke, the fire wasn't very big— Class D, maybe four hectares or so. We took our time checking our gear, tying our shoelaces, gathering ourselves for the task.

What we faced basically were two mountains, like two loaves of bread sitting side by side. In between the mountains was a ravine that as it approached the river to the west became steeper and steeper, until it was more like a rocky gorge. In the ravine was a ditch that in the wet months held a stream but was now bone-dry. The two mountains were like the sides of a funnel or trough draining into the ravine and then the river. But we approached the fire from the east, where the inclines were still fairly gradual, and we were on the opposite side of the ravine, following con-tour, so that the fire was across from us at roughly the same altitude.

Though we should have been able to see the flames on the opposite slope clearly, much smoke obscured the view. More out of habit than any-thing else, we figured the fire was burning up toward the further summit, and Saverio told me to radio in for another squad to meet the fire as it crested. I unhooked the radio from my belt and started a transmission. That's when I first noticed something wrong with the radio unit. The low-battery/recharge light was blinking on and off, and it took me three trans-missions to get our request across. The last I looked the low-battery light was not indicating need of a recharge. But that's when I realized I hadn't recharged the radios since the Polish girls had been here. That was maybe too long. A sense of dread washed over me, but there was nothing I could do about it. I hoped it would be okay. Not saying anything to the others, I hung the radio back on my belt.

The squad and I began clearing a firebreak along the hiker's path we'd been following on the slope opposite the fire. The middle of the hill wasn't the best place to clear a line, but it was already too late to try to use the ravine as a containment line and the grade wasn't all that steep so we thought the line might hold. While were clearing and widening the path, Tonino and Saverio moved on further west, downslope, to get a closer look at the fire. As soon as they were gone, Renato said he was going to check on the fire's easterly spread and turned back up the hiker's path in the direction we'd come from. As he headed away up the trail, I noticed there was a small green duffel bag slung over his shoulder, the kind we stored water pump refill tanks in; I thought it odd, since none of us had a water pump that day, then I forgot all about it.

Me and Nico, Pietro, Cesare, Luchetto, Enzo, Massimo, and Tancredi—we spread out and worked on clearing a fire line. It was a matter of widen-ing the hiker's path, clearing bushes, digging trenches and cutting down trees, and it was exhausting work. We were working quickly, too, and maybe we got a bit sloppy. At one point Enzo turned back, looked at the fire line and said, "That wouldn't stop a baby in a carriage."

"It's gonna crest no matter what," Pietro said, looking up the slope toward the summit of Maggiore. The top of the mountain was about six hundred meters above us, but the view was obscured by trees. "I don't know why they think we can stop it midslope."

"As long as the winds stay like this we should be able to," Tancredi said.

Luchetto shrugged. "We'd better dig a decent line," he said.

"Even if we dig down to China," Cesare said, "I don't think this'll work."

"Yeah," Massimo seconded, bracing his shovel between his knees so he could spit on his hands, "and I'm getting blisters already."

We all nodded our heads but kept clearing the break. We did the best we could—especially Nico, who was putting a lot of effort into today's labors. The others noticed too, and at one point Enzo said, "Hey, Americano, I think we finally taught you how to dig a good fire line!"

"It's about time I got the hang of it," Nico replied, shoveling a spadeful of earth high over his shoulder. He stopped for a moment and added loudly, "And I learned a lot more than this from you guys." He sent me a smile and an enigmatic wink.

We ignored the main fire, which we figured was burning up and away from us on the opposite ridge, and concentrated on clearing the line. After about twenty more minutes had passed, my radio crackled, but the voice was so garbled I couldn't make anything out of it. I said loudly into the mike, "I can't read you, I cannot read you, over and out," and hung the radio back on my belt. The battery was dead.

Luchetto looked at me with his eyebrows raised. "What's the matter?"

"The radio's shot," I answered. "No power."

"You couldn't hear anything?" Cesare asked.

"Just garble," I said.

"It was probably nothing worth hearing," Massimo guessed.

"Probably," Enzo said, "Tonino just wanted to bust our balls."

"And Renato," Pietro added, "where the hell is he?"

"He said he was going back up the path to check the easterly spread," I answered.

"Seems like he stopped to smell the roses," Pietro said.

"Or more likely," Enzo said, "he's cuttin' some Zs in the back of the jeep."

We shrugged our shoulders and went back to our digging. Every once in a while the wind would blow a puff of smoke in our direction; it seemed to get thicker each time. We kept widening the line. I guess we'd been working on the firebreak for another fifteen minutes when we heard yelling from below, and before long Saverio came running up from the ravine waving his arms. Some of us started moving down to see what he wanted, but he waved us off.

"Stop! Turn around! Go up the slope!" There was an urgency to Saverio's voice that we couldn't understand.

"What is it?"

"Why are you still here?" Saverio asked like he was mad at us.

"We're clearing the break!" Enzo answered, annoyed.

"Just like you told us to!" Tancredi added.

Saverio's voice turned cold and reasonable, like a parent who has to explain something serious to a kid. "The fire's burning down the south slope. It's gonna cross the ravine any minute. Why didn't you move back like we told you?"

I spoke up. "The radio unit's bad," I said, "We couldn't hear you." I shrugged my shoulders like it wasn't my fault, but Saverio and the others looked at me as though I'd just knocked a soccer ball into our own team's goal.

Just then Tonino appeared out of the smoke from downslope and ordered us back up along the hiker's path. We grumbled. We'd just spent the last hour cutting a decent fire line, and now we were being told to abandon it. We didn't see what the big deal was—there wasn't a flame in sight—but we reluctantly did as we were told, dragging our shovels in the dirt behind us. After we'd followed the path back for about three hundred meters, we met Renato returning down the path from the opposite direction.

When he saw us, he scowled. "Where the hell do you think you're going?"

"Back up the path, Tonino's orders."

"You can't go that way," Renato said.

"Why not?"

"Because I said so," Renato replied.

"But Tonino said. . . ."

"I don't care what Tonino said," Renato insisted. "You can't go up the path."

Well, we could insist too. We dug our heels into the ground and waited for Tonino to catch up and resolve this. It took him two or three minutes to reach us.

"What are you bunching up for?" he yelled when he saw us gathered together in the path. "Get off your goddamn heels!"

We pointed to Renato. I noticed then that he didn't have that little duffel bag with him anymore.

Tonino looked at him and said, "Renato, it's burning down into the ravine. Probably crossed over already. We'll have to circle around the eastern bluff and stop it at the crest."

Renato pressed his lips together and shook his head firmly from side to side. "We'll circle around from the west," he said.

Tonino scratched his stomach and grimaced. "Then we'd have to cross the steep knobs along the Punti Cliffs," he said. "I don't like it. We'll circle around from the east."

"No," Renato said.

"The *cliffs* are to the west, Renato."

"We'll be north of the cliffs," Renato said.

"Not by much," Tonino argued.

Renato had daggers in his eyes. His voice changed. "We *can't* go east," he said.

As if to punctuate the words, a great blast sounded up the mountainside at precisely that instant, and two seconds later we were hit by a gust of hot wind and saw to our amazement a vast bank of fire a hundred meters high flare up from the ravine below us. For a great, long, scary moment, the flames seemed as tall as the World Trade Center towers. We immediately realized what was happening: the fire had blown up, massively—it hadn't bothered to burn all the way down the north slope into the ravine before crossing it and heading up the southern slope of Mount Maggiore. It had just jumped across. There'd been enough heat and air to boost the fire over the ravine altogether. The flames had taken a shortcut, leaping across and devouring three hundred meters of terrain in mere seconds, and the main fire was now only a few hundred meters below us and coming our way fast.

Tonino glared at Renato one last time. Renato tapped the face of his watch with one finger and shook his head no, and Tonino shrugged and moved off the path and up the mountainside. "Let's move, people!" he yelled. The rest of us abandoned the hiker's path and followed him up the hillside. It was tough going. The terrain was choked with trees and dense brush. Where there wasn't a tree or a bush, loose rocks or big cumbersome boulders stood in your way. We guessed that the slope eased a bit up above the tree line, but here the grade was steep and we had to climb like monkeys on all fours. We thought this was the hard part, but it was actually the easy part. The hard part would be sprinting through the grassy slopes that loomed above us toward the summit of the mountain.

We'd climbed maybe seventy-five meters when I thought I heard a small explosion on the hiker's path to the east—a brief metallic pop, like someone had discharged a large-barreled shotgun. A few minutes later a stiff gust of wind hit me and kept blowing, growing stronger and stronger. The air became turbulent and searing hot and another thunderous noise rumbled up from below, as though a locomotive had entered the valley. The wind tugged so hard on my shirt that my shirttails flapped like flags in a tornado. My belt got caught on a branch and something slapped against my face and then I couldn't see anything in the smoke. I loosened my belt and the radio fell to the ground.

Tonino was giving orders to speed up.

"I dropped the radio!" I yelled.

"Leave it, Matteo!"

Another gust of wind hit us and cleared the smoke.

"Look!" Saverio called to us.

Downhill, not 150 meters from where we stood, the entire valley was aflame as though an incendiary bomb had been dropped. I felt my bowels loosen and ache sharply in my gut; the sight instantly instilled us with fear. It was like suddenly realizing you're driving the wrong way down the wrong side of a highway.

"Drop unneeded equipment!" Tonino ordered.

We didn't need any orders. We were running now, frenziedly scrambling toward the summit. What stood between us and safety was fifty meters of trees and bush, five hundred meters of steep grassland and a wall of thorn- and vine-entangled rocks at the top ridge. It crossed my mind that we weren't going to make it, and I realized with a certain strange and sudden nostalgia that less than an hour ago, in the jeep on our way to the burn, we had all been singing songs—stuff everybody half-knew, American standards, contemporary Italian pop pieces or old tunes by the Beatles. Perhaps if we had known some of us were going to die we would have chosen something different—an anthem maybe, something mournful yet rousing. But we didn't know. Tonino had been banging the steering wheel as he drove, punching the horn in time with the end of the chorus. Enzo, swung around in the passenger seat to face those of us sitting in the jeep's rear cabin, used a flashlight as a conductor's baton. The rest of us were wedged shoulder to shoulder on the black vinyl bench seats in the rear, grasping at the broken leather hand-straps and bracing ourselves against Tonino's turns. What had we been thinking? Enzo swinging the silver flashlight, Saverio with crumpled love notes in his pockets, Pietro scratching his Total Soccer lotto forms, Massimo fingering the silk scarf around his neck, Renato scowling at Tonino's driving, Cesare and Tancredi bickering about something, and Nico Americano, hat in his hands, the frayed copy of some novel jutting from his breast pocket, keeping secrets to himself. Perhaps we all were keeping secrets—keeping them to ourselves, keeping them from others, keeping them from ourselves.

About halfway up the slope, just beyond the tree line—exactly where I am standing right now with Mezzasoma and the fire inspector—that's where I saw Nico yelling and waving his arms beside some low flames burning on the grassy incline above him. I remember coming up the hill out of a bank of heavy smoke rising from the ravine and seeing the fire in the grasses ahead of me. I thought it was a spot fire at first, but I wondered how a spot fire could have gotten established so quickly and at such an odd location. Nico was standing there on the broad mountainside waving his arms and yelling something that couldn't be heard over the roar of flames coming up behind us. Luchetto, Cesare and Tancredi were somewhere up ahead of me, I remember, but the other guys—Enzo, Pietro, Renato, Saverio, Massimo and Tonino—were coming up the rise from behind and they began skirting to the right, east of this new fire that had somehow started on the high slope. They had no idea it was Nico's escape fire and in fact had never heard of a backfire referred to in such a way. The escape fire was burning up and to the right, which meant roughly north-northeast, like the main fire. And was that Tancredi in the black? Was he trying to put out the fire in the grass? What was Nico saying? Did he want us to help put out this spot fire?

The guys would have nothing of it. They ignored the American, sped right past him. Saverio slowed down for a moment and told Nico to keep moving up the slope, but Nico shook his head. Enzo actually took hold of Nico's shirt to pull him away, but when Nico tried to push Enzo toward the spot fire, Enzo broke free and continued uphill.

For some reason that I will never understand, Tancredi had immediately trusted Nico, or else he instinctively understood the concept of the escape fire. The idea was this: burn the grass in front of you before the fire behind you catches up. Step into the black—onto the ground that you just burned—and hunker down. Then when the fire behind you catches up, all it will find is a patch of already burned ground with you safely in the middle of it. That, I say, was the idea, but all I could see at the time—all my fright would allow me to see—was a grass fire burning at Nico's feet.

Me and my fear would have nothing to do with this. I could feel the main fire burning at me from behind. It was so close I could hear nothing but its roar, for it screamed absurdly in both my ears. *Up the slope*, my body said, *up the slope*. I made a run for it.

Nico saw me make a move and rushed toward me, and before I knew what he was doing he had dragged me into the burned-out area, swept a leg under my ankles and knocked me to the ground. Though I struggled mightily, he kept a grip on both my legs with one arm, and then a shadow passed over me, something covered my head. I quickly knocked it off with my arm.

"Let go of me!" I yelled at Nico, trying to flail my legs free.

"It's too late, Matteo! Cover your head!"

I heard a crinkling sound and grabbed at something like tinfoil; Nico had unwound a fire-resistant cocoon and was trying to cover us up with it, I realized. The trees nearby wavered ferociously and I saw leaves wrinkling black, devoured by the heat. Nico was right, it was too late. The flames reared all around us in the grass and the surrounding foliage. When the heat became unbearable I covered my head and stuck my nose into the dirt. The fire enclosed us.

I thought of fires across the land burning like candles at a wake, and for the first time in years I prayed to God. I realized that fire was a primal force of the universe, that stars were fire, that fire was light, that on the first day God had created fire, that fire was the word of God, that words were illuminations, that I had not uttered one pure word of truth in my entire life. . . . I thought of Nero playing the fiddle while Rome burned, and for a moment I understood that gesture—not its utter evil depravity but its capriciousness and insouciance—and I saw my mother cleaning the kitchen before bedtime and remembered how, when she finished, she would come to my bed to read me stories about blonde damsels and silver-clad knights and fire-breathing dragons.

Eventually, in minutes that were years, the roaring died down. I listened as the fire gradually moved off to the north and east, and after another minute it was as quiet as a pond.

Nico released my legs. I realized we'd been pressed closely together beneath the synthetic cocoon. We rose slowly, tentatively, testing our limbs, as though we had slept for a very long time.

When I looked around I thought it had snowed. The mountainside as far as I could see was covered in a sheet of bone-white ash with even whiter ashes hovering in the air like tiny pieces of origami.

I turned and saw Tancredi nearby us, sitting on the ground. He was covered with light-gray soot from head to toe. Only his blue eyes shone eerily.

"Where are the others?" he asked in a cracked voice.

Nico shook his head solemnly. We were alone in the field of ashes; we were ashes.

To the northeast we saw the fire cresting on the mountaintop, the winds blowing the huge flames back and forth like giant orange flags. We stared, but none of us dared move. After a few minutes the flames subsided, threw off a thick column of smoke, and moved over a ridge out of sight.

"We should look for the others," Nico said. We knew we should, but we were powerless to do anything but just stand there. We were as petrified as Il Carpiglio's statues in the gardens behind Palazzo Sangiusto.

There was a shout from below and a figure ambled up the mountainside. It was Tonino. His uniform was soaked wet with sweat and dirt. One of his sleeves had been burned off.

"Are you three all right? Where are the others?" he asked us.

"They were going up the slope . . ." Tancredi said, trailing off.

"We all need water," Tonino said. "There's a stream in the gorge on the other side of the ridge." He began climbing, and we slowly followed him up. The ground was burned clean and the rocks were sauna-hot. Nearer the summit, the mountain was rockier and almost bare of vegetation, except for some patches of low grass.

"Maybe they made it up this far," Tancredi said.

No one answered. We knew the chances were slim.

We reached and crossed the summit and had begun heading downslope when we noticed the burned deer about halfway down the rockslide. "Look!" someone cried. But it wasn't a deer, it was a man. It was Renato. Luchetto and Cesare appeared behind him, following closely. They were trying to get him to stop and sit down. We moved over toward them to cut Renato off.

He was burned foot to head, his clothes melted onto his skin. He was a black mummy with a red-pink slit for a mouth. It was a miracle he could move at all. We gently got him to lean against a boulder to rest, but as soon as Renato saw Nico, he lunged forward and grabbed at the American's shirt.

"Americano!" Renato gasped, managing to pull on Nico's collar.

Tonino put himself between them. "Calm down, Renato!"

"The Americano!" Renato repeated, suddenly lunging violently at Nico and trying to punch him. But Renato was massively injured. His punch missed and Renato fell with his own momentum to the ground and gave out a pitiful groan of distress, the yelp of a dog hit by a car on the roadway. We gathered around him in a circle. Barely conscious, he reached for Tonino and tugged on the front of his shirt. "Antonio," he said, "I guess we showed 'em?" He gave a short laugh, then continued in a barely audible whisper. "They said they wanted fireworks for this one"—Renato tried to lick his lips—"so I gave 'em fireworks, eh?" Before anyone could respond, his head fell back and he didn't say another word.

The fire inspector claps me on the shoulder and shakes me out of my reverie. He has his theory down pat and the conclusion is simple, he tells Mezzasoma and me. The American's backfire killed Enzo, Saverio, Massimo, Pietro and Renato, and it also seriously endangered the lives of Cesare and Luchetto, who were extremely lucky to have found the pass leading through the bluff. Had the American not lit the so-called emergency backfire, everyone in the squad would probably still be alive today.

But as I stand on the spot where Nico lit the escape fire, I see that it is much farther east, and much lower down the slope, than I had envisioned it with my capricious memory. If this is indeed the spot, then it is highly unlikely the escape fire had anything to do with the deaths.

I say as much to the inspector, but he won't be moved. "It's ironic, isn't it?" he muses instead, ignoring my protests. "Here we have a guy who's supposed to be fighting a fire, but instead he lights a second one! And maybe others too."

"He did fight," I say.

"If that's what you call fighting."

"It's what I call fighting."

"I call it manslaughter one."

"But. . . ."

"Everyone's got their opinion. Yours is tainted by the fact that the American spared you and that other Americanophile, what's-his-name. . . ." The inspector begins flipping through his notepad.

"Tancredi," I say.

"Yeah, him." The inspector snaps his finger on a name in the notepad. "Last name Gapardo."

"Did you ask him about what happened?" I asked.

"He's already corroborated the facts," the inspector says.

"Has he been up here?"

"No, won't come near the place. Refuses. But that's okay. We used maps."

"That's not the same thing," I say.

"No, you're right, it's not," the inspector counters, "it's actually better, more objective. One can use one's head and not get bogged down by foggy emotions—or spooked by this godforsaken landscape."

If I were a man, I would punch the inspector here and now. But I am not a man. I am a timid ghost frightened that I am lost in my own story.

Into the Black

"There's your proof," the inspector says. He points to one of the flags in the landscape; it is to the east, about five hundred meters below us.

I stare at the spot but can't place it on the itinerary.

"That is where the canister was found," Mezzasoma explains to me.

I've never heard anything about any canister before, and Mezzasoma sees the question on my face.

"The gas," Mezzasoma says. "The canister of gas we found off the hiker's path."

When the words sink in, I feel myself turn pale; I suddenly understand why the *contadino* died. He must have started the fire at the foot of the south slope, then come up the ravine to plant the canister to ensure that the fire would catch on this north slope. Yes, he might have done things backward like that, rather than plant the canister first. It would have saved him a good couple of kilometers of hiking. But he grossly underestimated how fast the fire would burn. If he had tried to follow the hiker's trail back down along the ravine, he would have been going right back into the fire. And when he realized what was happening, he was pushed off the trail up the rugged mountainside. He was found northwest of the ravine, toward the river, at nine hundred meters, so he must have gotten trapped, like us, when the flames jumped across the slopes. He was headed for the river but got caught in the fumes on the cliffs. The poor stupid fool.

"It wasn't Nico," I say.

"We have the evidence," the investigator says.

"But Nico didn't have any canister with him," I say.

"Maybe he concealed it in his backpack," the inspector says.

"No," I say.

"Then how do you explain its existence?"

"I don't know," I say, looking directly at Cavalier Mezzasoma.

Mezzasoma looks away. He doesn't want to go near this.

"Well, then," I say loudly to the inspector, "how do you explain the *contadino*?"

When the inspector can't answer, Cavalier Mezzasoma glares at me and grumbles, "He was an idiot, nothing more." I look back at the inspector, but Mezzasoma diverts our attention: "Look!" he says. He leans over and picks up something. "Look." He opens his fist to reveal the tender green needle of a baby pine tree. "It's beginning to come back." I look at the tiny green needle, hardly wider than the wrinkles on Mezzasoma's palm. It is as green as Katja's eyes, I say to myself.

The inspector hasn't answered my question, and I glower at him. "How do you explain the *contadino*?" I ask again.

"You tell me," he says. It is the first intelligent thing he's said all day.

"He was nothing but a man hiking in the mountains," Mezzasoma says. He drops the pine needle and takes me by the arm. "Matteo, we should go now."

I begin to pull my arm free, but Mezzasoma tightens his grip and steers me away. "Tell him," I whisper to Mezzasoma.

"We're going now, Matteo."

"*Tell him*," I say under my breath, but I know no one will.

Chapter 33

I was never asked to testify at the tribunal inquest in Napoli, and the findings in the end were inconclusive. Judge Ceruta-Levitas decided that there
was simply not enough evidence to charge the American with any wrong-
doing—neither on Mount Maggiore or anywhere else. Though arson was
still suspected to be the cause of several fires in our sector this summer, no
reliable evidence was recovered from any of the fire scenes. The prostitute
who claimed he had seen the American the day before the Marathon fire
was determined to have been a heavy heroin user, and his testimony was
thrown out of court. Nico's notebooks, which the judge refused to make

public, were apparently full of cryptic musings but absolutely no indication of intent to commit arson. And Nico's watch collection was thought to be just that, a watch collection, nothing more. No wires or batteries or diagrams of incendiary devices were found. In short, the state had no credible evidence, and the American was set free and asked politely—for by all accounts Nicolas Fowler had risked his own safety in the service of extinguishing fire and preserving the Mediterranean ecosystem—to leave the country. I never saw or heard from him again.

Throughout the country October rains begin falling, washing away the hillsides burned this summer; surveyors move in to measure the land and begin staking lines for more construction. A modified version of the legislation to allow construction on recently burned areas "only if the land is deemed too expensive or dangerous to regenerate" passes through the Assembly. The rule does not apply to state parks, national forests or ecologically endangered wilderness areas, which are still protected by strict standards; but by next year, if they hurry, land developers and builders will be able to smile upon their new real estate creations.

When I'm not slicing meat and cheese at the deli where I now work or attending classes at the university where I'm studying toward a degree, I wander through the city or take my new *motorino* out into the countryside. Sometimes I see the smoke of fires on the hillsides: somber gray, smoldering, at times mistlike, hugging the slopes and valleys; at other times rising up in heavy white-brown plumes as though from smokestacks of industry.

The smell of smoke—of wild brush afire—is beautiful to me. When I encounter it now on my daily meanderings, I react as others would upon entering an arbor of jasmine and magnolia: with a deep, savoring inhalation. Smoke is pure perfume, as wonderful as frangipani. And because it is a familiar smell, I find it comforting, like the sweet incense that greets you in church; yet its underlying heady musk stimulates, rouses me deeply. The smell lingers in the air teasingly, tantalizingly. It is a temptation, it is temptation itself. I must suppress the urge to follow it.

When I was about ten or eleven years old, my family went on vacation to Calabria one summer to visit relatives. My uncle had a small villa out in the countryside. It was a bleak place, the sunlight blinding, the land dry and on some windy afternoons streaked with reddish sand blowing north from the Sahara desert on the African sirocco.

I had a cousin about my age, maybe one or two years older than me. One day he took me excitedly by the elbow and pulled me outside the house. He had stolen a box of matches from my aunt's kitchen.

We went out behind the toolshed and took turns rubbing the match tips against the rough black striking line. There'd be a spark, then a small smoky flash near the fingertips. The fragile orange flames were barely visible in the sunlight. Puffs of sulfur swirled in our heads.

We began lighting leaves, twigs, strips of paper—anything handy—and were surprised when a small pile of hay and dry grass suddenly leapt upward into our hands and faces. Then there was another smell, something foul and old and evil that turned out to be the odor of our own burned hair. We were delighted. We lit rags and boxes and hay and grass and leaves and paper in the sunlight behind the toolshed and stomped out the unruly flames with the soles of our shoes until pieces of thin, curling, orange-edged paper-ash floated around us like black confetti. We'd probably have stayed out there all day if our parents hadn't called us in to eat lunch.

In the late afternoon, while our parents sat on the front terrace smoking cigarettes and drinking *fragolino* and *grappa,* my cousin and I went back outside behind the shed. Though my cousin had a fresh box of matches, we quickly tired of the tiny, brief leaf-and-paper fires that had thrilled us earlier, and we looked inside the toolshed for new ideas. The shed was filled with dusty wine bottles and wine caskets and rakes and shovels and equipment for the olive press. Corks didn't burn well, but the spider webs hanging in the corners seemed to melt at the merest hint of heat. All you had to do was wave a burning match near the spun filaments for the web to break and fall away, seemingly disappearing. We burned the spiders too, and a big brown cricket we'd cornered inside the shed. The stench of the burned insects was putrid and unfathomable.

The gasoline can rested on a cement block in one corner. The liquid sloshed in the metal container. My cousin carried the can outside and tipped a spot into the ground and lit it. We were very careful. We cleared a circle of dirt and poured a cup of gasoline into it and were amazed that the ground, the very dirt, seemed to burn. This flare-up was different from the others, we also noticed. Because it was now nearing twilight, the flames were brighter and harsher and more stubborn, and the gasoline fumes were like nasty thoughts hissing inside our heads, making us giddy and careless. We poured the gasoline in a line and watched the flame creep fuselike along it. We poured a longer line, with a small pile of leaves and grass and twigs at the end that at first smoldered, then took to flame, then spent itself. I don't know how many hours we spent behind the shed before we were called back to the house.

I spent a bad night. Despite a long bath, cotton pajamas, a midnight snack and Mom's kisses, something nagged me all night long, and I turned and tossed ceaselessly on the small squeaky cot.

At dawn the next morning, when the sky was still black on the western horizon, I went outside. I couldn't find my shoes and didn't want to wake anybody, so I went out barefooted. The grass was damp and the stones cool to my feet and there was a smell in the air like a fireplace when it rains.

Behind the shed the gas can lay empty on its side. The grass was singed black in patches, and in a circle of stones was a pile of ashes and half-burnt twigs. That was all as we had left it. What alarmed me was the haze in the air, a haze that, in the growing morning light, was becoming harder and harder to deny.

Then I saw the woodpile. Once used to feed the outdoor pizza oven (its apertures cemented closed now, to prevent animals from nesting inside), the woodpile had been sitting about for several years. Someone had occasionally tossed fresh branches and kindling atop the pile, but the wood on the bottom layer was rotting, probably infested with ants and termites. And somewhere along the middle layer, I saw, the pile was smoldering. The logs were covered with a film of gray-white ash, and when I blew the ashes away I saw that the wood was glowing red and orange. There were no flames, just a long, slow smoldering, the way charcoal burns. The logs had been smoldering all night long.

I went back to the house and filled the watering can from the spigot at the side door. I carried the can to the woodpile—the rocks and stones sharp now under my feet—and wet it down. Out past the woodpile a field began, and I saw how the fire could so easily have taken to the grass and spread to the forest at the far end of the field. I was dizzied by the immensity of what might have occurred.

"Do you smell smoke?" my father asked to no one in particular at breakfast that morning.

"Probably the neighbors burning their garbage," my uncle replied.

I kept my head lowered and sprinkled sugar on my buttered bread.

My mother looked at me and asked, "What were you doing outside this morning?"

"Nothing," I said. "Playing. I watered Auntie's flowers."

"Why, thank you, Mattolino!" my aunt said, giving me a kiss on the head. "Well, you smell like an ashtray!"

"I cleaned the ones out on the terrace," I lied. Both my parents and my uncle smoked heavily.

"Oh, don't you go touching those dirty things," my aunt said. And then to my uncle: "Really, Giuseppe, you should empty those things out once in a while—or better yet, stop smoking altogether!"

Later on, when I showed my cousin the woodpile, he blanched and pulled nervously at his hair. He was sure his father would unstrap his belt for such a thing, so we spent the whole day tidying up the area, being sure to erase every last trace of burnt grass and charred wood. No one ever found out, as far as I know.

Fire on Mount Maggiore was designed and typeset on a Macintosh computer system using QuarkXPress software. The body text is set in 10/13 Galliard and display type is set in Flexure. This book was designed and typeset by Kelly Gray and manufactured by Thomson-Shore, Inc.